All That Glitters

by Ericka M. Williams

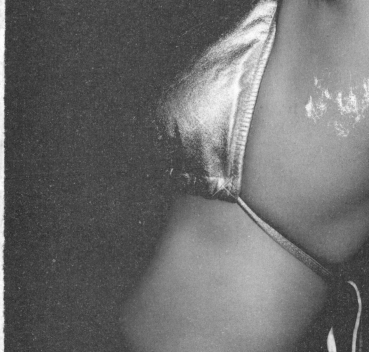

A Life Changing Book in conjunction with Power Play Media
Published by Life Changing Books
P.O. Box 423 Brandywine, MD 20613

Library of Congress Cataloging-in-Publication Data;

www.lifechangingbooks.net

ISBN - (10) 1-934230-94-4 (13) 978-1-934230-94-7
Copyright ® 2007

Dedication

Dedicated to Nadja Sydney Thompson
You were an Indian princess
In a world of your own
You stood out in a crowd
The world was your throne
How could you have left us
When your beauty was so fulfilling
Forget you, I did not
Salute you, I am willing
Thank God you were my cousin
You taught me, watched me grow
I will love you forever
My heart will never let you go

Until we meet again
I will think of you till the end

Michael Smith, you have been more than a friend, but a rock and a shoulder for me to lean on many times. Thank you, thank you!

To Nadja, I miss you tremendously and wish that you were still here.

Life, I love you too too much. You came into my life and gave me love when I needed it the most. I want to live my life with you. You know how to love me better. Thank you for our daughter Saniya.

Tori, you are the best son that a mother could ever ask for. Words cannot express how thankful I am for you and how much strength you have given me. You are a star.

Thanks to my new family at Life Changing Books. Azarel, what can I say. Thanks for helping me get this project together. I couldn't have done it without you. Leslie Allen, thanks for all your help as well. Davida Baldwin, thanks for the great cover. Leslie German, thanks for your great editing skills and advice. A special shout out goes to my publicist, Nakea Murry, and all the LCB authors. Anyone I forgot to mention, please forgive me.

To everyone, who did not judge or hate, but knew my heart and my loving spirit, thank you too. Blessings and Peace to all.

Ericka

Acknowledgements

First and foremost, I would like to thank my Lord and Savior Jesus Christ who chose me to love, cover, and keep. Being a child of God has given me the strength to share my trials and use them as a testimony to help others. I will never be ashamed. Nothing but the Blood has carried me thus far...thank You for my son, the light of my life next to You.

I would like to thank my mother, for being a strong woman and putting up with me as a daughter. I wish that we could have overcome our differences and been able to enjoy each other. Forgive me for all the pain I have caused you.

I would like to thank my father, for instilling in me to never give up and smile no matter what. I would like to thank my sister, Laura, for being a great example of a fly girl for me to follow in her footsteps. I would like to thank my brother, Deryle, for loving me beyond understanding.

I would like to thank all of my friends who have been true and supportive, who have stuck by me through the ups and downs, to name a few...Brigitte, Cynthia, Dee Dee, Erica, Grei, Jenturea, Karen, Kim Pauldon, Koko, Shelly R., Shelley S., Windy, Victor, and Clarence. To Anthony Griffith, thank you for all the scriptures. To Kendra and Lamartz, I love you both. To my godchildren, Simone, Sherelle, and Briana follow your dreams, I love you. My stepchildren Seven and Star, I love you both. To all the children in my life, I hope I have been an inspiration to you.

To all of my family, I wouldn't be me if I did not have a part of you in me. Family never dies.

Chapter 1

INSANITY

"I can't believe I'm going out with this fat, ugly-ass muthafucka," I mumbled to myself, hopping into Jarrod's car. *Damn, I've faked it before, but if I pull this one off, I'll deserve an Oscar.* I frowned and shook my head. Fuck it, I gotta do what I gotta do because my looks sure won't pay the bills. The more I stared at him, the more I thought about my rent being due in two days.

"Yo, Mika, what you wanna eat?" Jarrod asked.

I looked over at his fat ass and smiled. "Whatever, I'm not picky. Let's go to City Island."

I was gonna make him spend mega bucks for being so offensively gruesome. I really didn't care where I ate as long as there was a bar nearby, because I needed a drink badly. I planned on gettin' ripped, so that I wouldn't remember anything in the morning. I'd been out with ugly men before, but nothing could describe how ugly Jarrod was. The more I thought about his tar colored skin, big pink lips, and all the pimples that covered his face, the angrier I became. That's what I get for listening to my girl, Asia, who talked me into going out with him in the first place. I only agreed because she said Jarrod liked to spend money. So for now, I was gonna make sure I got more than just a lobster dinner and a bad view of his fucked up face.

"Why are you so quiet?" he grunted.

"I just got a lot on my mind."

The last thing I wanted to do was to hold a conversation

with him, so my plan was to talk to myself until we got to our destination. After several minutes of driving in silence, we finally pulled up to the restaurant. As we got out the car and walked toward the entrance, I noticed that he had on some corny ass played out Stacy Adams shoes, and they had the nerve to be multicolored and turned over. *What in the hell did I get myself into?* I couldn't wait to talk to Asia so I could curse her ass out for setting me up with this clown. Too bad I needed the money.

My night got even worse because as soon as we sat down at the restaurant, he started making cheap passes. The conversation was garbage and I couldn't wait to get the night over with. He kept saying, "So what's up with me and you?" and "I'll give you anything you want." I wanted to tell him, just give me a bag to put over your head, but I didn't want that to ruin my chances of gettin' some paper. It's nothin' wrong with a man who's not cute, if he had style, good conversation, or if he made me laugh, but this cat was straight dead. Besides, I loved an ugly man with finesse, 'cuz they normally treated you better than pretty boys, and they also made you feel like a queen. I was mad as hell at Jarrod for not havin' any game.

All throughout dinner, he continued to talk, but most of the time I just ignored him, hoping he would get the hint. When my food came, I made sure that I took several large bites, so I could finish quickly. The thought of being with him made me even sicker.

"Can we get a room? I just wanna spend some private time with you," he said, wiping his mouth with the cloth napkin.

"Sure, but time is money," I snapped.

He flashed a smile that still didn't make him look any better, "I got you."

After paying the bill, we headed straight to the Marriott hotel on 57th St. in Manhattan. I almost drank a whole bottle of Cristal on the way there, so I wouldn't be in my right frame of mind. The last thing I wanted was to remember

All That Glitters

fuckin' an over-groomed rat. The only thing about him that I liked was his brand new C Class Benz. Hell, I would rather make love to his car.

When we got the hotel, I sat down in the lobby and immediately covered my face. I didn't even want the hotel clerk to see me with this monster. The entire time he was at the front desk, I kept diggin' in my purse, like I was lookin' for something, and then I would put my head on the chair like I was exhausted. The clerk looked at me a few times, but I acted like I didn't feel well. I even played it off by rubbing my stomach a few times.

"Are you ready to go upstairs, baby?" Jarrod asked with a huge smile.

The sound of him calling me baby, instantly made me bite my lip. I didn't want to be called any fuckin' pet names. "Sure," I responded.

As soon as we got to the room, I was ready to make it happen, so I could bounce. I didn't want to waste any time on phony foreplay. I plopped down on the bed and instantly started taking off my clothes. When I glanced at him, he was staring at me and already breathing hard. I swear it looked like he was humping the bed the way he bounced up and down. Then, I almost passed out when he started licking his dry-ass lips. I thought, *damn, put your tongue back in your mouth, I'm not a piece of steak, you fat muthafucka.*

Several seconds later, he unzipped his pants and pulled out his dick. He must've thought I was gonna suck it, but he was sadly mistaken.

"Take your pants all the way off," I ordered. "And put this condom on while you're at it."

He tried his best to get me to put it on, but I wasn't try-ing to look at his dick, or even touch it for that matter. There was no way that thing wasn't gonna be covered up before going inside my treasure. I tried to make myself believe that I wasn't really gonna do it to him, but to the condom instead. Sadly, it didn't work.

Ericka M. Williams

3

I shook my head as he got butt-naked and exposed his ashy, flabby skin. His black ass was so flaky that I wanted to give him a bath in baby oil. It didn't make any sense that I was goin' out like this, but money is money and I had to have it. I didn't want him to get on top and give me a flake shower, so I stood up, pushed him on one of the full size beds, and jumped on top of his stiff dick.

Two minutes later he was sweating like a faucet. It was beyond disgusting. This was a hard one to fake. I just wanted him to hurry up and cum. He started putting me into different positions, and before I knew it, we were doing it doggy-style. All I heard was, "Ughhh…Damn, this pussy is good. Do you like that, baby?"

Between his dry ass skin that seemed to be fallin' off his body and the sweat that dripped on my back, I screamed to myself, "Hell no!" But before I could say anything, he gave one last moan and his body jerked continuously. *Damn, I'm glad he came.*

He finally pulled himself out and got up. I immediately jumped up as well and dashed to the bathroom with my clothes in hand, and got in the shower. I had to wash everything about him off my body. Twenty minutes later, I put my clothes back on and came out ready to make an excuse about having to leave. However, before I got a chance to speak, he was already dressed and said something that surprised the shit outta me.

"Yo baby, I got some business to take care of out of town, so take a cab home and I'll call you tomorrow. I wanna take you to a party my man is havin' in Virginia."

He kissed my cheek, dropped some money on the bed, and started walking toward the door. I was speechless. I never expected him to beat me to the door. "Hold up. You gonna make me take a cab all the way back to Jersey? Englewood is gonna be like fifty dollars."

He peeled off a few more bills from his stack and handed it to me. "Call me baby. I told you, I would take good care of you." He looked at me and smiled before he turned

All That Glitters

around and walked out the door.

Did he just try to play me? I wondered. That fat mutha-fucka. I was glad I didn't have to walk out of the hotel with him, even though I felt like he could've at least shot my ass home real fast. I'm sure he felt like he had one up on me. I snatched the money off the bed and started counting it. All together, I had seven one hundred dollar bills. My new small stack of money wasn't bad for fifteen minutes of pro-tected sex. I placed the money inside my purse, and walked out the room feelin' that my goal to make money had been accomplished. That was enough money to fuck him on a broke ass day. When I got to the lobby and walked outside to hail a cab, I thought about who I could get with next to get my phone bill paid.

I mentally ran through my contact list on the long ride home. I finally got to my house about four in the morning and Shani and my son, Kian were asleep. Even though I had taken a bath at the hotel, I decided to take a long, hot bath to scrub myself extra hard. After soaking for almost an hour, I dried myself off and applied my favorite lotion. I went to bed thinking how happy I was that I could finally pay something on time.

━━━━━━━━━

"Mommy, I'm hungry," my son said, waking me up. It felt like I had only slept five minutes. I rolled over and looked at the clock, which read 11:23 a.m. I put the pillow over my head and tried to act like I was still asleep. I loved my son, but sometimes the *motherhood thing* could be hectic. Deep down I knew the only reason why I had him in the first place was because his father and I were on the verge of breaking up. I wanted us to stay together. I thought the baby would make everything better, but it didn't, and now I couldn't stand his bitch-ass.

"Mommy, I'm hungry," Kian repeated. He got on the bed and lifted up the pillow.

Ericka M. Williams   5

"Kian, go ask Auntie Shani to make you some break-fast."

"Okay," he replied, running out the room.

Shani's my younger sister. We're four years apart and the complete opposite. I was considered the black sheep of the family, and she was the good one. She was also a Muslim, who'd never been involved with a street nigga, but I loved 'em of course. My mother always said that Shani had morals and respect, but I had another word for that, boring! Where's the drama? Where was the excitement? The fatal attractions? I loved my sister, but she made me sick. My mother thought that everything she did was right, which made the things I do- *all wrong*. I guess they didn't think partying all night was acceptable since all my sister did was attend classes for her law degree, work in her col-lege admissions office, and spend time with her boyfriend, Fuguan. Again, that life was boring as hell to me. Shani and I got along most of the time, except for when she for-got that she wasn't my damn mother.

As I continued to think about how she got under my skin, I fell back to sleep. A few hours later, I woke up to the sounds of Danny's voice in the living room. I wasn't in the mood to see his ass. *Shit, it's not even his weekend to keep Kian,* I thought. Danny loved to come over without calling like he still had it like that, which pissed me off. Knowing I had to deal with his ass was messing up my mood. I threw on some sweats and walked toward my door. The closer I got, the madder I became. I just didn't feel like seeing him today. I wished there was a way to get him completely out of my life, but unfortunately, I knew that wasn't gonna happen. He was Kian's father, so no matter what, I was stuck with the nigga for life.

When I walked into the living room, Danny was sitting on the floor playing with Kian, but I acted like he wasn't even there. I walked up to my son, bent over and kissed him on the forehead.

"Did you get something to eat?" I asked.

"Yep, Aunt Shani fixed me some Lucky Charms," he responded, throwing the ball back to his father.

I looked at Danny and rolled my eyes. He gave me a smirk. Danny knew he was good looking. I loved his tall 6'3' frame and medium build, but it was his charisma that made him even more attractive. His skin was dark as midnight. I thanked God everyday that Kian got my caramel complexion. Danny also had the gift of gab, and could talk the panties off a nun.

I strutted into the kitchen where Shani was doing her homework and sat down. "When did Blackie get here?"

She shook her head as if to say, "Here we go," and reported that he'd been here for over an hour.

"I told you that when he comes for Kian to let them go out. There's no reason for Danny to come in here."

Before Shani could respond, Kian came runnin' into the kitchen. "Mommy! Mommy! Daddy is gonna take me out to get some ice cream!" he said, excitedly.

"That's so special," I replied, giving a fake smile. I didn't want my son to know how much I hated his father. As soon as Kian ran back into the living room, Danny walked into the kitchen.

"What's up, Mika?" he asked. I ignored him, and didn't even look his way. "Mika Turner, what the fuck is wrong with you? You can't even say hello?"

"Obviously not," I snapped.

"You need to grow up, girl," he replied.

"Look stupid, if I wanted to speak I would've done that when I first saw your ass, so just leave me alone. I'm really not up for your shit today. Anyway, I told you when you want to see Kian, just come and get him. Don't lounge around here. Nobody else wants to see you but him, so either take Kian with you, or leave solo!"

"Why don't you stop acting like a bitch, and grow up for your son! You just mad 'cuz I don't want yo ass."

"You know what, get the fuck outta my house!" I yelled.

"Look, I know it's not my day to keep Kian, but I got

Ericka M. Williams 7

some family in town, and they want to see him. I'll bring him back tomorrow," Danny said, with authority.

Before I could respond, he turned around and walked out with me following close behind. "You better bring my son back first thing in the morning!" I screamed, as we walked into the living room.

Kian immediately started crying, and looked at me as if I'd done something wrong. Danny picked him up and walked out, slamming the door in the process. I ran to the door and opened it forcefully. "And don't be slamming my damn door!" I shouted.

"Mika, when are you two gonna stop acting like children? It's not right for Kian to always see you two at each other's throats," Shani said, walking up behind me.

I was so pissed off, that I slammed the door too. "I didn't hear you sayin' anything to Danny? How come you always preachin' to me? I'm not the only one."

"Because you're my sister and you know better. All this fighting is going to affect Kian." She watched as I paced back and forth. "Look, I know you and Danny still love each other, but neither of you want to admit it. Regardless, Kian is the one who's being hurt the most. One minute you're cursing each other out and the next he's spending the night. Watch, by next week you'll be telling me that Danny is taking you out to dinner."

I sucked my teeth and looked at my sister, who reminded me of a chubby, Vanessa Williams with her light brown hair and hazel eyes. "Shut up, Shani. Danny hasn't spent the night in months. I'm not messing with him anymore and I mean that." I continued to pace back and forth. "Every time I fall for his shit, I end up gettin' hurt. He always makes me think that he wants to get back with me just so I'll sleep with him. Fuck Danny!"

Shani looked at me and shook her head. I knew that meant she thought I was lying.

"You don't have to believe me, you'll see," I responded.

I walked out of the living room and back to my room

because I knew that I was getting ready to cry. I closed my bedroom door and turned on the radio. Ironically, *'No More Drama'* by Mary J. Blige was playing. Like I really needed to hear that song. I laid on the bed and looked up at the ceiling. A single tear rolled down my cheek and dropped into my ear. I started thinking about how close Danny and I used to be, and how now we were like strangers. When I saw Danny out in public, I acted like I didn't care about him, but in reality, I still loved him. As much as I didn't want to, I couldn't help it. I didn't want to be in a relationship with him, because I'd been down that road before. It's just that the feelings I had for him, wouldn't go away.

Even if we got back together, it would never be the same, so why bother. I spent six years of my life with him and it didn't work out. However, that hadn't stopped us from messing with each other every now and then. It had only been two months since we last slept with each other. We kept going back and forth, but never went all the way to commit to each other. It's hard to do that once you've let the relationship go. The foundation had been torn apart and it probably would never stand again. I should've listened to my mother when she told me that Danny wasn't gonna marry me in the first place. Unfortunately, I didn't believe her, but mothers always knew. I just knew Danny would always be by my side. No one could've convinced me that he would hurt me the way he did.

When we broke up over a year ago, I thought my life was over. I started buggin' out for a while, and when I started thinking about killing him, I knew I had to get it together. Luckily that's when Mark came into the picture. Mark was my boyfriend, but not officially. He wanted me to be his girl, but I couldn't commit to something like that because I still wanted to run the streets. He hated the fact that I went out with other dudes, but also knew it was all about gettin' paper.

The phone rang interrupting my thoughts. I didn't even bother to look at the caller ID before picking it up. "What's

Ericka M. Williams

up?" I answered.

"Why do you sound like that?" Mark asked. "Oh let me guess, Danny right?"

"Of course, he just left with Kian."

"You want me to come over?"

I let out a heavy sigh. "You already know."

"I'm on my way," Mark replied.

It's funny that me and Mark messed around in the first place because we were cool friends for so long. We used to work together, and I used to hang out with him and his ex-girlfriend all the time. When Danny and I were together, he really didn't pay Mark any mind since he didn't have any real paper. Being broke was a sign of a loser to Danny. He always trusted me with Mark, and didn't mind our friendship. Besides, Mark wasn't the type to mess with another man's girl anyway, but I always knew he liked me. When Danny and I broke up, he would come over every other day to make sure I was okay. He was there for me more than my friends and family were.

Then one day out of the blue, I took advantage of him. I didn't do it purposely, but I needed someone to take my mind off of Danny. Most men didn't want to hear your sob stories about your ex, but that's all Mark heard from me for at least three months. He listened and went through it with me, not once making a move. It got to the point where I began to wonder why he didn't. I guess I became attracted to him because of the fact that he wasn't sweating me.

After the first few months of staying in my room and crying all day and night, I started spending all my time with Mark. That first day we had sex, he didn't fuck me, he made love to me nice and slow, which was something I needed after all the drama with Danny. I realized, Mark accepted me for who I was and never complained, so I should've been ashamed for what I was taking him through. I loved him for being there for me, but honestly, I just didn't want to commit to him right now.

Forty minutes had passed, when suddenly my bedroom

door opened. I smiled as Mark walked in smelling good as usual. He always wore nice cologne, and kept a fresh hair cut. Like Danny, Mark had a tall 6"1' frame, but was slightly larger in size. I was glad he wasn't too muscular because dudes like that turned me off. I actually liked a little belly to rub and hold on to while I slept. He kind of reminded me of the singer, Tyrese a bit because his smile was so sexy.

Unfortunately, Mark's paper couldn't compare to Tyrese's or Danny's. I was used to shopping everyday and going to the nicest restaurants. Danny took good care of me, and spoiled me from the age of seventeen. I had all the latest designer bags, clothes, and iced out jewelry. Danny had even given me a 1996 sky blue 535-BMW when I graduated from high school. It was so hot, and I definitely thought I was the shit, but little did I know it didn't belong to me legally, because his slick ass had the car in his name. When we broke up, he stopped paying the payments because he knew I couldn't afford it. Since, the car note was $585.00 a month, I wasn't that interested in impressing people to make me and Kian starve just to drive it. So reluctantly, I gave the car back. I'd been walking and bumming rides ever since.

Mark, on the other hand, couldn't do shit like that for me. We did dinner and a movie every now and then, but shopping sprees were out of the question. His salary at UPS just didn't make it happen. Shit, he didn't even have a car himself. He usually had to drive his momma's car, when she gave it up.

Mark sat down beside me, and gave me a hug and a long kiss. He had those soft kissable LL Cool J type lips.

"What's wrong with you, why did you sound so evil on the phone?"

"I don't really feel like talking about it," I replied.

"Well, when you're ready to talk, let me know. Put this movie in," he said, handing me *Rush Hour 2*. We had probably seen the movie at least twenty times, but I didn't care. Chris Tucker always made me laugh and right now, I could use it. I refused to think about Danny's stupid ass anymore.

I stood up to put the movie in the DVD player, but as I started messing with the buttons, I suddenly began to get horny. I smiled to myself thinking, *I know this is gonna make his ass happy*. I stood in front of Mark, and did a sexy little dance before slowly taking my clothes off. Before long, I was standing in front of him exposing my perfect 130lb body. I wasn't voluptuous, but shapely enough to have a sexy pair of hips and a nice round ass.

"Do you like what you see?" I asked Mark, who had a wide smile.

"Hell yeah. You're so beautiful."

Before walking toward him, I grabbed the remote to my CD player and hit the power button. I didn't want Shani all in my business, so I knew the sounds of Omarion would drown out what was about to go down.

I walked over to Mark and took his sneakers and all of his clothes off. I then got on top of him and we immediately started kissing. He caressed and kissed me all over my body. I loved that he was so gentle. He always made sure I was satisfied. Mark was two years younger than me, but knew what to do in the bed. When we first started having sex, I thought he would be intimidated by me, but surprisingly he wasn't. At first, I used to treat him like a little boy, and didn't take him seriously at all. However, he quickly changed all that.

I looked down at his beautiful skin and ran my hands across his chest. I loved dark brown men. I wasn't prejudiced against light-skinned brothas, but there's just something about a ginger bread man. I wanted to melt his body and lick him off my fingers like a Hershey's kiss. As soon as Mark began to softly lick my nipples, I was startled by a knock on my door.

"What?" I screamed. I knew it was my annoying sister.

"I'm going to the store!" Shani yelled.

"So what Shani? Damn, aren't you grown?" I couldn't believe she'd interrupted us to tell me that shit.

All That Glitters

"Well, can I borrow a few dollars? I didn't get paid yet," she replied.

I can't believe this shit. I knew if I tried to ignore her she would continue to knock on the door, so I jumped off the bed, reached in my purse and grabbed three dollars. I was pissed as I opened the door slightly and tossed the bills out.

"If that's not enough, too bad. Next time don't interrupt me," I said, closing the door. I wasn't sure about Mark, but the mood had disappeared for me. When I looked at him, he gave a slight smile. I guess he already knew the outcome.

"Put the movie in, baby," he said.

Two hours later, I looked over at Mark who was sleeping like a baby and probably dreaming about Halle Berry. That thought instantly took me back to the night before when I had a dream about Mark and Danny.

In my dream, it was a sunny day and me, Mark, and Danny were walking down the street. The two of them were on each side of me and I was holding each one of their hands. We stopped at the corner to wait for the light to change, and I turned to Danny and gave him a kiss. Then, I did the same to Mark. We were all laughing and talking before walking into a jewelry store, where they both started looking at engagement rings, and before long both of them were on one knee.

I started laughing, and I couldn't believe I had a crazy dream that I was with both of them and that they both wanted to marry me. My best friend, Asia would probably say, I should try it for real. I think everyone at one time in their life, has been in love with two people at the same time. It was hard because Danny and Mark each had qualities that I liked. I just wished I could pick out the good qualities in both and make one perfect man. I would be straight. I guess life would be too easy if we could do that. *I'm always in love with two men at the same time.* I guess it was good to keep one on standby. Then, to top it off, I was also dating guys just for what I could get out of them. Some might say there's a name for a woman like that, but I didn't consider myself a prostitute. I was only twenty-four years old and just having fun. *Shit, you only live once.*

At that moment, the phone rang. "Hello," I said quietly. I didn't want to wake Mark up.

"I'm pickin' you up in ten minutes. Boogie got a friend for you to meet," Asia announced.

"I can't go, Mark is here sleep."

"He's sleep?" she asked loudly into the receiver.

"Yeah, didn't I just say that," I responded in a low tone. I didn't want Mark to wake up and try to get me to stay in the house like he normally did.

"I don't care. Be downstairs in ten minutes," Asia ordered.

I thought about it for a moment and decided not to miss out on any potential money. I couldn't afford to do that any-way. "Hurry up, but I can't stay long." I knew Mark was gonna kill me.

I snuck into the bathroom and quickly got dressed. I put on a pink Akademics sweat suit with some Icey White Nikes. My reddish brown hair was in twists going back into a long ponytail, so at least I didn't have to worry about that. I changed my hair color every six months and got a fresh weave, or different style every few weeks. Keeping a new do was a must.

Within ten minutes, I was dressed and out front waiting for Asia to come pick me up. Asia was wild as hell, and really didn't give a fuck about anything. That's why she couldn't keep a man. Hell, I didn't even think she wanted a man. From all the shit Asia did, she made me look like an angel. I couldn't blame her for what went down in my life, because I chose to run with her. It wasn't like she was pulling my arm.

When I first smoked weed at the age of twelve, it was compliments of Asia. At fifteen, when I took my first drink, Asia was making the drinks in her basement. She was Bad

Girl #1 and I was proud to admit that I was Bad Girl #2.

A few minutes later, Asia pulled up to my house and we headed to One Fish, Two Fish on 96th and Madison, in Manhattan. Once we arrived, the nigga I met, named True, was cool. He was laid back, not arrogant or cocky, and I liked that, but he just wasn't my type. We sat separately from Boogie and Asia, and made small talk about current events in the news and the entertainment industry. Near the end of dinner, he asked the famous question, "So do you have a man?"

"No, why?"

"Because I like your conversation and I want to take you out again," he answered.

"What's your situation?" I asked. I wasn't really interested in him like that, but I was just making conversation. His light complexion just didn't do it for me.

"My girl still lives with me, but she's about to move out."

I shook my head. "I've heard that too many times. How come men don't wait until the girl moves out before they try to move another girl in?"

He got up and sat next to me in the booth. I surely wasn't going to faint, he didn't have that type of effect on me.

"I'll make her leave tonight if you want me to."

I was really turned off now, with a capital T. "You would do that just for me?" I asked.

"You wanna come home with me and see? She ain't gonna be there tonight anyway."

That blew it. "No, I gotta go. My son is at home waiting for me." I stood up and gave Asia the signal without even giving him a chance to respond. "Asia, come on I gotta go home to Kian."

She looked at me and smiled. She knew once I said that, I wasn't feeling the dude who I was with. I didn't even bother to tell my date goodbye before I got up and walked out the restaurant.

On the way home, Asia told me about a girl she knew, who took True up on that offer once before and that they

Ericka M. Williams

had gotten a surprise visit by his girl, who he thought was still out of town. I could've punched myself for leaving Mark for that bullshit. I punched Asia on her arm for not telling me that shit earlier.

"Don't set me up with any more losers like that," I said, opening up the car door once we reached my house. "Especially if they look like a member of the fuckin' Debarge family. I prefer a mocha type of dude."

"Shit you're crazy. The only color you should be interested in is green," Asia replied.

"Shut up and call me later," I replied shutting the car door.

When I walked in my room, Mark was laying in the bed watching TV. He looked like he was mad at the world. I walked over to the bed, and bent down to give him a kiss that he didn't return.

"I didn't want to wake you up," I pleaded.

"Mika, why you gotta be so full of shit?" Mark asked.

"Baby, you were sleep, so I just went out with Asia for a few. What's the problem?" I asked, knowing I was dead wrong.

"The problem is that you have somebody who loves you, treats you right, and respects you right here, but that's not enough for you." His voice cracked a little, but if he knew what was good for him he better not start crying. I couldn't deal with a man who was too soft.

"Mark, don't start." I wasn't in the mood to hear this shit. "I only went out to eat."

"Mika, you think 'cause you look good, and all these niggas be sweatin' you, that you ain't gotta respect anybody."

"No, we look good. Don't we make a cute couple? We look like Tyrese and Halle Berry." I tried to pacify him.

He looked at me with disgust. "Mika, I wish you would stop letting these niggas fool you into thinkin' they'll treat you any different than they do all their other chicks. They don't give a fuck about you."

All That Glitters

"I don't give a fuck about them neither, but I do give a fuck about you." I slid in the bed next to him.

"Whatever Mika, keep searching the streets for what you already got, and the streets will be all you end up with."

"Yeah a'ight. Are you threatening me?" I said jokingly, and pulled his shaft out of his boxers.

Despite me holding on to his dick, he didn't crack a smile. "You'll see."

He could act mad all he wanted, but I knew he wasn't gonna stop me. "No, you'll see that I'm about to make it leak." I put his dick in my mouth and sucked like a pro, until I made it squirt.

Chapter 2

TRAPPED

The next morning, I was awakened by a knock on my door. When I sat up and looked at the clock it was only 8:15 a.m. *Damn, what does Shani want now?* I looked over at Mark, who was still knocked out next to me and completely naked. I pulled the covers over him, threw on a T-shirt, and opened the door. My face almost turned white when I saw Danny standing in front of me with Kian. I didn't know what to do. Before he could walk in, I stepped out and closed my bedroom door behind me.

"Hey baby," I said to Kian, giving him a kiss on his forehead. I slid my hand through his curly hair, while trying my best to ignore the strange stares from Danny.

"Why are you looking so crazy? You got a nigga in your bed or something?" Danny asked.

"That's none of your damn business. Why?"

At that moment, Shani came out of her bedroom and took Kian by the hand. "Can you two converse in a civilized manner please?" she said, as she took Kian into her room.

No sooner than she closed her door, Danny grabbed my arm and pulled me down the hall into the living room. I tried to pull away several times, but didn't have any success. *Damn, I didn't want him to know about me and Mark.*

"Look at the type of shit you do in front of my son, Mika! I don't want him seeing a whole bunch of bare-assed niggas walking around here. So if you're gonna be trickin', take yo ass to a hotel," Danny shouted, pushing me onto

All That Glitters

the couch.

I couldn't believe the nerve of his stupid ass. I wanted to punch him in the face, but we definitely would've been fighting.

"Wait a muthafuckin' minute! Who are you to tell me what to do in my own muthafuckin' house? Do you pay rent up in here?"

"Yeah I do. You pay your rent from all the muthafuckin' money I give your ass every month!" he yelled.

He was an asshole, but he was partially right. "Well, you don't tell me what to do in my house. Do I know how many hoes you be havin' up in your joint? Don't worry about what the fuck I do!"

I got up to go back in my room, but he body slammed me on the floor. He was leaning over me and was about to slap me, but I started scrambling around on the floor trying to get away. "Get the fuck off me!" I started screaming.

Something must have crossed his mind because he instantly took his hands off of me. I guess he didn't want to risk Kian seeing him. As he looked at me like I was crazy, I could see Mark approaching us, but I didn't say anything. However, Danny must've felt his presence and quickly turned around. When he noticed it was Mark, he backed away from me and started laughing.

"Get the fuck outta here. You and Mark are fuckin'? Wow! Mika, are you doin' charity work now?"

I looked at Danny and rolled my eyes, but didn't respond. I also looked at Mark who only had on a pair of boxers. *Why the fuck did he come out here like that?*

"So have y'all been fuckin' the whole time? I thought you were just friends?" Danny asked. He took a few more steps back and looked back and forth from me to Mark. I watched as he opened and closed his fists a few times. At that point, I wasn't sure what was about to go down. "This is funny. I guess you been playin' the nice guy role, huh? Make a nigga think you won't try his girl," Danny continued as he stared at Mark with a scowl.

Ericka M. Williams

Mark definitely seemed to be at a loss for words. I thought Danny was gonna try to play the tough guy role and smash Mark. Instead, he went from thinking it was funny to fronting like he didn't care.

"Maybe you should leave now," I suggested to Danny.

He ignored me and tried to intimidate Mark with words. He instantly started talking like he was Tony Soprano. "Mark man, I don't think you should get involved with this here because it doesn't concern you, and I would hate for you to have a problem with me, kid. You can fuck Mika all you want, that's old pussy to me, but we're gonna have a problem if you disrespect my son." His head moved up and down, while he continued to open and close his fist.

I couldn't believe he was talking about me like that. I was also surprised when Mark held his ground. Danny's reputation had a lot of niggas intimidated.

"Danny, I would never disrespect Mika or Kian. But, I'm not feelin' you disrespectin' your son's mother. That's like disrespectin' your son."

Danny looked annoyed. "Mark, you over steppin' your boundaries, nigga. How I talk to Mika is not your fuckin' concern."

Mark continued to stand his ground. His facial expression remained stern. "Mika is my concern."

Danny laughed again like Mark was being a fool.

"And…just so you know, I wouldn't let Kian see anything that he shouldn't see. He's never even seen me and Mika in bed together," Mark replied.

Danny really looked like he was trying to hide the fact that he was hurt. "You a fuckin' hoe, Mika," he said, as he turned, walked out, and slammed the door.

I tried to stay calm and told Mark that I needed some time alone to talk to Kian. I wanted to make sure he was all right. Mark obliged, got dressed, and I told him that I would call him later.

He probably hadn't even gotten in his car yet before I started crying. I was hysterical. I went to my room, jumped on the bed and buried my head in the pillow. I knew Danny was right about me exposing my son to a lot of different men. Even though Mark was the only one I was having sex with, after Kian went to sleep at night, it still wasn't right. Besides, Kian thought Mark and I were just friends. I was guilty of hanging out and partying sometimes, but I didn't expose my son to just anything.

Plus, I was always too scared to do anything. I didn't want to jeopardize my chances of someday getting back with Danny. Just in case. I knew if he thought that I was sleeping with a lot of men he would never get back with me. Even when he heard rumors about me talking to a dude, I always denied it.

I started thinking about what Danny said, and went from feeling sad and guilty to feeling angry. *Damn, did he mean what he said about me? Or is he just jealous? Things between us just keep getting worse and worse.* So much shit had happened that I didn't think there was a Band-Aid big enough to fix the scars that had been put on our relationship. Lord knows I wish there was. I quit feeling sorry for myself and went into Shani's room to check on my son. Surprisingly, Kian was calm. Shani had her TV up extra loud so he must not have heard me screaming.

"Baby, you okay?" I asked.

"Mommy, I want you and Daddy to stop arguing. Who was that in your room?" Kian asked innocently.

Even though I was shocked that he asked me that question, I wasn't gonna lie to him. "That was my friend, Mark."

"Mark was in the bed with you, Mommy?"

"No, we were watching movies late last night and I fell asleep on the bed, so he slept on the floor. You know Mark is my best friend like Asia, but he's a man." So much for not lying.

"I think he likes you," Kian asked, looking like a darker version of Ginuwine.

"Look boy, that's enough. I'm gonna go take a shower

then take you outside. Is that alright with you or do you have more grown folks questions for me?"

He jumped up and down on Shani's bed. "Yaaay. I wanna go to the park."

"I know you do. You would live in the park if you could."

"Only if you would live there with me, Mommy."

"Wherever you go, I go. Do you love your Mommy?" He nodded yes. "And I love you more than the whole world." I hugged him and left the room. I didn't even bother to look at Shani because I wasn't in the mood for her shit.

I took a shower and got dressed. While we were at the park, my plan was to talk to Kian a little bit more about his feelings. I'd been so wrapped up in my own pain about Danny, that I hadn't even thought about how all this was probably affecting Kian. My son was the one who really kept me strong and also kept me going because I knew I had to be there for him.

When I walked into the living room, Shani had already gotten Kian dressed. When I looked down, my innocent looking son was playing on the floor with one of his cars. Sometimes he seemed like a child, while other times he acted like an old man.

"Mommy, are you okay?" Kian asked, looking up at me.

"Yes baby. Are you ready to go outside?"

He nodded yes and quickly jumped up. I put on his shoes and coat, and we walked outside hand in hand. He looked so cute in his Sean John wind breaker, a baseball cap and Jordan sneakers. As we got on the elevator, I stared at him and smiled. He looked just like me and his father.

On the way out of the building, my crack-head neighbor, Kiki held the door open for us. I gave her a dollar and told her that she should apply for a job as a doorman since she was always doing it. All I got in return was a huge laugh.

It was a nice day out and as soon as I felt the sun sweep across my face, I started feeling better. I grabbed my baby's hand and thanked God for him. As we started

All That Glitters

walking to the park, I thought about what I would say to him about me and his father, but as usual he beat me to it.

"Mommy, why are you and Daddy always arguing? Do you love my Daddy?"

I wanted to say, "Because your father is a bastard who ain't worth shit." Instead I said, "Because sometimes people don't agree on things. Me and your Daddy are not the same. He's one way and I'm another. Now don't get me wrong, we love each other, but we don't like each other anymore." I realized that I sounded just like my mother when she told me the same thing as a child about my own father.

"Well, grownups are supposed to know how to act and you and Daddy don't know how to act and it gets on my nerves." I couldn't help but laugh. "So could you stop acting like that?" he added.

I lied to my son for the second time in one day, and told him we would try. I picked him up, put him on the swing and started pushing. When he got high in the air, I sat on the swing next to him and smiled. He looked so content and happy to be with his mother.

I thought back to when I first got pregnant. I really didn't know what I was getting myself into. Even after I had Kian, I still had it easy because my mother was still living in the apartment with me. She would always watch Kian for me while I went out, which gave Danny and I a lot of time for ourselves. We always used to go out to parties together, and were known as the party couple. Everything was beautiful for the first three years of Kian's life, and believe it or not, we were a real family.

Then, when my mother moved out and gave me the apartment, I was stuck in the house, and Danny started showing his true colors. He started doing his thing with other females because he always knew where I was. Shani was living on campus in undergrad, so I didn't have anyone to watch Kian, and everything changed, drastically. Danny turned into a male hoe. He gave me so many problems

Ericka M. Williams

that when Shani moved back home, I decided not to move with him like we'd planned. He eventually used that as an excuse to break up with me. The only good thing is that he never neglected Kian; he's always spent time with his son, and gave me money to support him.

"Mommy let's go on the Merry-Go-Round!" Kian said, interrupting my thoughts.

I took him off the swing and raced him to the next ride. He sat down and I told him to hold on tight while I spun it around. My beautiful baby was laughing and having so much fun. When he smiled, I saw Danny's face, and at that moment, I was happy too. It felt good not to have any serious issues on my mind. I looked at Kian and immediately felt safe. It may have been backwards, but I felt like he would protect me.

"Kian, are you ready to go home?" I asked.

"No, can we walk to McDonalds?"

Before I could answer, I heard several kids talking loudly. I turned around to see who the kids were and noticed it was crack-head, Kiki and her clan; she had two boys and a girl. I felt so sorry for those kids. They always looked dingy and starved. Their clothes were too small and their hair was never combed. *What a shame.*

When Kian ran over to play with them, Kiki came over and sat by me, and automatically started her shit. "Ooh Mika, your hair looks so nice." Crack-heads always seem to compliment you all the time, like you were gonna give them money for making you feel good.

"Thanks Kiki," I responded.

She said that she wanted me to take her to get her hair done because her man would be getting out of jail soon. She was getting high with him when he was home, but he would do all the robbing and stealing to support their habit. Now, she was the one out on the street selling her body. Even though, I was looking at her, I wasn't really listening to her eight million stories. It bothered me to see the way she looked. I didn't like to see people in bad situations, especially when they had kids. I always wondered how they got like that. Kiki was pretty back in the day too. A lot of guys liked her, but I guess she just got hooked up with the wrong person.

Looking at her situation made me look back on some of the guys I'd messed with in the past, and most of them were in jail. Two of them were dead, both murdered. Niggas always got caught up in the game and ended up dead or in jail. My mother always told me I must've had a death wish because of all the danger that I constantly surrounded myself with.

I realized that I was daydreaming while Kiki continued to ramble on about nothing. At that moment, I finally got the urge to ask her something that I wanted to ask for a long time. I just wasn't sure how to put it. "Kiki, do you realize what you've done to yourself?" I asked her.

At first she looked at me like she knew exactly what I was talking about. It was almost as if I had hit a nerve, but then she played the dumb role. "Mika, what are you talkin' 'bout girl?"

"I'm just sayin' Kiki, how long have you been smokin'? And I don't mean weed." At first I thought she was gonna lie and say that she'd quit.

"Uhm, I guess about eight years. Since I was about eighteen, but it's been off and on," she responded, in a trembled voice.

I thought to myself, *off and on my ass.* "So do you realize what you've done to yourself? I mean do you look in the mirror and see how your cheeks are sunken in? You must realize how skinny you are when you take your clothes off. What's going through your mind?"

"Mika, I don't even pay attention no more," she said, with her head down.

"Damn Kiki, how can you do this to yourself?" I felt myself getting upset and wondered why she didn't seem to care. I couldn't understand how she could be so taken over by drugs that she could ignore the fact that she was

Ericka M. Williams

destroying not only her own life, but her kids lives as well.

She replied very nonchalantly, "Mika, everybody goes through shit and has downfalls, but I'm getting myself together. When I'm ready to stop I'll stop." She was getting defensive. "I don't know why everybody has to be in my business all the damn time. It's my fucking life! If I wanna smoke, I can smoke can't I?"

I had this crazy look on my face, but didn't speak.

She stood up. "Mika, when you get a taste of the base then you can talk to me, but until then you can't criticize me! I haven't met anyone yet that only smoked crack one time. I know a seventy year old woman who was so upset that her grandson was addicted, she tried it herself. She couldn't believe a drug could be powerful enough to make someone steal from their family. Ask me where that lady is now. Grandma is on the corner, suckin' dick for crack. Crack will have you out there too, Mika. Shit, do you wanna try it? I'm gettin' ready to cop some in a minute."

This bitch has lost her mind. "Kiki, there ain't no helping you, so smoke 'till you muthafuckin' choke, I don't give a fuck."

"Fuck you Mika," Kiki replied.

I looked at her with rage. "I don't know who would fuck your dirty stankin' ass anyway." I had no idea the conversation would end on that note, but I had to let her have it because she had some nerve talking to me like that. Plus she looked like the walking dead. I could never walk around dirty like that. *Addiction is a muthafucka.* My mother always told me that she thought I was addicted to dick and she was right. I surely can't do without it.

I told Kian we had to go and we started walking out of the park. After walking a few short blocks, we ended up at his favorite place, McDonalds. As we sat down with our food and started talking, I asked him what he wanted to be when he grew up and he said he wanted to be like the rapper, Game. All I could do was shake my head. It wouldn't have been so bad if he would've said, Will Smith because even though he used to rap, his paper was extremely long. But no, my son wanted to be like 'Mr. Blood Nation' himself. *Damn. Shani said that I let him watch too many rap videos.* For once, I knew my sister was right and from now on he was gonna watch re-runs of 'Mister Rogers.'

All of a sudden, I heard a loud voice from behind. "There's my boyfriend!"

I turned around and saw Asia walking toward us. When she reached the table, she bent down and planted a huge kiss on Kian's cheek before sitting down. "Hey girl, I was coming from doing my laundry when I saw you and Key come in here."

I let out a slight laugh at the nickname she gave my son. "Asia, I have to tell you about the shit that went down this morning."

Before she could respond, Kian butted in. "Mommy, Daddy said you shouldn't curse in front of me and if you do I should tell him. But don't worry, I won't tell him okay?"

I looked at Kian and bit my bottom lip. I wanted to tell him where his Daddy could go, but I wasn't in the mood to even think about his father. "Anyway Asia, I got mad things to tell you. Do you see this? My own son is telling me what to do...so what's up for tonight? I need to get out and have a drink, or two, or four, because my life is in shambles right now. It's mad hectic."

Kian interrupted again, "Mommy and Mark was in the room and Daddy and me came home and Daddy got mad and left and..."

"Shut up boy! And don't go telling your grandmother either. He loves telling my mother all my business," I said to Asia. She covered her mouth and busted out laughing. I couldn't help but laugh myself at his grown ass. "I guess I'll just have to tell you the story later."

"It's cool, girl. I can see you got a news anchor sittin' right here," Asia responded.

After Kian and I finished our food, we all headed outside only to see that Asia had a brand new rental car sitting out front, compliments of her new cat, Tippie. I knew she would tell me the story of her latest caper later on. She took me and Kian home and said she would pick me up around ten o'clock. We were going to a cook-out after party that our girl, Angel had told her about in the city.

I was sick of the parties in Jersey. If we hung out in Jersey, it was mostly at the little local bars, where every-body knew your name, like fuckin' 'Cheers'. Not to mention, everybody knew your business; and even worse there were probably rumors that I had sex with at least one per-son in each bar. On the other hand, when we go to the city we act up, because even though we knew a few people, we didn't have to worry about going home and hearing about what we did or how we were acting. It's a small world, so a lot of Uptown people from Harlem knew people right over the GW Bridge in Englewood, Hackensack and Teaneck.

I was feeling real good as I walked in the house, and was definitely looking forward to the party. I still didn't feel like talking to Mark, so when Shani told me he called, I just shrugged my shoulders. I didn't want to think about any men at that moment.

Shani was in the living room with her boyfriend, Fuquan when I walked in. Fuquan wasn't what I would call a sex symbol, but they made a nice couple. Besides, he was a good dude. Both Fuquan and Shani kind of looked alike with their pale complexions.

Kian rushed to the floor with some of his toys, and I sat on the loveseat, across from the happy couple. I called them that because they never argued, which made me sick. But I knew it was just a front. They probably cursed each other out when no one was around. However, I did like being around them sometimes because we had good conversations. Fuquan always enlightened me on the ways of worldly men, as he called them. He used to be a man of the world, but now he was a Muslim and had removed him-self from this mixed up society. He always had an answer for everything, so we debated all the time.

"So Mika, have you captured your rich prince yet?" he asked, sarcastically.

I rolled my eyes. "No, I haven't and I'm not looking for one either. I've decided to come up with my own get rich plan so that I don't have to depend on a man for the rest of my life. Besides, I'm through with those no good creatures called men. The only man in my life is going to be my son."

He opened his eyes wide. "Is this Mika talking? You mean the hunt is off? Don't tell me that you, of all people, have been defeated. I thought for sure by now you would've been living in a big house somewhere, with maids and cooks! Where's the man who's supposed to take care of you for the rest of your life?" Fuquan questioned.

"No, I haven't been defeated. I just took myself out of the rat race. I'm tired of competing with women for niggas who ain't worth shit no way."

"Exactly. See, you're wasting your time with the type of men you're dating because they'll never do anything for you," he responded.

What's wrong with waiting for a nigga drenched in diamonds and platinum? I thought.

Shani had to add her two cents, of course. "Don't listen to Mika, baby. She had a bad experience this morning, so now she hates men again. Ask her the same thing tomorrow, after she goes out tonight, and see what she says. I bet it'll be a different story." She stood up and started imitating me. "Ooh Shani, you should've seen the nigga I met at the party last night. He took me out to breakfast after the party. He's so cute...He got...He lives...Yeah, I'm gonna get this one!"

I threw a pillow at her and we all started laughing. I knew she was right. But that was okay because one day I was gonna really mean what I said to Fuquan. One day, I was gonna really be ready to give up on these sorry ass men and take care of myself. I just had to get my master plan in order first.

Ericka M. Williams

"Hey Shani, speaking of going out, can you watch Kian tonight? I wanna go get something to eat with, Asia." I knew by me asking her in front of Kian, she wouldn't say no. She loved her nephew to death.

Shani looked at me and shook her head. "Yeah, I guess," she said reluctantly.

"Don't waste your time tonight, sister," Fuquan added.

"I don't plan on it, *brother*," I responded.

We sat in the living room talking and watching old school videos when Bobby and Whitney's 'We Got Somethin' in Common' came on. "Isn't it a shame how money always marries money? They both should've married somebody poor, so it could've been four black rich folks instead of two. Black people have to start helping each other. I would have gladly married him to help the struggle!" I joked.

Fuquan let out a slight laugh. "I bet you would've, but only for the cause, right Mika?"

"Of course! Power to the People!" I responded, with my fist held high in the air.

Suddenly, the phone rang and when I looked at the caller ID, it was my mother calling.

"Hi Ma," I said.

"Mika Turner, can you tell me why you had a man in your bed when your son came home this morning?" she yelled in the phone.

I immediately gave Shani a dirty look. Whenever my mother called me by my first and last name, I knew trouble was brewing. "Because I didn't know that Danny was gonna bring Kian home that early." I knew we were getting ready to argue, so I went in my room. I was tired of Kian always having to hear me argue with someone. I walked in my room and shut the door. "Calm down, it was only Mark, Ma."

"Oh well at least it wasn't one of your hoodlums that you like to ride around and get shot at with."

What the fuck is she talking about? "Ma, I've never

been shot at in a car or anywhere else, and nobody says hoodlum anymore," I replied. "Can you stop acting like I'm such a bad mother?"

"When you stop thinking it's all about you then I will. Do you have any respect for yourself, Mika?"

I rubbed my temples back and forth. "Yes, I do. I would never do anything wrong in front of Kian."

"But if his mother goes to jail that will be fine for him won't it? He won't be hurt will he?" she asked.

What in the hell is she talking about? "What am I going to jail for, Ma? Look, you can say I'm a bad mother all you want, but I know I'm a good mother. I may go out sometimes, but I do spend time with Kian. Did you spend time with me when I was growing up?" I knew that was gonna hit a nerve.

"Are you crazy, Mika? Yes I did! Until your no good father lost everything and I had to work my ass off. You'll never be the mother that I was!"

"I hope not! Because whatever Danny does to me, I'll never take that out on my son! And you and Shani can kiss my ass!" I yelled as I hung up the phone. At that moment, I couldn't believe I'd just said those words to my mother. If she was in front of me, she would've smacked the shit outta me. But I was tired of being treated like a misfit. *Shit, I'm not crack-head ass, Kiki.*

Chapter 3

PARTY TIME

I put Kian to bed around ten o'clock, jumped in the shower, and did my hair. By the time Asia came it was eleven thirty, and I'd just finished getting dressed. We were both dressed for a mid-September chilly evening, and ready to show out. I had on a Lady Enyce jean suit and Asia wore a pair of tight Mecca jeans, which showed off her round plump ass. Asia had more ass than I did, but her face wasn't as pretty as mine, or so *I've been told*. She had that Spanish look going on because her mother was black and her father was Dominican. Asia was my girl, so I wasn't hatin' on her. It's just that her body got her the attention that my face got me. However, her huge 38D breasts made my 36C's look like raisins.

We decided to go to Ray's, a local bar, for drinks before heading to NYC. Asia and I knew a lot of people, so when we walked inside, major hellos had to be said before sitting down. We found a table in the back and ordered two Long Island Iced Teas. Just as I downed my drink, Danny's friend, Rodney, came over and sat down with us. He'd been trying to get with Asia for the longest time, but she couldn't stand him.

"What's going on, Ladies? Mika how've you been?" Rodney asked.

He gave me a sympathetic kiss on the cheek; the way you do a person who was mourning the death of a loved one. I guess he figured I was still mourning the loss of

Danny. His friends always did that, like they felt bad for me, about the way shit went down between us. I knew they were full of shit though. They were the first ones tellin' him to leave me. They were the ones who put in his head that he had other pussy sweatin' him, so he didn't need to be stressin' over the drama with me. They were the pussies, two-faced bastards. I didn't even feel like sitting near his wack ass, so I told him I was fine and lied about having to go to the bathroom. I picked up my drink and did the head jerk to tell Asia to come on. She immediately gave me a dirty look for leaving her with Rodney, and was right on my trail within seconds. I headed to the bar to get someone to buy me another drink. The one and only drink I planned to buy for myself was almost gone. As I approached the bar, I saw some forbidden fruit.

It was another one of Danny's friends. I received another, *I'm sorry your man fucked you over and left you like that* kiss on the cheek. However, this was one kiss I didn't mind getting. Jeff was one of Danny's friends who I always thought was fine and sexy. I would never disrespect myself by messing with him, but I wish I could, just once. Like Luther Vandross said, *If Only For One Night.* We did flirt with each other often, and I knew he would take it if I ever offered. I knew Jeff had a thing for me even when I was with Danny, but I just couldn't do that. I'd be playing myself.

"Mika, what are you drinking?" Jeff asked. He was looking at me with that, *come on, just let me get that once* look. I knew that wouldn't be a one time only deal if I went there with him, so it was best to leave well enough alone.

"Yeah handsome, lemme get a Long Island Iced Tea. Asia wants one too." I turned around and saw her looking dead in my face. Her expression said, she would've smashed her glass up against my head if I hadn't gotten her one. She knew how we rolled.

"Asia can get a drink only 'cuz you asked," Jeff said, loud enough for her to hear.

"Fuck you Jeff, you just mad cause I won't give you no

Ericka M. Williams

pussy," Asia shouted. "You wanna be all up in Mika's face, but when she ain't around you always all up in mine." She put her empty glass on the bar and turned her back to us.

"Mika, you know Asia is crazy, right?" he said defensively. I just ignored him and waited for my drink cause I knew he tried to talk to her when I wasn't around. *He ain't gotta front for me, 'cuz I won't be giving him any pussy.*

When our drinks came, he passed me my glass, and I passed Asia hers. I started sipping and within minutes, I felt a little buzzed. I wasn't drunk, but I was on my way.

"Mika, let's go back. Rodney is holding the table," Asia said.

"Cool," I responded.

We walked toward the back of the bar with Jeff following closely behind me. The moment Asia sat back down, Rodney leaned over and whispered something in her ear. She looked at me, and rolled her eyes; she was in no way interested in his shit.

Jeff started talking to me about his girl that I'd met when he and Danny did the double date thing, and kept saying how they'd just broken up. I was hoping he didn't bring up Danny and his new girlfriend, who I kept hearing about. I didn't want my evening to be spoiled.

All of a sudden Asia started tapping me. I turned around and who was coming through the crowd, but Danny himself. Him and a bitch! I felt a warm sensation come over me. I didn't know what to do, but I knew I couldn't let him see me sweat. He had the nerve to come right up to the table holding the hood rat's hand. He gave his friends a pound and said, "What's up Mika?"

I looked at him with murder in my eyes, "If you don't get the fuck out of my face, I'm gonna show you what's up muthafucka." As usual I blew my cool, but at least I didn't yell and make a scene. After I said that, he smiled and told us all to have a good evening as he walked away gripping his hood rat's ass.

Before I could say a word, Asia started carrying on, "Uh

uh! I don't believe him! No he didn't bring that bitch right up in your face."

I just loved when my friends rubbed shit in, like I needed salt for my wound. "Asia do me a favor and don't even talk about it because I'm two seconds from starting a scene up in here. I hate his stupid ass, trying to act like he's the muthafuckin' man!"

"Keep your head up," Jeff whispered in my ear. "Don't even sweat it. You know all he wants you to do is start a scene and make a fool of yourself. Just play it cool, beautiful. Act like you don't give a fuck, just like he just did."

For some reason, I felt like he was trying to play both sides. But I wish I could've taken his advice because I hated the fact that Danny could always get a reaction out of me. I always got emotional around him and he loved it. He knew I still loved him and that's why he thought he could do anything to me. Now, I knew he was the enemy. His ass wasn't interested in protecting my feelings, just hurting them.

Asia and I got up and went back to the bar. After seeing Danny and that bitch, I needed another drink. It was Asia's turn to get somebody to purchase the next round. As we walked up, Tubby Troy, the Ladies Toy was standing there.

"Hey Troy, you lookin' cute tonight. Why don't you get me and Mika two Long Island Iced Teas?" Asia said, in her sweetest voice.

"Where's my kiss?" he grilled. "With your sexy self."

She kissed him on the lips and whispered something in his ear. Within seconds, he was smiling from ear to ear and turned around to order our drinks. Being that this was my third drink, I knew I was headed for disaster. We waited for our drinks and posted up by the bar for a few minutes to see what else was poppin'. As we stood there, two old dudes, who looked to be in their fifties tried to step up and start a conversation. When the old prunes made their way, I kept my eye on Danny, who was sitting right by the bar. Strangely, he was looking at me too. *Damn, he's looking at*

Ericka M. Williams

me like he wants me or something. It was the perfect opportunity to act like I didn't care. The only problem was the old dudes were not the bait to use. Danny would've been calling me everyday with Viagra and Ben Gay jokes. The wrong ones always came around at the wrong time, trying to get some play.

"Hello Ladies?" one of them said, as his sidekick salivated in our faces.

"Beat it Grandpa," Asia snapped. They looked hurt and casually moved to the side, not wanting to look like they'd just gotten played. Even though they were disgusting, I didn't like the way Asia handled the situation. *Her ass is so mean sometimes,* I thought.

"I'm sorry we just don't feel like talking right now. Have a nice evening," I said, to the older guys.

They nodded and stared me up and down for a few seconds. I just *happened* to glance back at Danny's table to see if he was still clocking my every move, and his bitch was eyeing me down. She whispered something in Danny's ear and started laughing.

That was it! I walked over to them and put my hands on my hips. "If you have somethin' to say to me I'm right here, but believe me, you don't want it!"

Miss Prissy very calmly told me, "Mika, if you have a problem with Danny, I think you should handle it with him because I didn't do anything to you, baby. There's no reason..."

I cut her off and gave up a short sarcastic laugh, since she wanted to play the sophisticated, classy role. I had to play her, "Look bitch, you can save all the nonchalant shit, okay. If you fuck with me, I'm gonna bust yo' shit!" I turned around and walked back over to Asia whose mouth was wide open. We sat back down, but I was ready to leave. "Look Asia, I'm ready to go, 'cuz if I stay here any longer, I'm gonna knock that bitch's head off."

"Yeah, let's go before things get ugly," she replied.

We walked back to the table to finish our drinks 'cuz I

All That Glitters

didn't want to stand right in Danny's view. When Asia and I were ready to make our way outside, I didn't see Danny or his bitch sitting at their table anymore. Just my luck, when we got to the parking lot Danny had beat us outside, and his car was blocking Asia in. Great, this is just what I need.

Danny stood outside of the car talking to his stupid friends, while his girl sat in his 2001 Chevy Tahoe. I was thinking, *damn, step your game up*. I knew he had money, so where was his baller ride.

"Danny, we need to get out," Asia said to him.

"Tiffany," Danny called out. Seconds later, she rolled down the window. "Baby, move the car for me please."

I watched as she got out of the passenger seat, and walked toward the driver's side. She looked at me, rolled her eyes and said, "Oh, when the jealous bitch says jump, you jump?"

Before she could close the driver's side door, I was in the car on top of her. I started punching her in the face and before long, her lips were bloody and I was ready to go into overtime. I was about to start choking her, when I felt someone grab me, and throw me to the ground. I immediately fell back and hit my head on the concrete.

It took me a few minutes before I could get back up. But when I did, I heard Danny's car screeching in reverse. The car screeched again as he put it in drive, drove up the street, and around the corner. He must've done 55 mph flat out of that parking lot.

"Yo! Mika, You a'ight? Damn girl, I ain't know you had that in you," Jeff said, trying to brush me off. I couldn't say anything. I kept feeling the back of my head, checking for blood.

"Yeah, I'm good. Fuck Danny and his trick. Are my clothes okay? Do I have blood on my head? I think I got a knot back there." Asia and Rodney were in my hair trying to see my scalp.

"Mika, I'm proud of you. You ain't talk about it, you showed her you was 'bout it 'bout it, girl," Asia boasted.

Ericka M. Williams

They all laughed as Asia and I walked toward her car.

"Where y'all going?" Rodney asked.

"We ain't staying out here. We city bound," Asia answered uninvitingly. "Lookin' for a hot spot."

"What club?" Jeff asked. I guess he thought he might've had better shot with me at a different spot. "We'll meet y'all out there."

Asia lied, "Boogie Nights in the Bronx."

"What is that some Spanish or Italian shit? That shit sounds cheesy as hell," Rodney responded. He definitely lacked any type of swagger.

"It's Indian. They got belly dancers and the whole shit. See y'all out there!" Asia yelled, as we pulled off.

"Damn girl, why do you treat Rodney like that?" I asked rubbing the back of my head.

"His Beggin' Billy ass. He's a lame ass nigga, who couldn't fuck me for two g's," Asia replied. "Well maybe for two g's. But Jeff, that nigga can get it any day of the week. I just be brushin' him off 'cuz I know he really wants you. You better get that girl, he's on you hard."

"I ain't fuckin' wit' it." *It would be nice though,* I thought to myself.

I figured the rest of my night was gonna be all fucked up. I told Asia to take me home, but she talked me out of it. She said that if I went home, I would only keep dwelling on what happened, which was true, so I agreed to go to the party and have a good time and not think about it. I knew she really wanted to go to the party. By that time, it was 1:30 a.m. *Damn, Shani is gonna kill me.*

Minutes later, Asia and I started joking about the whole thing. Somehow I knew that it would hit me later on. I couldn't stop thinking about how Danny threw me on the ground and drove off. My head could've busted wide open. I could've been on my way to the hospital. I couldn't believe he had done that to the mother of his son, over some chick. *I guess she ain't just some chick.*

All That Glitters

The party was at a club downtown called City Lights. We parked the car, and stood in line for about twenty minutes before getting in. As soon as we walked through the door, I went straight to the bathroom. I had to let all of those Long Island's out. Within minutes, Asia and I came out of the bathroom shaking our asses, ready to party. The place was packed, and the music was just right. I was ready to see who was in the place with some money, so we made our way to the bar, I didn't want any more liquor. I felt bad enough as it was. As we waited for Asia to order a drink, I looked around the club to see if I knew anybody, but didn't recognize a single person. After waiting to see if anyone was gonna pick up Asia's tab, she finally decided to buy the drink herself. I guess all the ballers were sittin' down. Once she got her glass, we walked toward the lounge area to find a seat because most of the niggas with paper congregate there if they weren't at the bar.

We had a good view of everything that was going on, and it was the usual. Niggas buying Cristal or some expensive liquor for their crew, and girls flocking around them trying to get some of it. It was funny how, no matter what city you're in, the club scene was always the same scenario.

A few minutes later, Asia saw Butch, one of her so-called boyfriends, and went over to talk to him. I watched as they gave each other a hug and he handed her something. After doing a little bit of small talk, she walked back toward me.

"Girl, Butch said he's gonna hook you up with his friend, Renny," Asia said, with a huge smile.

I returned the smiled thinking about Renny, who was a fine ass Dominican brother with lots of cash of course. We'd been trying to get together for a while. At that moment, I was glad that I came to the party after all. In the meantime, Asia told me to follow her to the bathroom because Butch had given her a goody bag.

When we walked into the bathroom, Asia immediately darted into a stall, while I looked in the mirror and checked

Ericka M. Williams

my body for scars. I wanted to make sure Danny didn't leave me with a battle wound.

"Mika, come in here," she yelled.

"For what?" I asked with a crazy expression.

"Just come here for a second," Asia ordered.

I went in the stall reluctantly and saw Asia sitting on the toilet seat like a crack-head. As soon as I closed the door to the small space, she passed the folded bill to me like this was my norm. It had coke and a straw in it.

"Asia, I ain't messin' wit' that shit. That's the shit that drove my uncle crazy."

She laughed and kept her hand extended toward me. "Mika, you're buggin'. Just try it. Take two hits. One in each nostril."

"Why? I don't need any."

"Because it'll make you feel better. I can tell you keep thinking about Danny. Fuck that nigga. Try it."

"Yeah I need something to take my mind off of that nigga. What is it gonna make me feel like?" I asked looking down at the folded bill.

"Like you know, like you're on a cloud. Weed makes you silly, but this makes you feel like superwoman. Like you can do anything," Asia replied.

Hesitantly, I scooped up some coke and led my hand to my nose and sniffed. It burned like hell, but I did it three more times. I didn't feel anything at first, but then suddenly I felt happy as hell. Happy in a mellow way, relaxed. I suddenly didn't have any worries. Hell, I had enough energy to run around Central Park without a break. Several minutes later, Asia hit me in my shoulder. "Let's go," she said.

When we went back to the party, I was ready to dance. People were still coming in from outside, so we finally saw some more familiar faces. All the Uptown crews were in effect. They had their little cliques who always traveled, and made money, together. We saw Smitty from 123rd St., who was a lunatic, and the Harlem Knights, a motor-cycle crew from 146th St. who came in and turned heads. Bronx,

Manhattan, Brooklyn, Queens...all the boroughs were doin' it. The place was packed. The party felt like a Biggie video. There were a couple of celebrities in the place too, like Fat Joe, Lil Kim, and some basketball players. I was tired of sitting and star gazing and Asia didn't want to be in the same spot when Butch came back, so we started walking around. Suddenly, Little Kim's old song *'Crush on You'* came on, and we hit the dance floor.

When we did, we walked right into Angel. Angel was one of our friends who I'd met during my small stay at Howard University. She was from Harlem, who had gotten her degree and now had a good job as a Social Worker. *Damn, I should've stayed in college, or at least transferred to a school at home when I had Kian.* We said our hellos and gave our hugs, and Angel introduced us to the two girls she was with. I immediately grabbed Angel's hand and pulled her to the side and told her about my crazy day. She couldn't believe Danny would do something like that to me. The two of them had become real cool when we were in college, so she knew a different side of him.

As we continued to talk, the DJ played Biggie's song, *'Hypnotize'* and all five of us started dancing in a circle. I went in and did my little dance and they yelled, "Go Mika! Go Mika!" Crazy Asia yelled out to the same beat, "Fuck Danny! You don't need him!" I started laughing and stepped out of the circle.

Suddenly, a group of guys came over and started pulling some of us to dance with them. Apparently, Angel knew them, but I'd only seen one of them before. The one that pulled me to the side was real cute, stocky just like I like 'em, so I didn't have a problem dancing with him. I loved his beautiful honey colored complexion. We matched perfectly. He had short, curly hair and hazel eyes, but he didn't look soft or sweet. He wore a light blue knitted top, and nice fitted jeans, that didn't hang off his ass. I didn't like that sloppy shit. Niggas rockin' their boxers as fashion was ignorant to me. The most important thing was the nice

Ericka M. Williams

41

pair of Pradas on his feet. I couldn't take a man with cheap ass shoes. The link he had around his neck was hot too, and his diamond stud reeled me in, for sure. The charm on his link was a Scorpion iced out with diamonds. I smiled because I could smell money comin' out of his pores. I thought to myself, *Here I go again.*

He moved close to me and whispered the usual "What's your name...pretty girl?"

"Mika," I said, before turning around and dancing real sexy. Of course my sexy moves invited him up on my ass.

He put his arm around my stomach and pulled me close to him. We moved together and then he whispered, "I wanna talk to you after this song." I turned back around and faced him to check him out again. Damn he was sweet. He looked official and rugged. I loved the rugged type. Like Fantasia's song says, *'I need a hood boy, wife beaters and jeans...'*

When the song finally ended, he took my hand and led me off of the dance floor. I wanted to find out more about him, so I told him I'd meet him at the bar in a few minutes. Once he walked away, I ran over and snatched Angel up. "All right you have twenty seconds to give me the run down on that cutie. What's his story?" I asked her.

"His name is Tamar, and he's from 116th, but he's been hustlin' down in Chesapeake for the last three years. He has a house down there and he owns a soul food restaurant."

"Where the hell is Chesapeake?" I asked.

Angel smiled. "In Virginia."

"Okay that's good enough for now, I'll be back." I started walking away then turned back around, "Wait! Who is he fuckin' wit'?"

"I don't know, but the last I heard, some girl from the Bronx named, Yanira was living with him," she reported.

"Find out," I demanded, and started to walk back over to the bar. Before I knew it, somebody grabbed me from behind. When I turned around, it was fat ass Jarrod from

All That Glitters

the other night. He looked terrible, but at least he wasn't ashy this time. Oh boy, I thought. "What's up," I said to him. "When did you get back from your trip?"

"A few hours ago," he said, with a lustful look in his eye. "What are you doing after the party? You want to go with me to the hotel again?"

"I'll call you on your cell when the party is over." I lied. I quickly turned around and walked away before he could say anything else. I would make sure I was long gone before the party was over. I was planning on having breakfast with Tamar if his conversation was up to par.

I spotted Tamar talking to Butch at the bar and I walked over to them with a sexy strut. Two seconds later, I tapped Tamar on his shoulder. When he turned around, I noticed a bucket with a bottle of champagne inside and two glasses sitting in front of him.

"Peace Butch," he said, as they each gave the other a hand clap. "Mika, follow me."

I loved a take charge man. I followed him like he was already my man. He even looked better than Danny and probably had more cash. I would've loved to show this one off. We found a small table and sat down. He didn't say anything at first. He just smiled, popped the bottle, and filled my glass first. He finished filling his glass, took a sip, and continued to scan my body.

"So what's up Tamar?" He laughed because he knew he hadn't told me his name.

"What else did Angel tell you about me?" he asked.

"Oh she just said that you were a nobody without any money. And that you were married with four kids." I started laughing.

He moved his chair closer to mine and took my hand. "Well if that's true, I'm getting ready to get a divorce so I can marry you."

"Yeah okay, so can we go get my diamond ring?"

"You can have my wife's ring, I can't afford to buy another one."

Ericka M. Williams

I laughed again. "And where are we gonna live?"

"In my Neon," he said, with a straight face.

He was funny. I liked that. He asked me where I lived and I told him Jersey. He said he didn't have any place to stay that night and asked could he go home with me. *Here come the games,* I thought. I told him that I didn't let just any man sleep in my bed. Before he could respond, Asia walked over and dragged a chair from the next table. When she sat down, I introduced them and then gave him the sucker test.

"Can you go get my girlfriend a glass?" I asked in a sexy tone.

He flashed a smile. "No, your girl can go and get her own glass. Get some bubbly, sweetheart and then let us have some time alone. I want to talk to you, not you and your friend," he said, looking at me like he wanted to eat me.

Asia instantly looked like a sad puppy dog. Normally, she would've said something slick, but she must've sensed that he was dead serious. She got up and strutted away, trying to shake her ass in his face, hoping he realized what he overlooked.

I guess she wanted to stay with us and try and steal the show. We were competitive like that sometimes, so I wasn't mad at all. Asia always went after my men. Even when we were young, she messed around with my first love, Gary who took my virginity. Although everybody found out and told me that Asia wasn't my friend, I took up for her. Asia just seemed to want everything I had. She would always try to be best friends with whatever boyfriend I had at the time, and would do little things to hurt me. I never understood why. It was as if she had a love/hate thing going on with me. But no matter what, I always made excuses for her when people talked about her disloyalty, and always forgave her. Asia probably wished Tamar would've snatched her up instead of me. I was glad that he didn't go get her a glass, because I'm sure she would've felt like he wanted to get with both of us.

"So Mika, I want you all for me...I want you to come with me back to Virginia," Tamar said, interrupting my thoughts.

"Oh, you live in VA? I thought you lived in your Neon?"

"Come on baby, stop playin'. Daddy don't have time for games. I checked you and your friends out, so I want to get to know you, but I'm not gonna be up here long. I'm leaving tomorrow.

I didn't want to seem too open or have him thinking of me as a trick. Now fat ass, Jarrod on the other hand, could think whatever he wanted. I liked Tamar's style.

"As much as I want to give you some tonight, I'll have to wait until you come back. I can't go down south with you, you might get me down there and treat me bad."

"I would never mistreat such a pretty girl. At least go with me to breakfast after this. I'll make sure you get home safe. You can give your girl my license plate number."

His nickname should've been, Game because he had lots of it. "We can go eat, I'm just not ready to stay overnight wit' you."

Suddenly, two of his boys came over and started talking to him. I wanted to say something, but decided to keep my cool. Besides, I didn't know Tamar that well to be causing a scene. Seconds more, Asia came back over, and filled her glass with some champagne. When she turned around to walk away, I told Tamar I would be right back. I wanted to take a stroll around the club wit' my girl.

As Asia and I walked past Angel and her friends, she shouted, "There goes them Jersey hookers, trying to steal our men!"

I put my middle finger up at her, and kept walking. There was always a lot of competition between New York and New Jersey women, over men of course.

"Are you leaving wit' Butch?" I asked Asia.

She laughed. "Why bitch, are you going with Mr. Smoove?" she smiled. "Hell yeah, I'm going with Butch.

Ericka M. Williams

45

We gonna get fucked up and fuck all night. He got that good coke."

Asia was crazy. I shook my head.

"That coke got me feeling good as shit. Sniff some more and your ass will be horny too."

"Nah, I like Tamar, but I don't want to fuck him yet."

"Bitch, you too goody goody, you ain't really no bad girl. Shani's speeches must be rubbing off on you."

"Nah bitch, I am a bad girl. You're just rotten to the core."

"Yup you're right," Asia admitted. "Aight, go get your new stuff before somebody else snatches him. You lucky I ain't see him first, because I woulda got his sexy ass. You know I would've fucked him real good. But I guess it's better that I didn't since Butch knows him. And you know Butch is my boo."

"Yeah, Butch and Boogie too."

"Hoe, you just mad, fuck you," she replied.

We started laughing and went our separate ways. I noticed Tamar watching us from a distance. I turned around and saw him looking right at me. In that short time, I was really diggin' Tamar. It wasn't just because I was feeling lonely and desperate over what happened with Danny. He had a hell of a sense of humor. I must admit, I was a bit open kind of fast, but I wasn't gonna sleep with him because I wanted to see if it could turn into more than a sex thing. I desperately needed a replacement for Danny. Someone who was on his same level. I needed a man with money.

Tamar and I left the club several minutes later, and walked around the corner to the parking garage. As we approached the garage, the guys that Tamar was talking to in the club were standing beside a Lexus and an Acura Coupe that were parked along the street. Tamar gave me the ticket to go get his car, and went over to talk to them. When the parking attendant came back, he arrived in a beautiful champagne colored convertible BMW. *A BMW?*

How you like me now Danny Boy? My mouth was wide open when the attendant hopped out the driver's seat. I looked around to make sure he didn't catch me lose my cool. I didn't run and jump in the car even though I wanted to. I waited for Tamar to saunter over with his bow-legged self. Uhm, he had no idea what I planned to do to him.

"What's the matter, Boo? Get in baby," Tamar said, as he walked toward me.

"Lemme drive? Since I know where I'm going."

"Go 'head baby. I like a take charge woman."

We jumped in the car, and I drove to an all night diner not far from my house. Once we arrived and took our seats, we talked so much we almost forgot to order. Before we knew it, the sun was coming up and we were still talking.

I found out that he was twenty-four and had a five year old son who lived in Harlem. He'd been living in VA for the last three years and he told me all about his restaurant. He said he was getting ready to open up another one in Harlem. I told him some things about myself and then we started talking about relationships. He didn't say anything about the girl Yanira that Angel had mentioned to me, and I didn't ask. However, he did say that he was seeing somebody, but that it was almost over. All I could do was laugh.

It was late or should I say early, when I was finally ready to go home. He made a minor attempt to take me to a hotel, and when I said no, he left it alone, which I liked.

"I'm calling it a night, but you better make it your business to call me tomorrow," I said. He smiled, and then I added, "I like you, which is why I don't want to spend the night with you tonight, Tamar. I want more than just your body."

"Sweetheart, we're both adults and I'm a man. Sex doesn't mean as much to me as it did when I was younger. Don't you think niggas get tired of trickin' with girls all the time?"

He talked a good game, but I could smell bullshit a mile

Ericka M. Williams

away. "Should I clap now or later?"

"You think I'm bullshitin' but I'm for real, man."

I laughed. "I would love for you to turn out to be for real, man. I'll just have to wait and see."

He looked at me and shook his head. "Oh boy, you one of those chicks who thinks she's a nigga? You feel like you call the shots? Do you think you got the power?"

"I got that pussy power." We both laughed. "Nah, I'm saying, men and women are no different. Sometimes women just want sex and that doesn't make them hoes, when a man can do the same thing."

"I see a lady in you. And you can say I'm just talkin' shit, but I really am too grown for games. I'm a business man, and I need a smart woman by my side. I'm gonna be honest with you, I'm glad you turned me down."

We continued to talk while he drove me home. When we pulled up, he kissed me and said he would definitely call me later. When I got out the car, I floated all the way up to my apartment. The night had ended way better than it started. Tamar made me feel like a queen, like black women are supposed to feel. It had been a long time since I went to bed with a smile on my face, and Tamar made it happen.

Chapter 4

EVERY WOMAN

I woke up the next morning when my mother called. She sounded real sick. She was coughing, and said that she had a high fever. I got Kian dressed quickly, and took a cab to her house.

On the ride to my mother's apartment, I thought about Tamar. I was hoping he'd call, even though I didn't really need the headache of a relationship right then, in addition to what I already had with Mark. I knew the routine with new relationships. In the beginning, the man did everything right. He calls you when he says he'll call. He comes over *on time.* He gives you whatever you want. Then, when you fall for him, all that goes right out the window, and he starts acting up. That's when all the lies and disappearances start. I stopped to think clearly…*Mark hasn't done any of that though.* He hadn't done anything to hurt me, and here I was treating him like shit. I hadn't even called him. I had finally found a sweet guy and still didn't appreciate him. I guess the fact that he was broke and still lived at home with his mother really bothered me. Besides, I was too old for that type of shit anyway.

When the cab pulled up to my mother's building, Kian and I quickly got out. I buzzed her apartment, hopped in the elevator and hit the number five on the panel for the fifth floor. When we got to her door, it was open. As soon as I walked into her bedroom, I found my mother lying in her bed with a bucket placed on the floor. She'd been vomiting a lot and looked very pale. I went over and kissed her on the cheek and gave her a hug, which we only did when someone died. Instead of love and affection we did arguments and sarcasms.

"Don't come too close, I don't want you to get sick," she said, in a weak tone.

"Hi Grandma," Kian said, from the doorway, "you look really sick."

"I know Kian, don't come in here." She tried to get up, but was too weak to lift herself. I told Kian to go play in his room that was fixed up just for him.

I lifted her up and fixed the pillow for her, and then sat on the bed. She didn't look good at all. She looked a bit old and worn out. Seeing her weak for the first time, I noticed that my mother was aging. I didn't know what it was, but it wasn't just her being sick. I never really wondered what it would be like to lose her. I never in my entire life even saw my mother in the hospital. I guess that's why I always thought of her as unbreakable. Now I was starting to see her as a delicate human being with real feelings, and not some super woman.

"Ma, call your doctor," I suggested.

"For what?"

"Mommy, you need to go to the hospital. Let me take your temperature."

"Don't tell me you're worried about your mother. Are you feeling okay?"

"Oh Ma, please. You know I care about you."

Before she could have a come back, I went into the kitchen to make her some tea. My mother always acted like nobody cared about her. I loved her dearly, despite the fact that we barely got along. It's just hard to show her because she was always criticizing me. I think she resented me because I was so street like my father, and she wanted me to be more like Shani. When I was eleven and my parents split up, my mother really didn't deal with men anymore. She dated a few times here and there, but nothing serious. I guess she didn't want to set a bad example for her two daughters by having a bunch of different men around. But little did she know, we wanted her to date. She didn't understand that she deserved to be wined and dined. She was too concerned with what people would say, but who cared what people said. I always told her that those people weren't doing nothin' for her, so who cared what they said.

In her time, women had to sacrifice happiness for etiquette. She always said that she didn't need a man, but I think she was just scared to get hurt again. That's why she focused so much on Shani and I. She only went out once in a while because she spent all her time being a good mother. What's sad is that, I couldn't see it. I took her for granted. I thought she was strong and could handle anything, partly because she always presented herself that way. I never worried about her because she acted like she didn't need anybody. Now I felt like we'd missed out on our mother/daughter relationship. I wished so much that we were closer.

Suddenly, I heard a loud thump and Kian screamed, "Grandma!"

I ran to the back and realized my mother had fallen on the floor trying to get out the bed. "Ma," I yelled.

"Mika, call 911," she moaned.

I ran to the kitchen and called the ambulance. Then, I called Danny and told him he had to come and get Kian because they probably wouldn't let him in the emergency room. I had to be there for my mother, for once. He said if he didn't make it before we left her house he would meet us at the hospital. I was trying to be strong and calm, like my mother. I put her shoes and coat on as we waited for the ambulance. Luckily, it arrived quickly. As soon as the EMT's came into the apartment, they put her on the gurney and we all walked outside. Kian cried the entire time, and I was nervous as hell. I needed Danny. I felt like he should've been there. He knew my mother well, even though they had their disagreements. He had been a part of the family for six years.

I looked into my mother's eyes, and felt for her. Everyone needed companionship and affection, and although I wasn't there for my mother like I should've been, I knew that I could not have given her the type of love that she needed. Everyone needed intimate love to make them feel special. She was so wrapped up in our lives that she made us feel guilty that we had lives of our own. She would always say my friends and boyfriends were more important than her. Growing up, I always wished that she had a man to love her.

My father was so busy trying to be slick and cool that his family took a back seat to him hanging out. All my mother did was sacrifice for us and she felt like she didn't get anything in return for all the wasted years of her life. It's sad because she felt betrayed and unappreciated. I always wanted to talk to her about her life, and what she'd really gone through with my father. I felt I was old enough to know the whole story.

The EMT's hand being shoved in my face brought me back to reality. He couldn't let Kian ride in the ambulance, so I had to stay back until Danny came. I immediately called to tell him to come to my moms and called Shani to tell her that Mommy was on her way to the hospital. I figured I'd have Danny drop me off there.

About fifteen minutes later, Danny pulled up with Tiffany in the car. He jumped out and grabbed Kian, and hugged him tightly.

"Is your mother all right?" he asked me, without looking me in the face.

"Damn, if you really cared you would've come here alone. I can't even get a ride to the fuckin' hospital 'cuz you had to bring your fuckin' stunt! Goddamn Danny, does your son get a minute to be alone with you!?"

"You could ride if you knew how to act. Here, call a cab!"

He threw twenty dollars on the ground, and put Kian in

the car so fast I couldn't even kiss my baby goodbye. I picked the money up and almost fell over when I bent down. Before I knew it, he was driving away, and the only thing I saw was a glimpse of Tiffany's smile. I couldn't cry, I was all cried out over him. I was weak with despair. My mother was being rushed to the hospital and I had to wait for a fucking cab! I stood outside of her house numb and lost. I few minutes later, I called Asia. Luckily she was in the area.

I stood outside looking like a lost puppy until Asia got there. When she pulled up, she was in a black Expedition moving her head to a Beyonce song. I knew the truck belonged to Butch. I guess she gotten rid of the rental Boogie got her. Normally, I would've wanted to hear the story, but this time I didn't even care. I was worried about my mother.

I guess Asia could see it in my face as I got in the truck. "Mika, she'll be all right. She ain't been sick. She probably got a bad flu or something."

"I hope that's all it is," I said sadly.

We rode to the hospital in silence, and when we arrived, I thanked her for bringing me, and then ran into the hospital to find out where my mother was.

I waited in the Emergency room for about three hours until they finally came and informed me that she had some type of viral infection in her lungs, but would be okay. After speaking with the doctor for a few minutes, they admitted my mother and assigned her to a room. I was exhausted mentally, but I was glad that I was there. Shani finally arrived on our way up to the room, and when she got there, we all sat quietly and watched a re-run episode of Good Times. I kept thinking about how Danny couldn't even come by himself to see about my mother, or be there for me when I needed him. He just threw the money on the ground.

A half an hour later, the Tyra Banks show was coming on, and the show was about teenage girls who were out of

Ericka M. Williams

control and driving their mothers crazy. The mothers on the show were upset because their daughters were acting too grown and dressing like hookers. Those little girls were off the hook. No one could tell them they weren't cute, but little did they know, they all looked a mess. The audience was trying to tell them to enjoy their lives and not rush their childhood because later on they would regret it, but like most teenagers they were too sassy and rude.

"These girls today are too damn grown. I am so glad my teenage years are over. I wouldn't want to be a teenager in this crazy time," I said. My mother gave me a look that said, *'Bitch, you've got a lot of nerve'.*

"Mika, you were just as bad," my mother replied. Shani laughed and nodded in agreement. I rolled my eyes at her. Hater. *She's just mad cause she ain't have as much fun as I did growing up,* I thought.

"Ma, I was bad, but give me a break. These little girls are ridiculous. At least I *snuck* around. They don't even care. They're broadcastin' what they do all over TV. Their mothers can kiss their asses for all they care. Look at the one with a two way. Now what does a twelve year old girl need with a two way? You know she doesn't call her mother."

"You're right. But you still have a long way to go too, and a lot to still learn. You really need to get *your* shit together," my mother said.

"I know. I just have to figure out my purpose in life."

"What you need to do is stop living in your own fairy tale world...But you've always been like that, in a dream world."

"I'm gonna go back to school, but I have to think about what I want to major in. I know I have to do something. See Mommy, I never put myself in your shoes before, but now that I'm a woman..."

She laughed. I continued anyway, "I see some of what you've been through and I see that life isn't as easy as I thought it was..."

All That Glitters

She interrupted me. "Yeah you thought that 'Danny the kingpin' was going to carry you off into the sunset."

"I'm sorry for anything that I did, Ma."

"You know how you can make it up to me?"

"How Mommy?" I asked.

"Have a daughter." We all started laughing.

"No...seriously, when are you going to grow up? I don't see you making any changes, or progressing in life. When are you going to face the fact that you're on your own now? It's time to get off your ass and stop waiting for Danny to come back...or another hoodlum to take care of you. You need to get in school or get a job. A real woman would do both, and stop hanging out in the street and start being a real mother."

I felt an argument coming on. I guess us having a decent conversation was too good to be true. "Why do I feel like you resent me?" I asked.

"You know what girl, you haven't changed. You still think you know everything but you'll see. See how you like it when the child that you carried for nine months turns out to be a selfish bitch!"

Now that hurt. I was upset because for one, she didn't have to call me a bitch. I guess I should've known we couldn't talk about a sensitive issue without it getting blown out of proportion. We should've kept the conversation simple, because there were too many bad memories from the past. I was just hoping things could be resolved. Damn, even when she was sick and in the hospital, she had to attack me. I was ready to leave. I left the room momentarily and called a cab.

When I returned, I lied. "Ma, Danny has something to do so he's gonna meet me downstairs and take me and Kian home. I'll come back tomorrow." I pecked her cheek real light.

"Yeah, I'll see what time you come, if I ain't dead by the time you wake up and get yourself together."

"Ma, stop. She'll be here early, right Mika?" Shani said.

I looked at Shani with tears in my eyes and walked out of the room.

I cried all the way home in the cab. Damn, just because I made a lot of bad choices growing up, my mother still wouldn't let us have a relationship now. She felt like I turned my back on her instead of realizing that all teenagers put their friends in front of their parents. But I was all she had, especially when Shani was in college. I needed a mother in my life that could be my friend some- times. I wish I had the type of mother I could call so we could get our nails done together, but I couldn't. We didn't have that bond and it was a serious void in my life.

She always bragged about how good a mother she was and how bad a daughter I was. It made me sick. Plus, she had to tell me how Shani wasn't half as bad as I was. But what she didn't realize was that I could've been much worse.

When I got out of the cab there were four cop cars out- side of our building. *Damn, what's going on now?* When I got upstairs a female officer was walking out with Kiki's kids, and I heard Kiki screaming for them. I stopped at Miss Simm's door, who lived next door to me and across from Kiki. She was always in everybody's business so I knew she would have the scoop.

"Miss Simms what happened?" I asked.

"Chile, that damn Kiki left them kids in the apartment by themselves and they were running around in the hall with no clothes on. Somebody called the child protective serv- ice, and they were waiting in the apartment with the police when Kiki came back. But that's not even the worst of it. Kiki came in there high as a kite girl, with two guys who had drugs and stolen property on them. That girl is on her way to jail."

I said good-bye to Miss Simms and went inside my apartment. I tried to think of other things, but I kept thinking about Kiki and my mother. When I walked into my room, I picked up the phone and called the hospital to get her room number. When my mother answered, I blurted out, "I love you Mommy and I'm really sorry."

Chapter 5

GAMES

Eight o'clock rolled around, and I was feeling lonely. I wished that Tamar could be here to cheer me up. I was sick of Shani and my mother always being against me. I called Asia to tell her about Kiki, and before she answered, my other line clicked. I hung up and answered the new call.

"Hello," the strange voice said, "Is Mika there?"

"This is Mika. Who's this?"

"It's Tee."

"Tee who?" I smiled. I knew it was him.

"It's Tamar. Stop being silly, you know who it is. What's kickin' chicken?"

"Oh now you wanna play. I ain't no chicken."

"All right then don't play with me and I won't play with you. What's up lady?"

"Nothin'. What's up with you Big Man?"

"Chillin'. Waitin' for you to come and stay with me."

"I'm waiting for the same thing. When are you coming back up here?" I asked trying not to sound desperate.

"I'll be back up there on Thursday and I'm coming to kidnap you."

"I'll let you know if you can take me out," I responded.

"Yo, you better stop playin' me like one of them soft niggas from Jersey. I'll be at your house Thursday night. I'll call you when I get in town. All right?"

"All right, Mr. Biggs."

"I'll talk to you in a few days."

"Damn, I can't get a little conversation? What, your girl is home?"

"Nah baby, I'm on my way out. I got business to handle. I'll call you back later," he said, sincerely.

I said, "Okay," after feeling like he was telling the truth, and we hung up. Seconds later, the phone rang again. It was Asia.

"I just called you. Damn, you're just getting home from Saturday night?"

"Girl, Butch ordered a private car that took us straight to Atlantic City. You know Butch gambles all the time. He's a high roller, so he had a free room and we went to the Tropicana Casino, saw some shows, and blew some g's- you know how it is. We had a car pick us up Sunday night. Renny wanted you to go, but you had left with cutie. But guess what, he wants to take you out tonight."

"Where?" I asked with sarcasm in my voice.

"We'll all go out and eat. Don't front now, you've been trying to get with him for the longest."

"All right, I'll be ready in an hour." I hung up before she had time to say anything else.

I quickly got dressed in a Baby Phat, pink and gold out-fit, with matching Baby Phat sneakers. Everybody knew that Baby Phat was my signature. I even had the Baby Phat cat tattooed on my thigh.

I was plotting on how to deal with my baby sitting issue when Shani and Kian walked into the house. She'd done me a favor and picked up Kian from Danny's. For some reason, I was still a little upset about what had happened at the hospital, so I wasn't speaking to her, but I still planned to go out, and wasn't gonna ask her to watch Kian. She wanted to see me beg, so my plan was to just leave.

Kian saw me all dolled up and said he wanted to sleep in my room. "Boy you're getting in your own bed. Go take your clothes off. I'll come in and help you put on your paja-mas."

"Mommy my stomach hurts," he whined. I knew it was

game.

"I'm leavin', so go get in the bed with Auntie Shani." He looked at me with disappointment and started whimpering.

"Kian stop being a baby. Go in my room and lay on the bed!"

"Mika, Kian is sick and you can't even stay home with him?" Shani asked standing in the doorway.

"He just wants some attention. He's not sick," I countered. "Just give him some Children's Tylenol. I'm just going to get something to eat, I'll be right back." I knew she wouldn't refuse to watch him.

"He may really be sick. You need to be more considerate. No man is more important than your son. Go give him the Tylenol, show your son that you care, damn. This is what me and Mommy are referring to when we converse with you." She walked away with her arms folded and rolled her eyes.

"I really don't feel like arguing with you Shani."

"Of course you don't! You don't have time to! The least you can do is give him the Tylenol, so he doesn't think you don't give a shit."

I stomped into the kitchen like a disgruntled teenager, and got a spoon and the liquid Tylenol. I made sure I slammed the cabinet door. In the background, Shani's voice resonated as she rambled on with her philosophical statements.

"All right damn, I'll be back early!" I yelled.

"You need to be back before morning if you're telling him to wait for you in your bed," she responded.

"You need to stop thinkin' you're my mother and that you're so perfect."

"You need to stop thinking I'm your nanny or your son's mother," Shani countered.

When I went into my room to give Kian some medicine, he was knocked out on my bed, clothes and all. I took his pants and shirt off, and slid him under the covers with his underwear on. He did that sometimes when he knew I was

All That Glitters

going out. I kissed him on his head and left. I didn't even say anything to Shani before leaving.

As soon as I walked outside, my ride was pulling up. Butch was driving his white rimmed Range Rover. He was paid, but looked like King Kong. Boogie, Asia's other dude was much finer than Butch. Boogie looked like Allen Iverson with the braids and all, but just had more weight on him. Asia had already reported that her other man, Boogie didn't spend as much money as Butch, but it was the *cute factor* that mattered to me.

I opened the door, got in the back and spoke to every-one. Renny was on the phone, so he just looked at me and nodded. I could tell he was talking to a girl because he was talking low and he kept saying, "Fall back. I'll call you back in a little while."

He finally got off the phone and smiled. "What's up sweetheart?"

"I'm good. How are you?"

"I'm horny. Can you help me out?" Renny asked.

I was caught off guard with that one, but I wasn't gonna let him think that shit was cute. "I can help you learn some class."

"I don't want class, I want ass," he replied.

"Well like Flava Flav said, I can't do nothin' for ya man."

"Oh well maybe we should turn around and take you home then."

"Yo Asia what's up?" I yelled. "Did you set me up on a booty call without me knowin' it? What's this nigga's fuckin' problem?"

"Renny stop trippin' damn," Asia said to him.

"Damn baby, I'm just playin'," Renny interjected. "You forgive me?"

"Whatever," I said waving him away.

"We ain't even hungry no more so we just gonna go and have some drinks," Asia announced from the front.

We went to the Mocha Lounge on 119th and 8th Avenue in Harlem. The place was dimly lit with cozy couch-

Ericka M. Williams

61

es all around. When we arrived, we sat down and ordered drinks. Renny kept talking to Butch about money, trying to impress me, or put a bid in like that was his bait to get me. He disclosed to us about how some young kid, that was hustlin' for him, came up short and that he'd put a gun to his head.

"I had to let him know I'm not to be fucked with," Renny bragged.

He seemed to think it sounded appealing, but I wasn't impressed. I was turned off. That wasn't cute at all, I didn't want to hear about that shit. I felt a bad evening coming on.

In between his wack dried out conversation, he checked his cell phone every five seconds, but it hadn't gone off once. Then he said, jokingly of course, "Are we gonna do bottle service, Butch or should we just keep ordering cheap drinks. I don't think Mika is ready to make the exchange."

He and Butch started laughing. I figured he meant that he didn't want to spend money popping bottles if I didn't seem like I would be fucking tonight.

I rolled my eyes and looked at Asia like I was going to kill her for not telling me that this muthafucka was such a clown. He lacked game, and charisma too. If he checked his cell phone one more time, I was gonna snatch it, run to the bathroom, and throw it in the toilet. I would've preferred being home lying in my bed with Kian next to me.

We sat there for about an hour until I couldn't take any-more of his fake image presentation. I said I had to go home to Kian, which was my famous out. When the bill came Renny proudly took out a knot of cash and counted it about fifty times. He then put a hundred dollars on the table, and put the money back in his pocket.

As we got up and started walking toward the car, I thought, NEVER AGAIN...I wasn't surprised when he said, "So Mika, we can't go to a hotel? I waited a long time to take you out."

62 *All That Glitters*

"You know what Renaldo, Renny, or whatever the hell your name is...you waited a long time just to sling some dick to me, not get to know me. You got a lot of bullshit going on with you. Shit that I don't have time for. Butch, take my ass home pronto," I ordered. I had an at-ti-tude for real. "You know what, here's fifty dollars toward my drinks," I said, grabbing my last fifty from my purse. "Use it to go buy a cheap jumpoff who will listen to you talk shit, and make you feel like a big daddy."

He tried not to take the money, but I stuffed the bill in his jacket pocket as he walked away. By now I was screaming at the top of my lungs, "I know you ain't used to having money, you must be new to the game. A real bad boy moves in silence. You put your own self on blast, tellin' me who's head you puttin' guns to. You ain't even a real nigga, chico."

Asia and I made up a new name for him, "Ferocious Wackadocious!" and cracked up laughing.

He threw my money on the ground and said, "Yo, Butch, take this uptight hooker home. She thinks I'm gonna beg for that ass, like it's *all* that."

Asia got even more upset than I did. "Renny stop trip-pin' damn, what the fuck is wrong with you, don't take no more Ecstasy again, ever. I ain't never seen him be on it like this. I guess his girl ain't been doin' him right." We gave each other a pound and continued to clown him.

"Bitch, you better calm down. You don't know me. I'll knock your fuckin' block off!" Renny had obviously had enough.

"You ain't doin' shit over here baby! You better watch where you throw threats! Butch, you better give your man a lesson in cool. He thinks he can flash some cash in my face and I'll start taking my clothes off. You must be messin' with eighteen year olds or somethin' but you don't approach me like that. You must be fuckin' crazy!"

"Yo, drop me off man, nah, fuck it, I'll take a cab home, let me out." We were about to get on the George

Ericka M. Williams

Washington Bridge back to Jersey. Butch pulled over with-out saying anything, and Renny got out.

"Good!" I shouted. *I should've listened to Shani and stayed home.* Minutes later, they dropped me off and I hur-ried upstairs. I wanted to talk to Mark. I hadn't spoken to him since Saturday, and the three days felt like three months. He'd been calling my cell and my house everyday, so I knew he would answer.

I called his house and was shocked when his answer-ing machine came on. I thought, *damn, it's one o'clock in the morning.* I hung up before the beep. *Where could he be at this time of night? He has to go to work tomorrow. I hope he ain't wit' another girl.* I called him again, but when he didn't answer, I hung up for the second time. What would I say if he answered? I could sing that Stevie Wonder song. 'I just called… to say…I love you…and I mean it from the bottom of my heart,' but decided against it. Instead, I put my pajamas on, got in the bed, and cud-dled up next to my son. At that moment I realized, he was the only real man who loved me.

All That Glitters

Chapter Six

APOLOGIES

I started the next day with a new perspective. I called a few colleges and had them send me catalogs. I didn't know what I was going to do with my life, but I wanted my baby, Mark for sure. I called his job and they said he was out sick. *Uh-oh! Why hasn't he called me?* I decided that if he didn't call me by tonight, I would go to his house and talk to him. The 'I don't care' game was over.

Shani had already left for school, and dropped Kian at my Aunt's on her way, so I could go see my mother. It was planned that he would spend the night with my Aunt because I told her I was going to look for a job the next day. When I called the hospital, my mother didn't answer the phone in her room, so I called the nurses' station. They informed me that she was having tests run all day, and that I should come in the evening, since I wouldn't be able to accompany her into the exam rooms. I asked the nurse to be sure to let my mother know that her daughter, Mika had called and that I was informed not to come. The last thing I needed was for her to say that I didn't want to come, even though I really didn't. I was gonna have to love my mother from afar.

Before I went to get the paper, I thought about who I could get to take me out to lunch. I picked up my phone book and started from the tab 'A' to find a man to call. Most of my girlfriends were at work, but I didn't feel like going out with a girl anyway. I didn't find anybody interesting under the A's.

Bernard was the first male in the B's. I hadn't spoken to Bernard in a long time. He was a cutie from the Bronx. And even though he had short money, he was cool. He worked at night, so when he didn't answer his cell, I decided not to leave a message. I'd never even gone out with him before. We were phone pals when we first met, but that got boring. I crossed his number out. I only kept current numbers in my phone. My book was for the ifs and the maybes.

Then there was Brad. I heard he was smoking crack. Plus there were two girls pregnant by him. *No Dice!* I crossed him out too.

I went to the C's where I found Chris, who was stuck on himself and too damn kinky. He did things that I wouldn't even do with my husband. I had to leave him alone when he told me he wanted me to do it to him with a dildo in his ass. *Undercover homo.* I crossed his name out too. Then there was Chuckie. I decided to call him, he was fun, cheap but fun. He worked at an insurance company. I'd met him about three months ago and we went out once. He talked about his ex-girlfriend the whole night, and I threw in my Danny stories. It was funny because her name was Danielle. When I called, the machine came on, "Danielle and Charles can't come to the phone right now..." I hung up and crossed his ass out twice. Oh well. It was hard to find a man without baggage.

I thought about calling Fatso, but quickly changed my mind. I didn't need to eat that bad, so I decided to call Wayne. Wayne was hot. I'd met him about two months after me and Danny broke up, just before I started messing with Mark. I was seeing him and nobody else for about three months, until I ran into problems with him. He had two kids, a boy and a girl, and a fiancé to go along with it, which was too much aggravation. I had to stop seeing him because I was starting to like him too much, and I knew he wouldn't leave his family. Even though I had game, I didn't believe in breaking up families. He was definitely *'The Man'* though. His mother had died and left him a large insurance policy, which he used to start a management company. He was doing real well, but it wasn't just the money that attracted me to him, he had respect and class. Someone who wasn't corny, just fun. I paged his cell and waited. Fifteen minutes later, the phone rang. That was his routine. He had to make me wait before he called back. He could've been sitting right by the phone and he still would've made me wait.

"Hello," I said, as cute and sexy as I could.

"Hey sexy."

"Hi Wayne. How've you been?" I was glad he couldn't see the big ass smile on my face.

"You know when I don't see you, shit doesn't go right," he said, in his deep voice.

"So come and get me then," I responded.

"Aw baby, I can't right now. I'm getting ready to go out of town on business."

"So take me with you," I pleaded. I sounded way too anxious.

"I'll see what I can do. I'll call you back in a few."

"I'll be here waiting." I hung up. I knew he wasn't going to call back and even if he did, I didn't want to be here. I sounded too desperate.

I went outside to see if Tyquan was on the stoop. He sold smoke. When I spotted him, I copped a bag from him. As I went back inside, he asked if he could come up and smoke with me.

"Come on," I said, sounding real desperate for company. I knew he liked me but he was only nineteen, and fine as hell. Another *just once,* I thought to myself. We went in my room and smoked the entire bag of weed, when suddenly R.Kelly's freaky shit, *'The Best Sex I Ever Had'* came on the radio.

"Yo, Mika, when you gonna lemme hit that?" Tyquan blurted out.

"Come on Ty, you can't handle this. This is too much for

Ericka M. Williams

your young ass."

"Mika, I done had mad chicks, even older than you." For some reason I believed him.

"Just lemme eat the pussy and if I don't eat it right, I'll give you some free weed."

"Come on, Ty. Don't play with me."

"I'm dead serious."

"Let me make it fresh for you," I responded, shocking the hell out of him. I went in the bathroom and washed up all along looking in the mirror asking myself, "Are you gonna go there with this boy? You're buggin'. You don't need to get this little boy open. All you can get is free weed." *Fuck it, let him taste it,* I thought to myself. I didn't want to seem like I was punking out, so I headed back into the room.

When I walked back in my Lil' Wayne look-a-like was sitting on my bed with his long, thick tongue hanging out his mouth. I tried to walk past him to change the cd, but he grabbed the inside of my leg and pulled me close to him. First, he kissed my stomach through my shirt. The strong youngun' that he was kept his arm wrapped tightly around my leg, so I had no choice but to feel what he was dishing out. Just his touch felt good, but I knew I was wrong, so I turned and twisted just a bit.

"What's up? You scared Mika?" he asked.

Before I could answer, he unzipped my pants and buried his face inside. He was breathing hard onto my sexy thongs. He grabbed my pants and brought them down to my knees and slid my thong right on top. Then he lifted one leg out gently, and then the other. Tyquan kicked my pants and underwear to the side and then forcefully turned me around to face him. Suddenly, his hands gripped my ass as pulled me to his mouth like he was about to eat a melon that was cut in half. "Damn," I shouted just as he stuck his tongue in like a pro. In and out he stroked, making me lose my mind. Just when I thought he'd given me all he had, he put one of my legs up on the bed while I stood straight up on the other leg. He was licking, sucking, and slurping like he was drinking all the flavor out of a 7 Eleven Slurpie. Damn. I was getting into it, bending my knees and going with the flow. I wasn't about to waste the nut that would soon come on his tongue. He had proved his point. I pushed his head away and told him to get undressed.

"Yeah lil nigga, you passed the test," I teased. I was horny as hell, and wanted to see what else he could do. "You got a condom," I asked, with my tits unleashing in his face.

Of course he had one.

Tyquan undressed, got on my bed, and he threw that condom on so fast, his dick was in me within two seconds. He was packing too, for a lil' dude. He did the side to side thing, then up and down, long and short motions. He was switchin' it up, and I was making sure my pussy was positioned everywhere his dick stroked. I could feel it bump against my walls, and it felt good as hell! It took him about twenty minutes to come.

"I set pussies on fiyah! Don't I?" he bragged.

Oh boy, what was this gonna turn into? Every afternoon, sneak visits. Nah, he got it this once, that was about it. I wasn't gonna be able to let him get it again, or he would start feeling himself. We would still be cool though. He did his thing.

I put him out shortly after and took a shower. As I washed myself, I laughed the entire time. *I should've never let him come up…nah fuck that, I needed to release some tension. His ass better keep his mouth shut though.*

I got dressed and called Dior to take me out to lunch, and he agreed of course. When I went downstairs to wait for him, Tyquan was still outside.

"Yo Mika, I'ma want that again," Tyquan yelled.

"Look Ty, I better not hear shit about this, or you're dead with me. We can do us, every now and then. You a cutie. I always be checkin' you out. You got a few twenties?"

Ericka M. Williams   69

Before he could answer, Dior pulled up in his 2000 Lexus Coupe, and I cut the conversation wit' Ty short. Dior was like my brother and we always had mad fun. He always spent money on me when I was with him, so I wasn't tripping off of Ty's little bit of money. Even though he lived by my grandmother's house, we grew up together. Now however, I had to be careful with his ass because he robbed houses for a living. Dior had been in and out of jail since the age of fourteen. Now at twenty-six, he couldn't find a job because of his past. He wasn't a bad person, but no one gave him a chance to try and turn his life around. He'd gotten a job at a computer company, but when they found out he was on parole they fired him. I felt sorry for him because when he was a teen doing devious shit, he didn't realize he was ruining his future. The criminal justice system is a joke. It is not designed to try to rehabilitate or train these men on how to survive on the streets the legal way. They get out of jail with no skills, like when they went in. This country needed to wake up because in a few years we were gonna have a bunch of middle-aged, homeless, ex-convicts reeking havoc on our streets.

"What's up D?" I asked with a smile.

"Mika, what's up baby?"

"Nothin' man. I miss you, where you been?"

"What's up with you and Tamar?" he asked, looking me dead in the face.

"What! How did you know about that?"

"Come on now, I can't reveal my sources."

"Stop playin', tell me."

"Can we go upstairs so I can get a quickie first?"

"No, stop playin'," I snapped. "I'm not in the mood." Dior and I had done it when we were in high school, but we were just close friends now. I could talk to Dior about all my man problems. I knew he still wanted me though.

"All right. I'm not in the mood either," he lied.

I really loved Dior because he really loved me like a sister. I just wished he would get his life together. He passed me the blunt he was smoking when he pulled up.

"Dior, you smoke too much."

"Shut up and smoke the blunt. Better yet pass the shit back since you're complainin'," he replied.

"Where are we going?" I asked.

"You want Red Lobster?"

"Yeah. So what ho are you fuckin' now?" I asked.

"Fuck you Queen." He called me queen sometimes. "I got a nice piece. Her name is Mona," he bragged. Dior whipped a u-turn right in the middle of the street.

"How many kids she got, five, six?" I joked.

"Why she gotta have kids?" He looked at me like he was offended, then admitted, "She got three."

We started laughing. "So Dior, how you know about Tamar?"

"Yeah, that's my man. He called and asked me if I knew you."

I started cheesing. "What? He's checkin' for me like that?"

"Girl, stop grinnin', you on his shit too."

"So! So what did you tell him? How do you know him anyway? What's his story? Is he..."

"Damn. Give me one question at a time," he said, holding up his finger. "I used to fuck with his cousin. Plus, me and him do business sometimes."

"So what did he say? What did you tell him?"

"He asked if you was a bird or a bitch with class?"

I sucked my teeth.

"Come on Queen you know how niggas talk. Don't take offense. He asked me what your order was and I told him you was my sis and you are thorough. I told him he gotta come correct. But on the real, be careful with that nigga, he's shifty. He's a cut throat and he don't care who he steps on. A lot of niggas don't like him. Word is bond. Don't go out with him in New York too much. And make sure his bodyguard is with him."

"Damn. What, he got a hit out on him?"

Ericka M. Williams

"Nah, it ain't like that...I don't think so anyway. I'd tell you not to fuck with him at all if it was like that. I'm just saying, a cat like that don't care about anybody but himself."

"Damn...Well this is my last hustler, I mean it. If this doesn't work out, I'm going straight. I just love street niggas. I need to go to Niggas Anonymous. For real though, if he turns out to be full of shit, I'm going to settle down with Mark."

"Tell it to somebody else Queen. I'm telling you right now, he's full of shit. He used to fuck with Danae."

"Danae Hudson?"

"Yeah. He beat the shit out of her too. He caught her fuckin' his man."

"Well that bitch is triflin' anyway. She deserves an ass kickin'," I said in a low voice. We pulled up to the Red Lobster, and for some reason I wasn't feeling too good. All the talk about Tamar had me shook. I changed the subject. "So anyway, did you find a job yet."

"Yeah. I start next week. I'm gonna be the president of Nike." He started laughing.

"Shit you should be, you got enough of their sneakers. I'm not playing Dior. Can't you be serious for a minute? Call my uncle. I told you he can help you get a job."

"All right, I'll call him."

"I'm serious D, what are you gonna do when you're seventy years old?"

"Here you go with that Social Security shit again. What are you an undercover recruiter for Social Services? I know. I'll call okay, when YOU get a damn job. You ain't no better than me."

"I'm telling you because I'm not coming to visit you in any more prisons. That reminds me, stop at the store so I can get a paper, I'm looking for a job," I said, in a more serious tone.

"You better cause retired hookers don't get Social Security either. What do you think you're gonna get the Gold-digger's Insurance?"

All That Glitters

I hit him in his stomach and we both laughed. "That's a right, I'll just be sixty with a ninety year old Suga Daddy. And watch your mouth, I'm not a hooker, I'm a gangsta bitch."

"Mika, you are wildin'. Don't worry, I'll take care of you when you get old. We'll probably end up together anyway. But for right now kill the lectures. I got a plan. I'm gonna stack 500Gs and stash it, and then work for a couple of years."

"Whatever Dior. I'm not gonna argue with you, you're too damn hard-headed. I just care about you. I don't want you to end up in jail again. I love you baby. But you right, I need to get my shit together too, before I start tellin' you what to do."

"I love you too, Mika. Let's go eat."

―――――――――――――

After spending some quality time with Dior, at the restaurant I knew where I needed to go next. "Take me past Mark's house," I asked, "he lives in Teaneck."

Dior didn't comment. He just hit the highway going 80 miles per hour. He knew me messing around with Mark was a waste of my time, but said nothing. When we arrived at Mark's place I asked Dior to wait while I rang the door-bell. Mark came to the door in a pair of boxers, and didn't look happy to see me. I hadn't planned to stay but when I saw him in his underwear, I got paranoid. Maybe he had a girl upstairs. He stepped out on the porch instead of inviting me in.

"What's up Mika? What do you want?" he asked, with his arms folded tightly.

"Is it like that?" I had to put my game face on. "Look Mark I know you're mad at me and that's why I came. I want to talk to you."

"So you came to visit?"

"Yeah. What do you think I came for?"

Ericka M. Williams

"To see if I was home. If you're staying why is Dior waiting for you?" he asked, looking over my shoulder.

"Oh! Let me tell him to go ahead." I ran over to the car and told Dior I'd call him later. He nodded and gave a slight wave to Mark as he drove off. Luckily for me, Dior was the only guy who Mark didn't get jealous over because he knew how close we were. He had no idea that Dior and I had sex before.

I walked inside and went straight up to Mark's room, located in the attic. It was a nice cool out spot. Sometimes, I would chill up there for days, like I was on vacation. I just hated the fact that he lived at home. I felt embarrassed when I had to use the bathroom, and would run into his mother. She'd be lookin' at me all crazy.

Once inside, I checked his room thoroughly. On a sneak tip, I checked under the bed, and slid back the closet door when he wasn't looking. I was glad he didn't have company. I would've been real upset if he did. Mark laid down, put his hands behind his head, and started watching TV. He was gonna make me work for his forgiveness.

I sat down next to him, and kissed him on the cheek. "Mark, I know it seems like I've been avoiding you, but I haven't. I've just been keeping to myself. I had to spend some time with Kian. I know you think I've been running the streets, but I haven't. I've been chillin'."

He looked at me like he didn't believe me and looked away. I pulled his chin so he could look at me. "Mark I'm telling you the truth. I've just been chillin'. Anyway, that's not the point. The point is, I missed you all those days."

"Mika, I love you." Boom! He dropped the bomb. He had never said it before. But I couldn't say it back. "I know you don't love me that's why I can't deal with this anymore. Messing with you ain't good for me anymore, I'm in too deep. I always have to compete against these clowns who only want you for sex. They don't treat you with respect like I do, but yet I'm the one on hold. You gotta have that street life. I may not be able to go in my pocket and give you five hundred dollars to go shopping, but I'll never hurt you. It's been a while now and you're still doing the same shit, and my feelings keep growing for you. What if you decide to go back with Danny, or what if you let one of those other clowns make you his girl? Then what the fuck am I supposed to do? Forget about all the times I was with you?"

"Mark, don't think like that. I'm with you all the time, it's just that we needed a little break. I had time to think about things. What happened was real ugly...Danny really tried to play me and I felt bad that you were there to see it."

"So what? I'm gonna start disrespecting you now because he did it? Look at what he gave up. Mika, you're beautiful."

I stopped him by kissing him. I was horny and I didn't feel like talking about what happened. I pulled his boxers off, wrapped my hand around his dick, and gave it a juicy kiss. I stuck my tongue teasing him, and licked from the bottom to the top. I knew how to shut his ass up.

"You want me to stop or you want me to keep going?" I asked sexily.

He gave me the look, and folded his arms behind his head and closed his eyes.

I put his whole thing in my mouth and slobbed on his knob. I moved slow at first and then started going all the way up and down. I could feel him moving to my moves. He grabbed my head and started helping me go faster. Up and down, faster, faster, faster, I went. He grabbed my head tighter and tighter. He was about to let loose so he pulled me from him. I tried to put it back in my mouth and he told me to climb up and sit on his face. I dropped my clothes on the floor and he laid on his back waiting for me to climb up on his face. I didn't want to disappoint him so I copped a squat. His tongue felt like a ruler, like a pointer teachers used to use to point at maps. He took a tour around my map and stuck his tongue in, around, and up and down. He was all the way in there, so far I felt like he could reach all the way up into my stomach. I had to change positions or I would burst.

I turned around and started licking his twins. I sucked on his two lollipops at one time. He was moving around and so was I as he licked the outside of me and sucked on my clit, officially. He had a routine, like a dance step. He went from my clit to my side, then right on in. I tried to jump off when I felt my waterfall about to explode. It was too late, so I just stayed where I was and let him take a drink, while I took one at the same time. He drank it till the last drop. I got on top of him and did the hoola hoop. I was bouncing up and down on that thing like it was the first time.

"Damn, baby, I love when you suck on my dick, and now this. What diddddd I doooo tooo deserve this!" he moaned.

"You love when I'm on top like this? I wish I had a lasso 'cuz I would have be swinging it around over my head, like this." I pretended to swing a lasso.

"Mika, I'm about to come!" he shouted.

I laid down on him and let my titties touch his chest. I was still on top, but leaning into him good. He grabbed my ass and pulled me in. I couldn't move, all I could feel was his piece jumping. Surprisingly, he wasn't done.

He flipped me onto my stomach, grabbed me by my waist and put me on my knees. His doggy-style had never been this good. We panted like dogs fucking in heat! Within minutes, he came all in me! And that pulsating feeling was enough to give me another one.

"Damn baby," I yelled and looked at him trying to figure out what had gotten into him.

I realized that I really had missed him. I decided that I was gonna try to treat him better, but not completely give up all my games yet. I was having too much fun.

All That Glitters

Chapter 7

RISKY

Early the next morning, I made breakfast, and called Asia to see if she would take me to fill out some job applications. She said she was tired, but that I could take a cab to her house and use the truck. She still had Butch's Expedition. It wasn't brand new, but I quickly took her up on the offer.

When I got to Asia's, I sat in her room and talked to her for a while. We laughed about Monday night, and she said she cursed Butch out for not saying anything to Renny. She said it turned into a big argument and he ended up taking her home. She called another guy thirty minutes later and went back out. I didn't know how she did it. Asia went out damn near every night. Shit, compared to Asia, I was a nun. I knew if I didn't have Kian, I'd probably be running the streets right along with her. Thank God for my child!

"You know what Mika? I might be pregnant," Asia informed me.

"By who? Please tell me not by, Butch. He's got too many kids all over the place as it is."

"It's between him and that kid I told you about named Stace."

"Oh yeah. Damn, Asia you just met Stace. You didn't make him wear a rubber?"

"I tried, but he said he was allergic to them."

I let out a huge laugh. "You fell for that? Damn, I never heard that one before." She was crazy. I always used condoms, except with Mark. Asia just didn't care.

"I know. I thought he was just saying that too, but he said it's the stuff that they use to lubricate them. It breaks his dick out," she said sounding stupid.

We laughed. "Bitch, as hot and horny as your ass is you don't need lubricated rubbers. You better stop fuckin' around and start making these clowns wear condoms."

"I know," she replied, "I gotta do better."

"Well, go take a pregnancy test," I said, headed to the door. I wasn't gonna let Asia's foolishness keep me from job hunting.

"I will slut," she responded, as I finally walked out.

―――――――――――――

I went to a few business offices, and some law firms to fill out applications for data entry, customer service, and paralegal positions. I was exhausted after five places. That was good enough for one day. After I finished it was still early. I picked up Kian from my Aunt's house and took him to the zoo. When we left it was close to the time that Shani got off of work. I picked her up from her job, because I knew her car was in the shop and I wanted us to go get my mother's test results. I stayed in the waiting room with Kian while Shani talked to my mother and then the doctor. Fortunately, my mother would be going home the next day and the infection had cleared up tremendously. The doctor advised her to quit smoking cigarettes to avoid having serious respiratory problems later on.

After we left the hospital, we went to Asia's house to take her the car back. When we arrived, Asia was dressed and waiting downstairs. She looked out of it when she got in the car. I knew something was wrong. I thought about what it could be all the way home.

"Girl, I thought you were sick. Where are you in a rush to?" I asked.

"Chile please, you're not going to believe what happened!" A tear welled in her eye.

"Oh boy, what happened now?"

"Renny and Butch got shot!"

"Get the fuck outta here!" I covered my mouth and looked back at Shani, who was riding in the back with Kian.

"Mika, Renny is dead," Asia continued.

"You're lyin'."

"I wish I was, but in a few days that man is going to be planted like a seed."

"You knew that shit was coming. Renny was asking for that shit. What about Butch?"

"He's in the hospital with a bullet in his side," Asia responded, like this was nothing major. "That's where I'm going now. I gotta pick his sister up first. Damn, we were just with them," she added.

Shit, why did she say that in front of Shani?

"See, you two better stop conspiring with these drug dealing criminals. What if you were with them when it hap- pened?" Shani added.

We both chuckled at that one. It sounded so cute and innocent. I couldn't believe she said 'conspiring'.

"Shani, I'd love to listen to a lecture, but right now I gotta go. I was supposed to have been there an hour ago but I couldn't find Mika. She never answers her damn cell phone. I gotta stay in good with the family because Butch will be going straight to jail from the hospital, and I want to be there when his stash gets divided." She grinned.

Asia is so conniving. "What the hell happened?" I asked her.

"I don't know the story yet. I wouldn't be surprised if it was Renny's big-assed mouth that caused it."

"Me either."

Several minutes later, Asia dropped us off and said that she would call me with the deal about what happened. I put on some house clothes and went in the kitchen to make dinner, but Shani had already started cooking.

"Mika, I know you don't feel like getting into it, but when

Ericka M. Williams   79

are you going to change your lifestyle?"

"When I can be comfortable with a new one."

"You act like you have no other choices. Like you're stuck in the fast lane, or even worse, like the way you live is the only way to live. I don't hang with criminals and I'm happy." She turned to check out my expression.

"Yeah, but I don't want to live like you. It's too boring. All you do is go to work, go to school, and be with Fuquan."

"Yeah for now. I'm preparing for my future. You have to work hard in the beginning but in the end it pays off. You think a bag of money is going to fall into your lap. And I hope you don't still think that Prince Charming is going to come in the form of a drug dealer and take you away to Never Never Land. You don't even realize how good it feels to be an independent woman and not have to ask a man for anything. It's a good feeling because then he doesn't think he owns you; and he knows that you can make it without him. Even though Fu is not like the knuckle heads you hang around, he's still a man, and if I depend on him for everything, he'll start to feel himself a little too much too. My life might be boring, but it's safer than yours. I don't hang with people who can get me killed or locked up."

"I hear you." I was trying to shut her up.

"Mika, I'm trying to make you open your eyes. You're my sister and I love you. Do you think I want to see you in a casket at your age? The truth is I don't want to have to raise your brat!" We started laughing. As much as I complained about Shani, she was a beautiful person and I'm glad she was my sister.

"But Shani, you think I just hang with these people and don't try to talk to them. I try to show them that I understand. I try to encourage them to get out of the game."

"Your name ain't Jesus. You can't save anybody. And if you want to help somebody, help yourself first. Go back to college and then help someone who wants to be helped. Be a teacher or a psychiatrist. At least get paid for it. Oh excuse me, you do get paid right?" she asked.

"It's not always like that damn, I'm not a hooker. I do have male friends, it's not all about sex all the time. I'm thinking about going back to college. These niggas out here are gettin' so fuckin' cheap. They ain't comin' up off that paper like back in the day when Alpo and Richard Porter were getting it."

"Yeah, well they're still dying and going to jail the same. Come on Mika, I thought you would've learned when Rich got killed. You were too young messing with him. They could have kidnapped you instead of his brother. You weren't even twenty years old, messing with a drug kingpin. The drug game is not a joke and you're getting older now. You have a son to raise. Ain't nothin' wrong with having fun, but the street game is played. The only survivors are the hustlers who've managed to clean their money by opening businesses or getting in with the entertainment industry."

I shook my head. "You know what Shani, you're tellin' the truth. I wasn't going to tell you until I got accepted somewhere, but I called some colleges and they're sending me brochures."

Her eyes opened wide. "That's good Mika. I think that's the best thing for you to do. I'm glad that we're having a civilized conversation and not arguing. I just hope what I'm saying isn't going in one ear and out the other. You have to think about Kian too, not just yourself."

"I know. I know. Shani, thank you for caring about me. It's just that the devil on my left shoulder says 'Don't worry so much! Live! Go for yours! Get *all* the money!' Then the angel on my right says 'Now Mika you've gotta cut this out.' What's a pretty woman to do?" She looked at me like I was crazy and shook her head.

"Girl, I am really convinced that you are off your rocker."

The phone rang, and I answered on the first ring. "Come outside," Asia said.

"Shani that's Asia, I'm going downstairs to see what

Ericka M. Williams

happened. The moment I got downstairs, I saw Asia pacing back and forth. She met me at the front door of the building like she had something important to say.

"I need a package. Let's go upstairs to Dawniece's apartment," she announced.

"For what?"

"The bitch sells coke, crack, E pills and weed. She probably even sells prescription pills and dope too. Come on."

I followed Asia reluctantly, up to Dawniece's apartment. I'd never even knew that she was selling drugs. For some reason, I felt a little uneasy, but Asia knocked on the door like the police.

"Who is it?" a voice yelled.

"Asia and Mika."

"Mika?"

"Come on, she's down too, open the door," Asia explained.

We walked in and there were four people, three guys and a girl in the living room sniffing and smoking crack. It smelled crazy in there. Dawniece was acting all high and jittery. Seeing her Ike that, shook me up a little.

Asia spoke up quick, "What's up with all these people in here, you buggin'. Hurry up and give us a sixty. I ain't trying to go to jail."

"Nah, those are my brothers, my cousin and his wife. I don't be havin' it like that in here. Here you go. Mika, you live right downstairs, you can come up anytime. I didn't know you sniff."

"I don't, I tried it for the first time the other night. It wasn't bad."

"Yeah, it starts off good."

Asia cut the conversation short. "All right, we out," she said, walking with speed toward the door.

Asia and I went downstairs, snuck into my room, and closed the door. As soon as I started, I felt very relaxed. Too good to be true. I didn't know that I was about to add another problem to my life. The more I sniffed the crazier I felt. After a while, I was fucked up and couldn't move.

"Yo Mika, what's up. Don't be havin' no heart attack. Relax, you're doing it to fast," Asia said.

"I'm fucked up though," I stuttered. "I'm speedin' and I'm stuck at the same time. I feel good and crazy at the same time."

"I know it's like a rollercoaster ride. You love it and hate it at the same time. It makes you horny to. I told you, you can go for hours when you're on it," Asia explained.

Instantly, I heard Shani yell, saying the food was ready. I told her I'd eat later. Asia warned me that it would fuck up my appetite. I already knew that from seeing skinny ass Kiki. I stopped doing it for a few minutes, so I could calm down, then started back again. I was starting to feel horny too, so I called Mark. I figured I'd tell him to come over that night since Tamar was supposed to be coming tomorrow.

Mark came over about an hour and three more drinks later. Asia had gone to the liquor store for a bottle after Kian went to sleep. So, saying I was fucked up was an understatement.

As soon as Mark walked in my room, I hugged him and told him to gimme some dick. I immediately started helping him take off his shirt. Even though he wasn't sure why I was acting that way, he took it off and sat on the bed. I realized that the door was open so I closed it and went over to sit on his lap. I wasn't wasting any time. I started kissing him, but he wasn't trying to kiss me back.

"Mika, hold up for a second. Sit next to me for a minute. I wanna talk to you. Damn girl, how many drinks have you had, you smell like a lush." He patted the bed for me to get off his lap and sit next to him.

"What Boo? Why can't we talk later? What's wrong? What's the ma..."

"If you would chill for a minute, I'll tell you what's the matter. Mika, why didn't you tell me you had a fight with Danny's new girl?"

Ericka M. Williams

"Oh please. That's what you're talking about? That shit wasn't nothin'. I just knocked that bitch's face off. That's all."

"Yeah, but it happened when you were supposedly in the house, remember? When you were missing me so much."

Uh-oh, I thought, just before panicking. I couldn't lie well while I was high. "It happened Saturday night. That was the only night I went out. Come on now, that shit is petty."

"No, it's not because I want to know what you're going to do."

"About what?" I asked with a slight attitude. He was blowing my high.

"Danny?"

"What about Danny? Ain't nobody thinking about Danny."

"Look Mika, I'm tired of your games. You're always saying that you're tired of this and that, and niggas that just wanna take you to a hotel. You're full of shit. You always have to be on every set. You're not ready to settle down and raise Kian."

"So what's your point?"

"My point is, that I'm not waitin' around for you to kick the habit."

"Oh now I'm an alcoholic?"

"No, your ass is addicted to the streets," Mark replied.

"Damn, you act like I go out every night. I don't go out every..."

"Listen Mika. You know how I feel about you and you know how I want things to be. So what's up? Are you ready to be with me or what?" he asked, with a serious look on his face.

"What do you mean? I'm always with you."

"So you should be ready to be my girl then."

"I know I'm ready to give you some." I rubbed my clit.

"Mika, can you be serious for one minute?...Are you ready to be my girl? Because I'm tired of waiting to see if we're gonna be together knowing that you go out with other dudes."

I was stuck. The moment had finally arrived and I wasn't ready for it. What was I gonna say, that I wasn't ready yet? Or let me go out with Tamar first and see how it goes and then I'll know. I couldn't say that. He'd walk out and never come back. Why couldn't this have happened later. I'm sure one more month is all I need and then I would be ready. Ready to be a faithful girlfriend. I didn't know what was wrong with me. Mark was perfect. He was the type of man that I knew would make a good husband and father. The type to stay with you and do family things. He was the closest I had to a Prince Charming...I'd seen and gotten all there was to see and get from the streets. Oh well, here goes nothin'.

"Mark, I'll be your girl," I said. I was gonna give it an honest chance. It probably wouldn't work with Tamar all the way in VA anyway.

"All right baby, let's do it how it's supposed to be done. I knew you had feelings for me. You just wanted to play games. Watch Mika, I'm gonna make you so happy because I'm gonna love you right. Now I want some lovin'."

We made love, but it wasn't as good as it would've been before the conversation. My mind was not into it, and taken over by deep thought. I wasn't even horny anymore. I wasn't sure what I had committed myself to. I wondered if being Mark's girl was gonna be the same as being Danny's girl. I knew the answer was no. I knew people wouldn't be going out of their way to do things for me just because I was Mark's girlfriend. I knew I wouldn't have bitches trying to sleep with my man. Well, I won't go that far, there's always some hooker trying to get with your man whether he had cash or not. Being Mark's girl wouldn't mean that much in the street...but so what. I'm not trying to win any popularity contests. As I thought about it, I became more interested in it. It may not be so bad. I did have feelings for him and he deserved more of a chance than anyone else did. Mark had proven that he cared for me.

I had a date with Tamar the next day though. He was a mystery that I wanted to solve. I wanted to see what he was all about. My plan was to go out with him just to have a good time and then that would be it. I promised not to see him anymore. It wasn't like Tamar wasn't going to be any different than any other hustler I'd dealt with.

━━━━━━━━━━━━━━

On Thursday morning Mark woke me up to tell me that he was going home to get ready for work. He gave me a kiss and walked towards the door. He turned around and said, "I'll call you from work, baby. I get off at seven. I'll be over by eight because I wanna stop and get some clothes." I felt like I was in a car driving toward a brick wall, with no brakes. "Well, don't think you're gonna be sleeping over and waking me up at seven every morning. Kian doesn't even get up until nine."

"I can do what I want to now. This is my house." He started laughing.

"Yeah okay." He better slow his role.

I rolled over and went back to sleep. Asia called and woke me up about eleven. I was surprised Kian hadn't already woke me up.

"So what's up? What's going on with Butch?"

"Man listen, his ass is in some deep shit. They're trying to charge him with murder, tax evasion, weapons possession...you should see the list of charges they have against him."

"Damn, why murder? They don't think he killed his own friend do they?" I asked.

"No, but one of the kids that was shooting at them got killed too. The guy that he was with got away so Butch is taking all of the weight because he's the only one in custody. The tax evasion charge is because he had fifty thousand dollars in his car."

All That Glitters

"Damn."

"Mika, would you stop saying damn. His lawyer said he's facing at least thirty years if he gets convicted of all charges."

"Damn," I repeated just to make her mad.

"Well, I'll call you later. I have to take him some stuff from his house that he wants."

"All this flunky work better get you at least five thousand."

"Don't worry I'm gonna get more than that. His mom loves me."

As soon as I hung up, the phone rang. It was Fu for Shani. I thought she was at work. No wonder Kian didn't wake me up. I went to the kitchen and she had her books spread out all over the table. Kian was sitting there eating oatmeal. I gave her the phone and when she got off she said she had taken off of work to study for an exam. I figured I'd take Kian out so he wouldn't disturb her.

We took a cab to Mark's job and got his car. I was gonna have the car whenever I wanted now. It was nothing fancy. He drove a Honda Accord. I took Kian to the movies and when we came back Shani was still studying. She said that Mark had called and would call back. At that point, I decided to go and take him his car. Besides, I didn't want him here when Tamar was supposed to be picking me up. After going to Mark's job, he dropped me off and went back to work.

As soon as I got back in the house the phone rang.

"What," I answered real ghetto-like.

"That's how you answer the phone?" It was Tamar. I was all smiles.

"Hi Tamar, I just walked in, I thought you were someone else."

"What's the matter Boo? You thought I wasn't going to call."

"I knew you better call. Where are you?"

"NYC baby, I'll pick you up at ten," he replied.

Ericka M. Williams

"Huh?"

"Oh what's up, you got other plans?"

"Oh, uh-uh...I'll be ready." I hung up.

What am I gonna do about Kian? Shani has to study. I picked up the phone and called Danny, but he didn't answer. When I went to my closet to pick out an outfit, the phone rang. *Please don't let it be Mark,* I thought. When I looked at the caller ID, I let out a huge sigh. It was Danny.

"Hello," I answered.

"Yeah, what you want now?" Danny asked.

"Asia's boyfriend died and she's real upset. I need you to watch Kian while I go with her to his family's house."

"What that got to do with you?" he asked, in a sarcastic tone.

"That's my girl and she needs me, damn. Your girl won't let you watch your son, faggot?"

"Is that a good idea to call somebody names when you need a favor?"

"A favor? Watching your son is doing me a favor? Damn, I just told you my girl's man died and you can't watch Kian for me?"

"Yeah, me and my girl will watch him. Have his clothes packed. We'll keep him for the rest of the weekend. Oh, and by the way, Asia ain't got no man, she got a football team. Her ass is probably waiting around for some insurance money."

"Whatever. He'll be ready."

I hung up and put on my hot pair of brown Baby Phat boots, a brown pair of velour Baby Phat jeans and a brown Baby Phat sweater with the big pussy cat in gold studs on the front. When I looked in the mirror, I smiled at my fresh new China Doll weave, with the straight bang and long length. It was dark brown with light brown streaks. I knew I looked like a million bucks as I ran my fingers through it.

I had to think fast, because Mark was about to get off of work. I picked up the phone and called his job.

"United Parcel Service," some articulate guy answered.

"Can I speak to Mark Phillips?"

"Just a second."

"Hello?" Mark answered.

"What's up baby?" I asked.

"What's up doll?"

"I can't see you tonight," I said, trying to sound sad.

"Damn, you're starting your shit already? You couldn't even be faithful for a whole week," Mark replied.

Damn, I felt like he could see me all dressed up through the phone. I felt bad, but I wasn't canceling with Tamar. I crossed my fingers.

"Stop playing, Asia's boyfriend got shot and she's real upset. I'm gonna spend the night at her house. Danny is gonna keep Kian."

"All right. I wanted to spend our first day as a couple together. Oh well, call me from Asia's, and be careful doll, you know I love you."

"I love you too." I felt guilty as hell.

Damn. I couldn't believe that he'd fallen for that lie. Even worse, he'd told me to be careful. I vowed to be faithful after that night. I just wanted to do it with Tamar one time. He was sexy as hell, and I didn't want him to get away. It would be like my last night before getting married. Mark was a good man, so I knew he would probably marry me.

Chapter 8

THE MAN

I ran into the living room like a wild woman. "Shani listen, I'm going out with Tamar tonight. I told Mark I was spending the night at Asia's, so if he calls tell him I left already." Shani looked at me like I was crazy. "I'll be back in the morning. Danny is keeping Kian for the rest of the weekend," I added.

"Who is Tamar? Mika didn't we just have this conversation?"

"Shani, I know him okay. Fall back. I'm in a rush. I don't have time. I gotta get Kian ready, but I'll tell you about it later."

I quickly fed Kian and was packing his bag when the doorbell rang. Oh shit, what if Mark decided to stop by, I thought. I nervously opened the door with just my robe on, and breathed a sigh of relief when I saw Danny standing at the door.

"Waiting for me?" he asked, with a sly grin.

I sucked my teeth. "You wish."

"Come on Mika, just take the robe off and let me get some for old times sake."

"Kian! Come on, your father's here!"

Kian ran down the hall toward the door, and into his father's arms. I gave my son a quick kiss on his cheek and rushed them out the door before closing it.

"Asshole!," I said, to myself as I ran back into my room and put some light makeup on. Just mascara, lip gloss, and a little eye shadow was all I needed. I smiled as I put on my Dolce and Gabana perfume, in all the right spots. That's what I loved about seeing different men, the excitement of first dates. I was so anxious. It was like I'd won a free trip somewhere. The phone rang, and my eyes lit up when I saw his number on the caller ID.

"Talk to me baby," I answered quickly.

"Mika, are you ready?"

"Yup. You on your way?" I grinned.

"I'm outside of your building in the car."

"You said ten o'clock, it's only nine-thirty."

"So, I couldn't wait any longer to see you."

"Yeah I'm ready to see you too," I said. "I'm on my way down." I said bye to Shani and jetted out the door.

I smiled the whole way downstairs. When I got outside he was in a Lincoln Navigator with this big black guy driving. I got in looking for some type of welcome, but he was on the phone. Eventually, he got off and motioned for me to move closer under his arm, which I did.

"Where's my kiss?" he asked.

I kissed him on his lips. "What's up handsome?"

"Mika, that's my man, Les. He's my bodyguard. Yo kid, this my new wife, Mika."

Les looked like a mass murderer, but he did speak. "How you doin' Lady?"

"Fine," I answered, and turned to Tamar. "So where are we headed?"

"We're going back across the water. I got a few things to do and then whatever you wanna do."

"All right muhfucka don't have me runnin' errands with you all night."

He grabbed my cheeks and squeezed them real hard.

"You better watch your mouth. Pretty girls shouldn't curse, and if you're gonna be my girl you ain't gonna be talkin' like that."

"All right big daddy whatever you say," I said sarcastically. Another muthafucka who wants to run shit.

Ericka M. Williams

"I can see that you got a smart mouth. One of them know it alls that gotta get a spankin' every once in a while."

"Yeah muthfucka try and hit me, I fight back," I boasted. He popped me in my mouth and I started laughing. I couldn't front, I liked a take charge man. I wasn't with that physical shit though. Even the many times I hit Danny first, and got my ass beat, I still went down fighting.

We went straight to New York, and made three stops. At a candy store on 139th St, an apartment building on 143rd St, and a barber shop. I figured he was picking up money, even though he never came out and told me. After the last stop, he apologized and said that he was ready to hang out. We ended up at a Japanese restaurant, where they cooked on the table in front of you. We were drinking Saki, Japanese liquor, that was no joke. It must've snuck up on me fast 'cuz I was twisted after the second drink. We were cracking jokes on the cook and the other people at our table. Strangely, Les was right there with us.

Once Tamar was good and drunk, I started asking about the girl Angel had told me about. He said they had just broke up and that he was bringing her along with her shit back to New York the weekend he met me. I felt kinda bad when he said she was sniffing coke behind his back. Suddenly, he turned and asked, "You don't mess with coke do you?"

"Hell no," I said, with a straight face. It's not like I really did anyway. I only did it twice, I thought.

"So what did you do to her when you found out she was getting high?"

"I beat her ass!" he yelled.

"I better stop messing with you while I'm ahead," I returned.

"Look baby, I'm a fair man. I did too much for that girl to see her fall off. She was losin' mad weight, not taking care of herself...not to mention having sticky fingers. I gave her what she wanted and she took from me..."

He got quiet and I ran my fingers through his curly hair.

All That Glitters

His hair texture reminded me of Kian's. He put his head on my shoulder. For some reason I felt like I'd known him for a long time. We sat there talking, like we were a couple in love. We finally left the restaurant and wobbled to the car around eleven.

"You staying with me right?" Tamar asked.

"Where?"

"At a hotel?" he responded, with a crazy look.

I thought about it for a minute. I wanted to stay with him. "Yeah, I'm staying with you."

"All right, we're gonna drop Les home first."

"Okay," I responded, in a sleepy voice.

I put my head in his lap and went to sleep. My thoughts were sweet as I slept. I just knew Tamar was going to be the one. When I woke up, we were still driving. *Damn, he sure does live far,* I thought. As I looked out the window, the sun was coming up. I sat up and a few minutes later, it finally hit me. This muthafucka was taking me to Virginia. I nudged Tamar real hard and woke him up.

"Now, I know you're not taking me to Chesapeake! What type of shit is that? How do you know I don't have to do something. What about my son....You're buggin'. Take me home!"

"Mika, chill. I wanna take you to the place where you will eventually be living. I want you to see my house and see that I'm a man who is about his business. I want you to meet my life."

"What do you mean chill? You didn't even ask me. Plus, you told me we were taking Les home."

"He lives with me in Virginia." He started laughing.

"Tamar this is not funny. Who is gonna watch my son?"

"Ask your sister. You said you never have a problem with her watching him."

"Yeah, but she works and goes to school."

"So, tell his Daddy to keep him."

"What!?"

"Look, I just want to spend some more time with you

and I have to get back to VA. to handle something. Think about it. I could've just took you to a hotel and broke out in the morning, if all I wanted was some ass. I wouldn't bring you all the way to Virginia just to have sex with you. Call your son's father and tell him you went on vacation for a couple of days. Let him watch his son."

"I guess so. He is keeping him for the rest of the week-end."

"See baby, you knew you would want to stay with me too. I just want to concentrate on me and you and sending you back home as mine. As far as I see it, you're mine now."

Yeah, you and Mark. "Tamar, I do want to see your house and how you're living, but for real, that wasn't right. Why didn't you just ask me?"

"If you don't have a good time, then you don't have to see me again. Deal?" He held out his hand, and waited for my response.

"I guess." I was acting mad, but I'd already gotten over it. Instantly, I thought abut Mark. I had to think of a way to get in touch with him. Plus, I needed to call Asia. She didn't even know I had lied to Mark and told him, I was with her. I hope this trip is worth it...

When I arrived at Tamar's place, I got excited. His house was not exactly on the beach, but it had water behind it that led to the beach. It was like a cove. The house was nice, but not huge like I thought it would be. However, I did like the pool table, workout equipment, and the bar. Even the bedroom where Les stayed was nice. I also admired the huge master bedroom with the sliding doors glass doors that led to a wooden deck.

"So, do you like my house?" he asked.

"Yeah, it's really nice, but it could use a woman's touch."

"It had a woman's touch and the bitch touched too much." We both laughed. "You ready to move in?"

"You better stop playing before I send for my son and

all my shit. Besides, if I move in how are you gonna have all of your hookers visit you?"

"I'll have to take them to a hotel," Tamar joked.

"I know you would. You're just like the rest. A dog and a mess!"

"Nah, I'm messin' with you. I told you before, I've had pussy and I've had more pussy. I've had so much pussy I had to put some in storage. I still have some in the garage, wanna see?"

I rolled my eyes and lightly punched him in the stomach.

"Nah, for real I told you I'm not living like that anymore. I need a real woman who can stand strong next to me. Females think this life is all a big party. Money, champagne, houses and cars. All girls wanna do is party and play. Then when the cash gets scarce, so do they. Think of what it's like to always be looking behind your back. If you're not dodging the Feds, you're dodging a bullet. All because I want a better life. Because I don't want to die in the same place where I was born...in the projects."

"I understand," I said, realizing he was taking his conversation seriously.

"The Feds wanna put me in jail because I'm a young, black man with a house and three cars; but the government makes drug dealers by allowing the shit to come in and that's their way of locking a brother up. I'm not a killer, a rapist, or a child molester. I'm just trying to make a living. This whole fucking world is crooked. I'm just giving people what they gonna get from someone else if they don't get it from me."

"Yeah, but you got women neglecting their children, all for drugs." I am gonna make sure I don't get hooked on that shit. "So it doesn't bother you at all?" I asked, with a serious tone.

"Yeah, I think about it. I have to plan how I'm going to get out and do it right. When I was fourteen years old selling dope out of my sock, I didn't know what I was getting

Ericka M. Williams

myself into."

"You know I just realized that I don't have any clothes or underwear."

"Don't worry, Yanira left some underwear in the drawer."

"I'll smack you with my shoe. I'm not wearing anybody else's underwear."

"Yo, you fall for anything. Come on let's go to the mall."

═══════════════

By the time we got to the mall, I'd found out a lot of information on Tamar. We walked through Greenbriar Mall, holding hands, like we were a real couple. I was diggin' him, and hoped he was digging me too. He was cool, smart, and not unbearably arrogant. He was a little like Mark, but more street. Damn, *I still didn't call Asia,* I thought to myself.

"Hey girl, stop daydreaming."

"I was thinking about my baby...If we get with each other for real, how are you going to treat my son?" I asked bluntly.

"Like he's mine...I won't treat him any different than our other kids."

"You are such a playa."

"I'm for real. Yo, I like you. I'm gonna give you a chance. I want a good girl and you seem like you could be one, with a little guidance from me. You definitely ain't a dumb broad. I'm tired of girls, with no upbringing, who I have to raise and teach. Like Ya Ya, she had a fucked up childhood. Her mom is a fiend and her uncle raped her. I tried to show her a better life, but she didn't appreciate it 'cause she wasn't used to shit."

"So are you ready to get married?"

"I haven't found a female that made me want to get married yet...Oh, look at that piece of lingerie. Let's go in here." He grabbed my arm and pulled me into Victoria's Secret. A man always changes the subject when the 'M'

All That Glitters

word is brought up.

Tamar bought me five pairs of sexy underwear and two teddies. He wanted me to model one of the teddies in the store but I didn't. We continued through the mall, acting like husband and wife, and it felt good. I went into Against All Odds and got two Baby Phat sets of course. He said he was taking me to a party the next night at Playas Joint, so I went into Nordstroms and picked out a pants suit that was fat as hell. It was blue and with a matching cowboy hat. Before it was all said and done, Tamar had spent about $1,000.00 on me. I loved it!

When we got back to the house, the first thing I did was call Asia on her cell, but it went straight to her voice mail. "Damn," I said softly. I left a message saying that I was in Virginia wit' Tamar and that I'd told Mark, I was with her. Then, I called Danny's house to speak to Kian, and his bitch answered.

"Yeah, let me speak to my son," I snapped.

I heard her call Kian from another room and told Danny who seemed to be next to her, that it was "The Crab" on the phone. I hope she wasn't gonna make me have to fuck her up again.

"Mommy?" Kian said, sounding like he was glad I called.

"Hey baby, you havin' fun?"

"Yeah, my cousins are here playing with me."

"That's good, I'll see you Monday okay? Tell your Dad I'll call on Monday when I want him to bring you home, okay?"

"Okay Mommy, I love you."

"I love you too."

I wanted to call Mark next, but didn't know what I would say. When Tamar asked me who I was seeing I told him that it wasn't serious. I should've told him the truth. Some girlfriend I was. I knew Mark deserved better than me. He would probably never speak to me again. I knew Shani was probably worried too, but this time it wasn't my fault.

Ericka M. Williams

Tamar had kidnapped me. I'll call her when she gets in from work to let her know that I am fine, and having a nice time, I thought.

Tamar came out of his room with a new set of clothes on wanting to know who I'd called. I just shrugged my shoulders wondering where in hell he was going.

"Listen, I gotta go to Norfolk for somethin'," he said.

"And? I hope you're not going to leave me stuck in the house." I placed my hands on my hips.

"I'll be back. I'm not gonna leave you stuck."

"So when are you gonna take me around? I wanna see the restaurant and..."

"I'll take you tomorrow."

"I'm leaving Sunday." I wanted to see what he was going to say.

"No, you're not, you're leaving Monday."

I couldn't lie, I did like that control shit sometimes! "I have to get my son!"

"I know, Boo, but I want you to stay. What's one more day?"

"I'll think about it." He came over and slid in between my legs, as I sat on the stool. He kissed me on my neck. I wondered why he hadn't made a move yet.

"All right. I'll be back. What do you want me to bring you back to eat?"

"Chinese. Pepper Steak to be exact."

"All right baby." He gave me a kiss and walked toward the kitchen door that led to the garage. He turned around and said, "Oh, I set up a hot bubble bath for you." He opened the door and shut it behind him.

I jumped up and ran to the door. I opened it and said, "You're gonna give me some when you get back, right?"

He opened the door to his two door Benz and replied, "I'll think about it."

When he got in, I closed the kitchen door. I loved his game! I went into the master bathroom and looked at the step-down Jacuzzi. The bathroom was all black and fat to death. I took off my clothes as fast as I could and slid into the bubbles. *I'm gonna do him in this tub before I leave,* I thought.

I thought about how Tamar had it goin' on as I leaned back and realized there was a champagne glass on the ledge of the tub and a bottle in the stand next to the tub. It was too good to be true. I laughed. *He's probably gonna wine and dine me, send my ass home, and start acting shitty. Even if he didn't act up, what if I fall for him and he gets locked up or killed? Even still, I just can't leave Mark alone. He's my baby too. Damn, what am I gonna do?*

Chapter 9

FALLING

I got out of the bubble bath and put on the lavender terry cloth robe that was hanging on the door. I wondered how many women had been in that robe. Suddenly, I felt the urge to take a nap. I walked into the bedroom, laid on the bed, and picked up the remote. I didn't know what the TV channels were in VA, so I started at Channel 2 and kept going until I found something that caught my attention. However, my search didn't last long because before I knew it, I'd fallen asleep.

Several minutes later, I woke up to the feeling of someone unloosening my robe. I quickly sat up on my elbows and noticed Tamar at my feet. He opened my robe to view one of the cute little underwear sets that he'd bought me. He leaned over, opened my legs and crawled in between them. He started by kissing my forehead and making his way to my lips. Suddenly, he stood up and took his clothes off.

Tamar kissed my stomach and started moving down, further and further until he was downtown. He wasn't anxious like most niggas, he was smooth. I loved his style more and more, especially the way he licked me like a sweet lollipop. His eating game was unusual, real sweet. All of a sudden, music came on. *That slick muthafucka must've set it before he woke me up.* I closed my eyes as the sounds of R. Kelly filled the room, and my soaked ass moved to the beat.

Tamar was gentle and slow. He took his time trying to learn my body. At that moment, I knew he was the one for me. He stuck his tongue slowly inside of me. My muscles relaxed and I grabbed the sheets on both sides and put my head way back. "Damn, Tamar," I screamed.

I felt his wet kiss creep up my walls like he was painting with a paint roller, up and down, nice and slow. I felt the sensation coming and knew I couldn't stop it. He used the slow motion to bring my potion down.

"Damn baby, you coming already?" he asked with a smile.

"Shut up and keep kissin' it," I moaned and pressed his head inward. My body started jerking but he kept his position. He made his tongue stiff and let my juice run straight down his throat. I lifted my butt up off the bed just as he took two more licks and then wiped his mouth with the back of his hand.

"How you want yours baby?" I asked him smiling. I had never been satisfied like that before.

"Get up on your knees and turn around."

"Oh, you want it from the back huh?" I said seductively.

"Yeah. Mr. Nice Guy is gone," he boasted. He grabbed me by shoulders and pushed me to my knees. He stood on the edge of the bed and thrust his body into mine. Tamar almost knocked me down on the bed the way he tugged with force. He grabbed my waist and pulled me back up and put himself back in. Instantly, he started long stroking me. He hugged me around my waist to keep us close. I was on my hands and knees, serving my baby for a good half hour, he was gettin' it. He grabbed my thighs for the final ride and I knew it was time. He gave one last thrust, let out a "Goddamn!" and threw me down on my stomach. I laid still for several minutes with his joint still in. We melted into each other and became one.

It was different than the usual casual fuck. He poured his body into mine, and I was open to take him in. It was almost like being with Mark, like there were real feelings

Ericka M. Williams

there. If there was such a thing as overnight love, I'd found it.

When I finally came, he did too. Wow! *A simultaneous climax from the first round?* I might have to pack my bags Monday and come on down like Bob Barker on the Price is Right, I said to myself.

Tamar laid inside my nest for a few minutes and then finally pulled out. He smacked my hips and said, "I knew you would be a trooper."

I laughed. "Nah baby, I'm not an Isuzu, I'm a Ferrari."

He laughed and rolled over. Just then the phone rang and he got up to answer it. He stood in front of me, butt-naked. I looked him over, and knew he was sure of himself because he didn't even turn around and face the other way. He knew his body was tight. I knew it was a girl on the phone because he wasn't saying anything. Whoever was on the other line was probably asking him a bunch of questions or cursing him out.

Suddenly, I thought, *Shit, he didn't even wear a rubber.* At that moment, I thought about me and Shani's little talk the other day. Normally, I made guys that I didn't know wear rubbers, so I prayed to God this wasn't the one time when I should've.

"Yo, baby, I said I have company. I'll check you later," Tamar said, in a loud tone. He took a deep breath, hung up the phone, and jumped on the bed. As bad as I wanted to know what that was all about, I didn't ask any questions.

"Come here baby, you ready for part two?" he asked.

"Yeah, come on Daddy, let's release that stress you just got from that phone call."

He started laughing. "You should be a comedian, you're funny as hell...But don't sweat that call, it didn't mean any-thing."

"Yeah, that's what they all say. You better come on because the drug store is getting ready to close," I replied.

"Oh, so you think your shit is dope, huh?" he asked.

"You know it baby."

"Yeah well I'm not the type to get strung out no matter how good the dose is."

"Well, I guess this is going to be one of those rare occasions...I'm gonna get you hooked."

He started shaking like a junkie. "Come on baby, give me another hit..." I started laughing. "You know what Mika? I like you. You gotta a lot of game, just like a nigga."

"What do you mean I got ga...?"

"Ssh." He kissed my lips cutting me off. "Let me get some more of that drug."

He rolled on his back and pulled me on top of him. Damn, his body was solid and so was his dick. He was in and out in a shorter time than the last, but it was still good. It's a good thing I was on the pill because I wasn't one of those get pregnant by a stranger and have the baby as long as he has paper type of girls. The next time I had a baby I was going to be married. I climbed off of Tamar and laid next to him."

"So where's my Chinese Food?"

"In the kitchen, go get two plates and bring it in here," he ordered.

"All right, but don't get used to this because when we get married I want a maid."

"I guess I'll never get out of the game if I gotta have maids, cooks, nannies and shit."

"Okay you're right. Forget the nanny. I don't need anybody taking care of my kids."

"You're a mean Queen baby. You got it goin' on," he replied with a smile.

"I'm as bad as they come. I put my bra and a pair of his boxers on and went into the kitchen. I made two plates and went back to the room. When I returned, he was laying on his back butt naked watching videos on BET.

"Oh yeah, you get cool points for that bubble bath and champagne set up," I said handing him a huge plate of food. "That was real slick. Where'd you read about that in 'How to be a Mac'?"

Ericka M. Williams

"You ain't used to that romantic shit, huh?"

"I'm gonna sit back and see how long this romance shit is gonna last. And you better be good to me or my brother is gonna see you."

"Uh-oh, I know about those so-called brothers. Is this your real brother or somebody that you're real close to and fuck with from time to time?"

I started laughing. "No, it's not like that," I said in between bites.

"Yeah, right. Well, you better tell that brother that he ain't your brother anymore. That from now on y'all are just friends."

"I'm talking about, Dior," I said.

"Oh, that's my man. He's a cool brother, even though he's from Jersey...All right I'll excuse you this time...But don't let me get to that party tomorrow and have any of my boys coming up to me telling me they knocked you down. I can't stand when I hear that my girl used to mess with somebody I know. Niggas like to tease about that shit."

I thought, *uh-oh.* I didn't want any drama at that party. I hadn't even thought about something like that happening. I wasn't gonna sweat it though. I prayed he didn't know Fatso because he'd probably make fun of me instead of getting mad about that one. He might've known Wayne, but I wasn't concerned about that because I knew he would never say anything negative about me. Wayne and I weren't just sex partners when we messed around, we were serious or so I thought. I was more serious about him. I was seeing him for a couple of months until his wife called me one day and ruined my fairytale relationship.

I was startled by Tamar nudging me in my side.

"What?"

"I said what do you think about that?" I had no idea what he was talking about.

"What are you doing? Daydreaming about me? I'm talking about what's on T.V. They're talking about black people calling each other, nigga. So, what do you think

Rockhead?" Tamar asked.

"What do *you* think Nucka? You seem to have all the answers."

"I think it's all right because we don't mean it in a bad way. I got mad love for my niggas. Plus, we're messing with the white man's head by using it because we switched around a derogatory word that they used against us and made it peace amongst us," he replied.

"A lot of us feel that way, but many older people don't because they went through the civil rights movement. Plus, they feel that it's stupid because if white people used the word we will fuck them up." I sat my plate on the night-stand.

"Nobody told them to start that shit in the first place. Either way it doesn't really matter because it's just a word, and we don't have to use it how they used it. They're not the boss of me!" he explained.

We both started cracking up laughing. Then, out of the blue, I turned, looked at Tamar and realized I much I loved his conversation. "Tamar, you're retarded, but I like a man who can talk about more than cars, sports, bitches, and music."

"Oh, so you thought I was a verbally crippled muthafuc-ka?" he asked.

"No, but some niggas are."

"Oh, why you gotta say the N word, I'm offended."

I punched him in the stomach, and we started fighting playfully, which was foreplay for me. I pushed him off the bed and he got up and pinned me down. I felt his hard ass dick on my leg. Damn, this nigga don't quit. I gave up the fight and joined him in round three.

I was falling fast and hard for Tamar, and forgot that I promised myself I wouldn't, but everything was happening too fast. I looked down at him, as we did it good and hard, but we weren't fucking, we were making love.

Chapter 10

HIP HOP RULES

I woke up butt-naked and beat. I felt like all the energy had been drained out of me. Tamar was no joke in the bedroom. He wore me out the night before until I fell asleep. If I would've left it up to him, we'd still be doin' it. When I looked over he was knocked out, mouth wide open with dry spit on his cheek. I picked up the phone quietly and called my house.

The machine came on, so I left a message for Shani. "Hi Shani, don't be mad or worried, I'm fine. I'll be home Monday," I said, feeling guilty. "If you want to call me, hit me on my cell." I hung up. I hoped she didn't have my mother worried. Next, I called Asia but her machine came on too.

"Damn Asia, where are you? I've been trying to get in touch with you. Call me on my cell." I hung up and turned over. *Mark is never gonna speak to me again*. I laid across Tamar's chest and stuck my tongue in his ear. He jumped.

"What's up baby, you startin' it up so early in the morning?" he asked.

"No, I was just trying to wake you up." When he sat up on the bed and stretched, I turned the TV on.

"Gimme a kiss," he said, in a begging voice. He slid his arms around my waist and stuck his tongue deep in my mouth.

"Take that filmy chalky mouth to the bathroom and brush those teeth!" I yelled, wiping my mouth.

"After you give me some," he begged.

"Give you some what? I'll give yo' ass some toothpaste, but that's it. You're not touchin' me until we come in from the party tonight. I think you better join Nymphos Anonymous because you got an addiction baby."

"Only for you," he returned.

I gave him a smirk. "Tamar must we have game so early in the morning?"

"Okay, I'll stop, for now. So, what do you want to do today lady?"

"I want to go to your restaurant. Then I wanna go to Kings Dominion. I've always wanted to go there."

"That's like a two hour drive."

"So, Les can drive," I suggested.

He scratched his head. "We'll see about that."

We stayed in the bed watching TV for at least another hour, before we took a bath together. It felt like I was a star in the movie, Scarface as we sat in his huge Jacuzzi. He sat on one side and I sat on the other. As we talked, I imagined us married.

By the time we got dressed and made our way into the kitchen, Les had made breakfast. He hooked us up with pancakes, eggs, and grits. The food was delicious. After we ate, we hopped in a black RX 300 Lexus. I asked Tamar what happened to the car we were in the first night I met him, and he said that the lease was up and he gave it back. He said he leased most of his cars, and only owned one. The Navigator was his. He said the Lexus truck was originally for this girl who hustled for him, but she was locked up and the lease had another year on it.

"So you should let me take it home," I shot back.

He gave me a funny look. "I'll think about it."

We got to his soul food restaurant around three o'clock, and I was hungry all over again. He took me in the kitchen and introduced me to the cooks, and his mother who ran the restaurant for him. She seemed very nice. On our way upstairs to the office, he introduced me to the girl who was the hostess. She was very pretty and although it was her job to welcome the customers, I didn't get a warm welcome from her. I knew what that meant.

When we got in the office I instantly said, "See why you shouldn't fuck with the help?"

"Mika, it was nothing. I was with her one time after me and Ya Ya broke up. She must've thought it meant she was gonna be my girl, and when she realized it wasn't happening, she started buggin'. She's been actin' crazy ever since, I might have to fire her and hire you."

I shook my head. "Men can't be trusted."

"You gotta give a brother a chance though. You act like you been an angel all your life, like you ain't never hurt nobody."

His comment instantly made me think about Mark. *It's not that I've been an angel, but when you try to be good to somebody they take you for granted. It seems like a man will sweat you if you run around like him, but if he knows you're gonna be good he doesn't know how to act. I've been hurt and I'm not takin' any more shorts.*

"But see you gotta let your guard down. You're only gonna hurt yourself because you're going to come across a good man and not realize it. You can't do somebody wrong just because somebody did wrong to you."

"Well, when I meet the right man, I'll be good. My father left me and the first man I ever really loved did too. Last year, my motto became, "Fuck niggas!" I shot him a serious look.

"I understand that, but women hurt men too. I've had bitches break my heart," Tamar responded.

"Look, I'm gonna try not to carry my baggage to this situation with you, but every time I get hurt I give a little less to the next relationship. It's natural, to start protecting yourself."

"Let's just see what happens. Our destiny is up to us, not your last nigga or my last bitch and since they're gone, why should we let them fuck with our shit?" He moved real

All That Glitters

close to me, like he wanted something to go down in his office. "Now let's go back to the house and get ready for tonight. They're three other couples who are going with us."

An hour later, we were back at the house. Les was in the kitchen cooking with his girl. I was glad to know he had a chick. "Yo, Maggie, this is my new wife, Mika," Tamar said.

I hated that 'wifey' shit. *Give me a ring and then you can call me your wife.*

"How you doin' Mika, my name is Dee Dee. Stupid calls me Maggie because he claims I'm always in rollers and my robe." She laughed.

"Nice to meet you, Dee Dee," I said, giving her a slight wave. She was short and cute, with long hair resembling a woman mixed with Black and Indian. Suddenly, I was glad I had somebody to hang out with at the party; I wasn't going to be following Tamar around all night.

I kicked it with Tamar, Les, and Dee Dee for a couple of hours before I realized I needed some stockings for the party. I asked Dee Dee if she could take me to the store real quick. When she agreed, Tamar gave us both a funny look and said, "All right, don't make us have to come looking for y'all. Here, take the Lex."

Dee Dee grabbed the keys and smiled like she was glad to get away. We talked the entire time we were gone. I found out that she was a hairdresser and orginally from Norfolk, but most importantly, she loved to smoke weed. After her short bio, she rolled a blunt and begged me to smoke it with her. We hit it off real well. When we got back, I tried not to give myself away,but I was acting too silly. Everything Tamar said was hilarious.

"What's up, how do I look?" he asked.

"Ooh Boo, you look so cute." He really did. He looked like money. I giggled and gave him a hug. His linen suit was tight.

"You look classy too baby."

"Thank you," I said woozy.

Ericka M. Williams   109

"What's wrong with you man? Why you so sil...Oh, you and Dee Dee was smokin' that shit, huh? I should've known when you came in here gigglin' and shit. Oh boy, I guess y'all are gonna be good friends now."

"She's cool... I like her," I said, following him into the living room where Les and Dee Dee were dressed and ready to go. They looked nice together, even though his ass was big as hell.

"Yo Les, tell Maggie not to be corrupting my girl...givin' her drugs. I had to get rid of the last one over that shit."

They both laughed, and we all headed out the door. We left in two separate cars. Tamar and I were in the Benz and they were in Dee Dee's Audi. First, we went to eat at the Pirate's Reef Restaurant, which was a docked ship. We met the other two couples there. For some reason, one of the guys looked familiar. As soon as we were seated, the drinks were in effect. The table soon became live in no time. It became a battle of the sexes.

Dee Dee said, "Don't you hate when you call your man's cell and he doesn't answer. Then when you see him he claims that he didn't get the call because his battery was low."

We agreed, "Yup, yup! Word, right?"

Then Tamar said, "Nah, females think they slick too. You could be at their spot and another nigga calls and you know it because she got a stupid ass look on her face. Then when you ask her who it was it's, 'Oh, he's just a friend.' He's a friend, but you ain't never heard his name during your whole relationship."

I had to add somethin'. "That ain't nothin'. I found a hotel receipt in my ex-man's drawer and he tried to tell me he was so tired one day, and that there was so many people at his house he couldn't get any rest. So he went to a hotel." The girls shook their heads.

"Yeah, but you fell for it right? I know you didn't leave him," Tamar's friend Dap said. "I hate when females complain. It's your fault, you let us get away with too much shit." He held his glass high in the air.

"Oh is that so?" his girl asked with an annoyed look.

"Look, y'all are just as bad. I was tellin' Mika that today. I know mad scheming bitches. I got so many girl cousins and they run mad games on niggas," Dee Dee interjected.

"We got it from y'all," I said turning my attention to Tamar. "I hope you don't think you're gonna be acting up when I'm up in Jersey."

The whole table got quiet until Dee Dee spoke up. "Don't worry girl, I'll watch him while you're gone."

"Les, I'm gonna have to evict your girl, man," Tamar said. We laughed, ate, and drank some more, until it was time to go. Ty, Tamar's other friend said, "Why don't we let the ladies go together? Dee Dee knows how to get there."

I could tell that Ty's girl, Monet, was not thrilled about the idea. She had been fairly quiet most of the night. "Oh you're starting your shit already? All right, no problem," Monet said, with a smirk. "Come on girls."

"Shut up man. Ain't nobody trying to hear that shit!" Ty shouted. He seemed like a mean muhfucka.

Tamar asked me what I wanted to do and I told him I would go with the girls, I didn't care. He gave me the keys and money for drinks, and left out behind Les.

We met them there about twenty minutes later, and went straight to the bathroom, like ladies always do. We checked our appearances, re-applied our makeup, tightened our belts, and sucked in our tummies. We were ready to make our grand entrance. The place was really nice. It reminded me of Tavern on the Green in Central Park. There were two dance floors, a room with a long table with all types of finger foods. There was a lounge area with couches and a big screen TV. They were playing an old Mike Tyson fight on the screen. There was even an outdoor patio. We went to the bar and still didn't see our men. We got our first round and sat down at a table along the dance floor. When I finished my drink I was ready to ask Dee Dee some questions about Tamar.

Ericka M. Williams

"So, how long have you been with Les?" I asked innocently.

"Two years," Dee Dee replied.

"For real? Are you in love?" I asked playing detective.

"Yeah. He gave me some problems in the beginning,
but he's calmed down a lot since then."

"That's good."

"I know you wanna know about Tamar right?" She
laughed.

"I can't front, hell yeah! What is it with him? He seems
so straight up, but it seems too good to be true."

"Tamar is cool, but he's hard to call when it comes to
females. I've seen him be faithful and I've seen him be a
dog. Of all the girls I've seen him with, Yanira was the one
he really loved, but she fucked up. When he was with her
he seemed really happy. He was messin' with my girlfriend
and he played her. Don't say anything because Les would
kill me. Anyway, when I met Les he was with Tamar and I
was with my friend, Jackie. We all hooked up and it was
cool for a minute. We went out and vacationed often. Once
we were headed for Florida just to chill and two days
before we were to leave, she told me she was pregnant.
They had only been talking for two months. She said she
was going to tell him when we got there. I told her it was
best if she waited until we came back because she didn't
know how he would react, but she didn't listen. We got
there and the second night we were at dinner, asshole
decided to tell him in front of me and Les. And, to make a
long story short, he left her ass in Florida and Les had to
send her home on the plane."

"Why did he flip on her like that?" I asked with a confused expression.

"I'm saying, they had only been talking for a couple of
months and she announced it like they were a happily married couple. You don't do no shit like that."

Damn, I'd heard enough. I turned and started looking
for Tamar. The dance floor was packed and a lot of pimpin'

was goin' on. Where Tamar and his friends were was still a mystery though. We all started dancing when Biggie came on like we'd known each other for years. Next, it was 50 Cent and then Lil Wayne. They were playing all the bangers back to back. This guy went up to Keisha, Dap's girl, and started dancing with her.

Suddenly, Dee Dee grabbed my arm and Monet said, "Come on let's leave that bitch!" We went to the bar and while we waited to order, they gave me the run down on Keisha. They said they didn't like her because for one, she wasn't Dap's real girl. She was Dap's girl's best friend. They said he always brought her when he went out of town, so they didn't have to sneak around. Dee Dee and Monet were friends with his official girl, Regina, but they couldn't tell her what was going on because Les and Ty would go crazy on them.

I thought that was the craziest thing I'd ever heard. I wanted to say something, but spotted the boys, and pointed them out. They were walkin' away from the bar with three bottles of champagne and headed into the lounge area. We paid for our drinks and made it through the crowd to where they were. We saw them seated at a small table with three girls standing around them. What a lovely surprise. We ignored the girls and walked right up to them.

"Where the fuck y'all been?" Monet asked, with attitude. "Oh ladies, you're excused!" She gave the girls a look and they sucked their teeth and walked away.

"What's up with that?" Dee Dee asked, heated.

"That ain't nothin' but chicken head hawks circlin' around the smell of success," Ty stated arrogantly.

Tamar pulled me onto his lap. He handed a glass to me, and I placed it on the table.

"Yo, where's Keisha?" Dap wanted to know.

"Talking to Regina," Monet joked. "She's dancing, fool."

Dap went to look for her, and Tamar started kissing my neck. He appeared to be drunk, so I had an idea to get him back for the day before.

Ericka M. Williams

"Tamar," I called.

"What's up baby?"

"Don't be mad, but this guy I used to talk to is here and he wants me to go somewhere with him. If I don't catch back up to you, I'll call you in the morning."

He squeezed my arm real tight and pulled me close to him. He whispered in my ear, "If you think you're going to embarrass me in front of my boys, you're wrong. Do you know who I am, bitch?"

"Ooh, somebody's angry." I started laughing. "I had to get you back for scaring me yesterday."

"Oh, so you got jokes? That shit wasn't funny. I was getting ready to knock your head off."

I pulled him out of the chair and led him to the dance floor. I couldn't believe I'd only known him a week. We were in our own little world, like no one else existed. I pulled him close and grabbed his ass. He locked his arms around my neck and let me feel his body against mine. When I turned around, he came up close behind me. Seconds later, Biggie's song *JUICY* blasted through the speakers, so I sang along with Big Poppa. "It was all a dream, I used to read Word Up Magazine, Salt 'n Peppa and Heavy D up in the limousine. Hanging pictures on my wall every Saturday rap attack Mr. Magic Marley Marl..."

We danced for two more songs and I told him I needed to use the bathroom. I snatched Monet to go with me. I was starting to really like her; especially when I found out she was from Harlem, because most of my family was from Harlem. We talked, fixed our hair, and did the girl thang. When we came back they were gone.

So, we grabbed Dee Dee, leaving Keisha in her seat to wait for the fellas. We paraded around like the party was for us. We got more drinks and by then I was ripped. The DJ said he would play an hour of old school Hip Hop and it brought back memories. I screamed when the DJ played *'Bitches ain't Shit'* by Dr. Dre. "Bitches ain't shit but hoes and tricks lick on the balls and suck the dick," I yelled. We

All That Glitters

were dancing, and having a good time, but I felt funny. I yelled in Monet's ear, "Why are we dancing to this? They're talking about us."

"They ain't talking about me. I ain't no bitch or ho, at least not all the time," she responded. We both laughed. "I'm joking, you're right, but the beat is so dope that you forget what they're saying."

I got ready to walk off the dance floor when *'U.N.I.T.Y.'* by Queen Latifah came on. We both got hyped and started dancing and singing the words real loud, "Instinct leads me to another flow every time I hear a brotha call a girl a bitch or a hoe tryin' to make a sister feel low you know all of that gots to go...who you callin' a bitch U.N.I.T.Y," we yelled loudly.

After two more songs I was tired of dancing. We set out to find the men again, who were only a few steps away, dancing with some other girls. When Monet saw Ty squeezing some girl's ass she flipped!

"All right, bitch, you gotta go!" she shouted and snatched Ty's arm from around her.

"I know you ain't talking to me!" the girl shouted.

"I'm gonna show you bitch!" Monet got ready to punch the girl just as Ty grabbed her, and pulled her out to the patio. Tamar walked away from the other girl, grabbed my hand and walked out to the patio too. Monet cursed Ty out, and he kept telling her to fall back and that she'd better stop making a scene or he was going to embarrass her. I think it was the liquor making her bug out because she swung and punched him right in the jaw. All I saw after that was him, on the ground, on top of her. She screamed and tried to get up. Tamar went over and pulled him off of her. She got up looking a mess. Her lip was bleeding and her clothes were soiled and wrinkled.

"Mika, take her to the bar to get some ice and then meet us outside," Tamar ordered.

There were people watching us as we passed. Dee Dee ran up to us and asked what had happened. When I told

Ericka M. Williams

her, we both took Monet to get some ice. Besides the fact that she looked terrible, she was very upset. Monet tried to press her hair back down into place. It just wasn't working. We found Keisha and left.

We all got in our cars and went our separate ways. I got Monet's hotel number because she said she would be going back to New York in the morning. I told her I was thinking about making a reservation to fly back with her. I missed Kian and Mark, so I was ready to go home. I didn't want to stay until Monday. Plus, I wanted to leave so I could see how Tamar was gonna act.

When we got to the house I asked Tamar to make me a bowl of ice cream while I undressed. I was still drunk, but that shit with Monet had sobered me up a bit. I finished my ice cream, and drifted off to sleep, until I was quickly interrupted by Tamar undressing me. I was tired, but not too tired for sex, *his sex.* He scooped me up from the sheets and carried me to the Jacuzzi, which was full of bubbles. The warm water felt good as I sat down inside the soothing water.

Tamar took his clothes off and got in. "So did you like the party?"

"Yeah, it was okay."

"Yo, Monet is a crazy bitch. She always does shit like that, so don't let that situation bother you."

"Ty shouldn't have been squeezing on that girl's ass."

"Oh, it's a crime to dance with other girls? You wasn't mad."

"I didn't say it was a crime. I said, he shouldn't have been squeezin' asses. And I'm not your girl, so I can't get mad." I wondered if Tamar would've done the same thing.

"Still she shouldn't have made a scene like that. She should've pulled him to the side and talked to him."

Yeah, *he would've.* "So I guess it's her fault that she has a fat lip," I asked.

"Hell yeah it's her fault. She disrespected her man in front of a whole party. Hold up, I don't have shit to do with it, so let's just change the subject before you start getting mad at me. Show me some love."

He grabbed the back of my thighs and pulled me toward him. I loved fuckin' in the Jacuzzi. We did it forcefully, making our own waves. When he came, I went...right to sleep.

Chapter 11

QUEENS

The phone woke me up the next morning and scared the shit out of me. Tamar didn't budge, so I picked it up like I lived there.

"Hello?"

"Mika, it's Monet."

"What's up girl? How you feelin'?"

"I'm okay, but I'm getting the fuck away from this muthafucka. He's over here losing his mind. You still thinking about flying out with me?"

"Uh uh, what's your flight number? And what time are you leaving? I'll call there right now." She gave me the information and said the flight left at 3:00pm. "All right, let me call now, and I'll call you right back."

Tamar rolled over. "Where do you think you're going?"

"Tamar, I have to go home. I haven't seen my son since Thursday. "You gonna let me take the Lex?"

"Yeah baby, take it. I'll be up there by the weekend. If not, you can drive back down here."

I called Monet back and told her to cancel her reservation and ride home with me. Tamar watched me closely the whole time I was talking to her. "Are you gonna dream about me every night?" he asked when I hung up.

"Hell no," I commented. "But come on, make your queen some breakfast."

He picked up the phone and dialed, "Yo Les, you up man? Come up and make breakfast. Mika's leaving in a little while."

"Damn, how much do you pay him?"

"That man gets $1700 a week just to chill in a nice house rent free, travel, and all he has to do is cook and watch my back. I'd say my man is doin' well."

"Would you do his job?" He looked at me like I was stupid. "See, I know you wouldn't," I explained.

"Les ain't the hustlin' type. He's not a business type nigga. He's happy with that money. I'm the mastermind and he's the watchdog. I make in a day what he makes in a week." He got out the bed and stretched. "Let's go eat."

When we walked into the kitchen, Les was starting breakfast and Dee Dee was at the table with her scarf and robe on.

"What's up Maggie?" I said to her.

"Oh, he's rubbin' off on you…And you, Tamar, what were you doing dancing with that girl last night. I hope Mika got in yo' ass."

"No, she didn't. I got her trained, right Mika?" Tamar asked patting my ass.

"You got me trained? I just wasn't sweatin' it because I met a cutie last night too." Dee Dee and I started laughing and slapped hands. Tamar playfully slapped my face and told me to stop playing or he would cut my titties off.

"I thought you were gonna leave tomorrow? I wanted to take you around my way," Dee Dee said sadly.

"Damn, that would've been nice, but I gotta go see my baby, I miss him." I ate quickly, and snuck in the room to make a few phone calls. I called my house first. I instantly felt a lump in my throat when my mother answered.

"Girl, where are you?" she asked, ready to jump in my shit.

"In Virginia. I'm coming home today," I said softly. "Where's my baby?"

"His father brought him back last night and I stayed over here. He misses you."

"I know. I miss him too. I'll see you when I get back," I

Ericka M. Williams

said, before hanging up. I turned to see Tamar standing in the doorway. For a moment I thought the nigga was eaves-dropping; but then I realized he wanted one for the road, so I gave him a quickie. *Damn, he wants it every hour of the day.* I knew I was falling fast and hard. Plus, he didn't make it any easier by lending me the Lex. I knew I would have to hide that shit from Mark. I took a bath, got dressed and got my stuff together.

Before leaving, Dee Dee and I exchanged numbers. She gave me the number where she really lived, even though she was always at Tamar's house. She said she was normally home during the week because she had a five year old daughter. I didn't understand how she could spend so much time away from her baby. I wondered if she ever brought her daughter with her. I knew I couldn't leave Kian every weekend. Besides, any man I got serious with was gonna have to be interested in spending time with me and my child.

We left and I followed Tamar to pick up Monet. When we got to the hotel, she was waiting downstairs with a swollen lip.

"Where's my man at?" Tamar asked, acting like he did-n't see her fat lip.

"Damn, Tamar you can't say hello first?" Monet asked.

"Yea, what up Mo...Where's Ty?"

"He's upstairs in the room. I hope his ass stays down here in VA."

"You don't mean that girl. You know you shouldn't have flipped out like that. You must've had too much to drink and started thinkin' you was Super girl." He started laughing, but neither Monet or I found it funny.

"Tamar, I don't think it's funny, plus I don't feel like get-ting into it because you're going to take his side anyway. Y'all niggas think it's all a big fucking joke anyway."

"Don't cry now, bad ass."

"Fuck you, Tamar!"

"Fuck you too, bitch. If you wasn't my man's girl, I'd

smack the shit outta you."

I looked at him with a funny expression. I was both surprised and turned off by the way he was treating her. I
pulled him to the side. "Monet, I'll be right back...Tamar that
ain't right."

"Yo, fuck that bitch. I'm gonna find Ty a top chick down
here so he won't even go back to New York. I want my
man down here anyway, she's the only reason he hasn't
moved."

"The way it looked last night, he already got a honey
down here," I said sarcastically. He turned and ignored me.
"All right then, I'll call you when I get home." I gave him a
kiss on the lips and turned to walk away when he pulled
me close to him.

"Oh, now you're gonna let their problems affect us?
Don't do that. Here, here's some money for the week. It's
two g's. Now give me a real kiss."

I gave him the best kiss I could.

"Now go 'head, I'll see you soon, and don't be fuckin'
around....I love you."

"Yeah right," I replied before walking away. I didn't know
why he'd said that. I didn't like that fake love shit. Throwing
that word around wasn't cute. *Didn't he see the movie,
'Thin Line Between Love and Hate', with Martin Lawrence?*
He smacked my ass as I walked away and it made me
laugh. I had fun with him. He seemed like he would take
good care of me.

I walked back over to Monet, who looked upset. "You
okay, girl."

"I'll be fine the further I get up 95."

I knew she wasn't, but I figured I'd wait until she was
ready to talk. She started crying ten minutes before we
even hit the highway.

"What's up girl, you wanna talk about it?" I asked. I really did feel bad for her because I knew how men could be.

"It's men, they ain't shit. I know it seems like I overre-
acted last night, but it was because I'm fed up with him

Ericka M. Williams

always doing shit like that. If it's not a girl callin' him, it's a number in his pocket, or a girl in his car. Two weeks ago I saw the muthafucka with a bitch in his car and I couldn't catch up to the car. When he got home he tried to tell me it wasn't him. Like I don't know his license plate number. I'm sick of his shit!"

"Well, I'm not the type to tell you to leave your man because females are quick to say 'leave him girl' but when it's their man they can't leave. Maybe you need some time to decide whether you're more happy without him or more miserable with him. If you're having more problems than happiness, what's the point?"

"I hear what you're saying, but I've been with Ty for four years," she said, as tears continued to roll down her cheeks. "Besides, it's hard to find a man out here. Everybody's already taken, or they have a past that they can't let go of. And that AIDS shit ain't no joke either."

"True, but if he's cheating, how safe are you? Do you have any kids by him?" I asked.

"Nope, I don't have any kids," she said, seeming relieved.

"Well good. It's harder to leave a man when you have his kids so you better think about it." I pointed my finger at her like I was speaking from experience. "Think about all the girls who get stuck putting up with a man, who ain't worth shit, because she's scared no other man will want her and her kids?"

"I know. But even if I leave him, I may have the same type of problems with the next man. Especially if he has cash. Bitches will always be sweatin' him and shit."

"Yeah, girls will cut your throat just to get a buck. It's not always the best thing when your man has money. That's why I don't know if I should get serious with Tamar. I think he's cool, but I don't want the headache of worryin' about other bitches. I mean he's all the way down here."

Monet interrupted me. "Whatever you do, make sure you save some of the money Tamar gives you, because if you leave he's gonna take everything and try to break you down." Monet stopped and thought for a minute. I knew she felt strongly about what she was saying to me.

I tried to lighten the conversation. "I'm not gonna leave him yet. I'm gonna make him put me through school and then when I graduate if he's still acting foul I'm gonna break out." I laughed. She didn't.

"I'm going to go to school, meet a nerd, whip some shit on him that he's dreamed of all his life, and have him marry me. Then I'll have a little cutie on the side." We both laughed.

"You never know. He could seem corny, but be a stud behind clothes doors." I looked over at Monet wondering if I could trust her. I wanted to tell her about Mark. I knew I never thought Mark had it goin' on the way he did. *Nah...I decided against it.*

"I messed up," Monet confessed. "I had a good job working downtown and when I got with Ty he convinced me to quit. He kept saying, 'Why are you gonna work when I can give you more than what you make. I wanna spend all day and night with you.' You see what that got me, full dependency on his ass. I should've known better."

Monet cried once again, but I cheered her up. We talked the rest of the way home because the subject of men was a never-ending one. We exchanged numbers and vowed to start being independent and strong. I dropped her off in the city and rushed home.

═══════════

My mother, Shani, Fuquan and Kian were sitting in the living room when I walked through the door. Kian ran up to me, grabbed my leg and squeezed me real tight. I picked my son up and hugged him.

"How's my little man?" I asked, giving him a kiss.

"Fine. I missed you Mommy."

"I missed you too, baby. Hi Ma, hi Shani." There were

Ericka M. Williams

123

no hugs coming from that direction. No smiles either. They were anxiously awaiting the verbal interrogation.

"So Mika, didn't you know that when you have children you don't disappear with strangers?" my second mother commented.

"Shani, that was not a problem because Danny watched him. You act like you had to take off of work or miss school because I left you stuck with Kian. Besides, it was a last minute thing. I didn't know I was going away when I left the house."

"Well, when you found out you should've called. When you walked on that plane you knew you weren't going around the block," my mother added.

"I didn't fly." I was trying to stay calm. I wasn't in the mood to argue.

"So then how didn't you know any better?" my mother asked.

"Ma, can we leave it alone?"

"So, who is this Tamar character, one of your hoodlum friends?"

"He's a guy I met at a party, but I don't know his social security number yet, okay?"

"He probably doesn't know it either," Shani added. "But it wouldn't have been funny if you never came back now would it?"

"Shani, why must you be so paranoid?"

"Why must you be so loose?" my mother asked.

"Loose! I'm not loose, maybe you two should loosen up."

"You are so damned smart. You're gonna wish you had listened one day. You are too old to be playing these little games. I shouldn't have to be worrying about you," my mother replied.

I tried to ignore them and just let their mouths move, but couldn't blur them out.

"You know I've tried to bring you up to be a lady and you refuse to be one. You have a son for goodness sake,

Mika. These men you lay around with have no intention on marrying you. You think sex is the only way to a good life?" By now, my mother was right in front of my face pointing. "No man wants a woman who can't do for herself. Have something more to offer than your panties. By the time you're thirty-five, you'll only be able to get a man for a night." She walked into the bathroom and quickly closed the door.

As I stomped away, I heard Fuquan say, "Mika doesn't deserve Mark. She better stop hiding behind those weaves and tight jeans. Besides, she has a man who loves her for who she is, not how big her butt is."

Now he's going too far. "My butt ain't that big! They love me 'cuz I'm the shit! Now leave me the hell alone!" I yelled, from the bathroom to my bedroom walking and slamming the door. Seconds later, when the phone rang, I looked in horror as I saw Mark's number on the caller ID. Before I could yell to them to say I wasn't home, Shani was calling me to the phone. I hadn't even gotten my story straight with Asia yet.

"Hello?" I said nervously.

"Yeah, what's going on Mika?" I could tell he was pissed.

"Nothing," I said softly. I had guilt all in my voice, but I had to try to fix it. "I know you're mad but I've been through so much in these last few days, runnin' around with Asia." I crossed my fingers and hoped he hadn't seen her.

"Oh, for real?" By sound of his voice, he knew I was lying.

"Yeah, I'll tell you all about it. Come and see me."

"I'll be there in an hour," he said and hung up. Something was wrong. I called Asia and the bitch finally answered her cell.

"Where the fuck you been?" I asked, pacing the floor. "Look, Mark is coming here, did you see him this week-end?"

"No, I didn't see him. I would've told you. So, tell me

Ericka M. Williams 125

about your little vacation before he gets there. So what's up? Does Tamar have it going on or what?"

"Yeah, man. I'm driving a Lexus RX 300, bitch."

"What! Get the fuck outta here. What the fuck did you do suck his dick for three days straight?" She laughed hysterically. "You're not telling me that this nigga actually bought you a muthafuckin' truck in two days?"

"I'll tell you what happened, but come over here real fast so you can be here looking sad when Mark gets here. You're my alibi. I'm gonna say I was with you since Butch got shot and you were distraught and shit. Hurry up."

As soon as I hung up, my mother opened my door. I'm going home to my husband."

"What husband Mommy?"

"My television set."

"All right Mommy, I love you."

"Yeah right," she said, closing the door behind her. All I could do was shake my head.

Asia made it to the house in fifteen minutes flat. She looked worn out. I could tell she was still feeling nauseous.

"You better take a pregnancy test girl," I said, worrying about her just a bit.

"I know."

"You better stop running the streets or your baby's gonna come out with stilletos and a thong on."

"That was a wack ass joke Mika. But, if I am pregnant, I'll slow down...if I plan on having it."

"Oh boy, you're crazy."

"Look, when is Mark coming, 'cuz I'm going to see my new cutie, Plum."

"What kind of name is that? And what's up with Butch's case?"

"They call him that because he's dark like a plum, but he's so cute...He's young and dumb too...Butch's case won't be up for about six months. He's such a baby too. He calls me every damn day. I told him he should've been this good when he was home. His mother and his sister are already spending his money and they don't even know how much all of his million cases are going to cost. I'm making sure I get hit off too. That's why I been with them everyday, takin' them wherever they need to go, doing whatever they need to do."

"Damn, that ain't right."

"Mika, do you ever say anything else but damn?"

"Yeah, I can say get the fuck out!" I pushed her.

"Oh yeah, okay, I'm out!"

"Asia stop playing, you gotta wait 'til Mark gets here."

"So, tell me about the new car you got."

"He ain't buy it. It's a lease and it's up in a year. It was for a girl who was hustlin' for him, but she got locked up on some other shit and he has the truck, so I was like 'Yo, lemme take it home' and he let me."

"Bitch! Damn, I taught you too good. So you open on him right? Don't even front."

I smiled. "Yeah, a little somethin', but I'll explain it to you later. Right now, I gotta get my story straight."

"Look stop being a punk. You can handle it, 'cuz I gotta go get Butch's mother. They all saying they want me to have the baby, and Butch too, like he ain't got enough kids as it is. He's gonna do at least ten years, but his mother wants to go shopping. You would think the bitch hit Lottery the way she's been spending his loot."

"Poor Butch, he's in jail while y'all spend up all his money."

"I'm out girl. You better get your story straight. I would have waited but his ass is taking too long. Pull up your boot straps and do yo' thang girl, like I taught you. Just tell him that you went with me to Virginia to get some money from Butch's man because he owed him a lot of money and he needed it for his lawyer. That way you won't be completely lying. Don't worry, that man ain't goin' nowhere. He's never had a girl like you."

"Yeah, and he's never had a girl put him through so much drama and changes either."

Ericka M. Williams

"People love changes. It keeps them from getting bored."

"Not Mark, he's not for the games," I responded.

"Oh, I forgot to tell you, I saw Danny on Saturday with Kian and his so called girlfriend."

"What!? You know I can't believe that he can't spend time with his son by himself. He always has to have that bitch around Kian."

"So what does Kian say about her?" Asia asked.

"I don't ask him about her. I don't wanna know about that bitch!"

"How do you know she's a bitch? She may be a really nice person." Asia loved being an asshole. "And you don't want to ask about her because you're scared that Kian will say nice things about her."

"Don't you have somewhere to go? And since when did you become a damn psychiatrist?"

"All right bitch, handle your scandal." She got up and walked to my door. "I'll call you later."

"All right," I said, as she walked out the room. *Damn, she didn't look good at all,* I thought.

Chapter 12

REALITY BITES

When I walked into the living room, the family was sitting around looking at the television as usual. "Will I be safe in here or are there going to be more attacks on my character?" I asked sarcastically.

"Don't run from the truth, my sister, the truth will set you free," Farrakan's protégé told me. "You need to look into your soul and find your true self and that way you will be more content with life. You'll be more content with Mark because you'll realize that he is a true man. A true man doesn't have to control you."

"Preach, Fuquan baby," Shani added.

"Thanks for the wisdom Brother Fu, but I've had enough for the day. Come on Kian, come follow me in your Mommy's room. I missed you when I was gone." He quickly got up and followed me.

When we went into my room, I put Shrek into the DVD player while I finished unpacking. When I was done, I sat hugged up with Kian on the little love seat in my room. It reminded me of the relationship I wish I had with my mother. A lot of times, I wanted to hug her, but I couldn't because she acted like she couldn't stand me for some reason. Luckily, Kian fell asleep, just as someone knocked on the front door. I knew it was Mark. I picked Kian up and put him in his bed, then rushed to get the door.

I immediately got nervous when I thought about what I was going to say to Mark. I was glad that Shani and Fuquan had gone into her room so they couldn't see how nervous I was. I knew they would've had jokes. When I

Ericka M. Williams

opened the door, my baby stood there looking so good.

"Hi baby!" I said, opening my arms for him to hug me. Instead, he walked past them. "Oh, what's up? I can't get a hug?"

"Mika, cut the bullshit alright. Where've you been?"

"Come in my room, Kian is sleeping," I said, buying myself a few seconds to think.

When we got in my room. I closed the door as Mark sat on my bed and asked me again. "So, where were you? Are you gonna be straight up or what?"

"About what?" What could he know if he didn't see Asia?

"About where you were all weekend."

"Take your coat off," I ordered, but he shook his head. "Oh, you can't even take off your coat? Okay, no problem." I got mad and defensive. "I was in Virginia wit' Asia. She had to go to get some money from one of Butch's boys, for his lawyer. I told you he was locked up. Anyway, we were only supposed to be going for one night, but we ended up staying until today."

"And you couldn't call me and let me know you were alright?"

"I called you, but your machine kept coming on. I should be asking you where you've been."

"Mika, don't play me! You ain't leave no message. So, who's the kid?"

"What?!" I was stuck.

"Look, I know that you were in VA, but not with Asia. And I also know that some kid came up here and got you."

The look on my face read guilty, but I wasn't ready to give up just yet. "Mark, what are you talking about?"

"I just told you."

"Where the hell did you get that from?" I asked, pacing the floor.

"You really wanna know? Danny told me."

That muthafuckin' bastard! "And you believe him? Don't you think he's trying to cause problems between us?"

"Not the way it happened, no."

"Yeah, well I'd like to hear how it happened, so start talking.

"I was in the mall and I ran into Danny, his girl, and Kian. When Kian saw me he ran up to me and told me that he'd just seen Asia. When I asked him were you with her, he said no. Danny told me that there was no beef with us over what happened. Then he told me to watch you because you were with another muthafucka. I asked him how he knew. He said that he'd just seen Asia and she told him that you were with your new man in Virginia. I guess she was trying to make him jealous."

Mark looked at me like he was so disgusted. I felt two inches tall. I was caught out there and I didn't know what to say. I could've tried to make something up, but he didn't deserve that. I owed him the truth, but I couldn't give it to him because it was foul. I felt like a no good piece of shit because I saw the hurt in his eyes.

"Mark, he's lying. I was with Asia in Virginia. Maybe he saw her before we left or something."

"Mika, who's the nigga?" he said firmly.

"He's nobody," I blurted out. I gave up without a fight. "I'm not going to see him anymore, I mean it." I dropped a few tears. "Mark, the last thing I want to do is hurt you. I'm with you now."

"Yo Mika, on the real, I'm fed up with all your bullshit stories. I tried to wait for you to be with me because I thought that when we finally got together, you would be happy. I was more concerned with you being happy than myself. I wasn't happy havin' a girl who I couldn't have to myself and I'm not going to do it anymore. You think I don't have girls coming on to me?" He got up and walked toward the door. I was shocked. *Was this the day that I would lose him?*

"So, you can't accept my apology?" I whined.

"Nah, not this time."

I tried to stay calm, but I was starting to lose it. Mark

Ericka M. Williams

was my security blanket, he couldn't leave me. "So, what's up? You ain't fuckin' with me anymore?" I cried. This time it wasn't a show. I was hurt.

"Nah, because you a selfish bitch. You don't give a fuck about nobody but yourself. "

"That's not true." By now I was balling. "I love you, Mark," I said, pulling on his shoulder.

"Not the way I want you to." He walked to the door like he was done.

"Mark, don't do this to me. I wanna be with you. I'm sorry," I cried out.

I couldn't believe I was beggin' him, but I knew he was serious. I grabbed him from behind and tried to hug him, but he broke away. He walked swiftly toward the door. I jumped in front of him and started hugging him. I tried to rub on his dick, but he pushed my hand away and walked out. I sat on my bed stunned. *Was he for real?* I couldn't lose him. He was my future husband. I wanted to run after him, but I couldn't move. I cried a little harder and then got angry. I told myself that he'd be back because he just couldn't leave me. I called Asia to curse her out and her voice mail came on.

"You blew my cover, bitch!" I hung up. I called Mark to ask him to come back, but he didn't answer. I called about fifty times back to back and once again, he didn't answer. He must've got tired of me calling and turned off his phone after the first twenty-five calls because eventually all the calls went straight to voice mail. "Mark, I'm sorry. I love you," I said on every message.

I hung up and tried to call Danny's bitch ass, but his voice mail came on as well. "You better mind your fuckin' business and stop spreadin' mine, you pussy muthafucka." I slammed the phone down and went to bed, steaming.

I was mad at the world for hatin' on me. Shani, for being right about Mark eventually leaving me. Asia, for having such a big-ass mouth. Danny, for being a bitch-ass nigga and for always being in the fuckin' mall. And Tamar, for thinkin' he was all that to just up and take me to Virginia. Come to think of it, the muthafucka didn't even call to see if I made it home alright. Faggot.

━━━━━━━━━━

I woke up Monday morning about ten o'clock with my clothes still on. My weave looked like an old mop, and I had dry mascara on my cheeks from crying. I went in Kian's room, but he was still sleeping. I went in the kitchen and turned the TV on. I looked through the weekend mail and a catalogue from Rutgers University had come. *Good. I'll go back to school and forget about all these mutha-fuckas.* They were messing up my life. I looked through a few different majors: Social Work, Education, Communications, and Psychology.

I was doing good for a little while, making myself believe that I was busy. I read the brochure, called some other schools, and filled out some applications. Then, of course, my mind began to wander. It began with a simple question, "What am I gonna do now?" I was tired of meeting niggas. Where was the man who had his shit together? Who worked a legitimate job, and was also ready to settle down. WHERE IS THAT MAN? My life was falling apart. I was ready to start crying again, but quickly stopped when the phone rang.

Please be Mark, I prayed. "Hello?"

"You could've called me to let me know you made it home safe?" His sexy voice actually made me think he cared.

"You could've called to see if I made it home, Tamar." *Asshole.* I was really mad at him.

"Well, I see you made it. So, was everything cool with your son and your sister when you got back?"

"Yeah." *Nah, he didn't really care.*

"So, do you miss me?"

"Yeah," I said, with no feeling.

Ericka M. Williams

133

"Well, at least try to sound convincing. What's wrong with you?"

"Nothin', I'm just tired." I wiped the tears that fell from my eyes.

"Alright. Well, I just called to make sure you made it. I'll call you later. I'm diggin' you girl. I want us to have something. Take care of that truck. Alright, baby?"

"Okay baby." I started smiling. *I forgot he let me take the truck*. Tamar was gonna be my next baby, if I couldn't get Mark back. *Fuck it, you gotta be able to move on in life.* "Are you coming up to New York this weekend?"

"I'm working on it okay? Call me later." He didn't even give me a chance to respond before he hung up.

After getting off the phone, I went in Kian's room and woke him up. I wanted him to go with me to Dawniece's house for a minute. Even though, I wanted him to stay home, I didn't feel like hearing Shani's mouth.

When we got upstairs, I gave Dawniece forty dollars and she gave me some coke in a little baggie. We hurried back downstairs, and I started doin' that shit again. *Damn. What the fuck is happening to me?*

The sad thing was that I felt like I needed it to solve my problems. I knew that a truck wasn't going to replace Mark's love for me and that I had gotten myself into something with Tamar that would probably end disastrously. That was the story of my life, danger and disaster. I should've had a warning sign on my back, *'Don't fuck with this bitch, she's nothin' but trouble*. Ask Mark Phillips, he's a witness."

I got fucked up alone, and decided I would go out with Asia later. When Shani came home I was dying to get out of the house. I hadn't paid Kian any attention all day. I had so much other shit on my mind and the drugs weren't helping. I was feeling upbeat and happy every time I took a *hit* and then when the high started coming down, I would feel like shit. I began to realize that that was how the drug trapped people. You would feel great and then two minutes later feel like you were gonna die. It was making me feel depressed as it wore off, so I kept going in the bathroom all day. I called Dior and his mother said that he was locked up. She said that she was on the other line, but to call her back and she would tell me what happened. "Damn, damn, damn," I said to myself.

I called Asia and she said for me to pick her up at nine. It was only seven, so I took a short nap. I got up at eight-thirty and threw on some jeans with a tight shirt, and some black boots. I really didn't feel like going out, but we were only going to a comedy show at a bar in the Bronx. Dawniece was hanging too, so we picked up Asia, then Peaches.

The street that the bar was on was packed with BMWs, Lexus', and every Benz you could name. Normally I would have been excited too because the more nice cars in a parking lot meant a good chance that we would meet one of the drivers, but I was in a crabby mood and everybody noticed. I knew what it was, sniffin' that shit all day made me depressed. Now I needed some more coke to lift me back up.

Asia made an announcement before we got out of the car. "Alright ladies, there are a lot a prospects in there...enough to go around. First one who claims a catch, everyone else HANDS OFF! Oh, and if Mika keeps acting like a bitch don't fuck with her!" We all started laughing.

"Yo Dawniece, hit me with a twenty, I need a picker-up-er," I said. We all sat in the car and had a small coke session. This was the second time that I had done it with Asia, but she had no idea this was turning into a small habit for me. We were all fucked up off of that shit by the time we got inside.

When we walked in, heads turned. We walked through the crowd and found a small table to the left of the stage. When we sat down, the waitress came to our table and took our orders for drinks. We took off our coats and got comfortable. I tried to keep my mind off of Mark, and the drugs were helping a little.

Ericka M. Williams

135

I looked at Asia and she looked just as crazy. "What the hell is wrong with you?" I asked her.

"I'm stuck. I feel like I'm frozen. I can't move," she replied. Being that we all felt the same way, we started laughing.

"Yo Dawniece's shit be almost raw and uncut. You better slow down Mika, you ain't used to this shit yet, " Asia continued.

"Yeah, well it's your fault I started doing this shit in the first place. You always trying to get somebody to do something bad."

"You sound like you're five years old or some shit. Just shut the fuck up, and enjoy it."

"I wanna go home," I said.

"Stop buggin, Mika," Dawniece responded. "Y'all bitches are ruthless."

As the show started we quieted down, but I didn't feel comfortable though. I kept checking my pulse to see how fast my heart was beating. I had to keep drinking to calm down. Out of the four comedians who performed, two of the men were good and the lady was funny as hell because she got on "men" of course. I enjoyed the show, but I was ready to go when it was over. I was just out of it, and couldn't function right. It felt like my equilibrium was off.

After another hour we were all ready to go. Nobody got much play and the play they did get was from the wrong niggas. There wasn't that much mingling. It was simply a dry night.

I got home and went straight to bed, but I couldn't sleep. That shit had me buggin'. When I checked the caller ID, I noticed there were no calls from Mark. Even the voice mail on my cell phone was empty. I turned my room light off and stared at the ceiling. *Why is it that we never miss what we have until it's gone? Why is it that we always want what we can't have? I knew there wouldn't be any answers falling from the sky, so I closed my eyes after telling myself that things would get better. If Mark never came back, I would just have to get over it,* I thought. It won't be easy but if I survived Danny, I could survive Mark.

Chapter 13

NASTY MEDICINE

By Tuesday morning, I had a new attitude. I wasn't going to let Mark or any other man, for that matter, mess up my day, but I had to stop sniffin' that shit. It wasn't even fun anymore. It was becoming a crutch every time I got upset about something, and I knew that wasn't good.

I sluggishly made something for Kian to eat, helped him get dressed, and played with him while I watched my usual shows: from Maury to Montel, then Judge Hatchet and Tyra Banks. That's what most of my mornings consisted of. I called a few of the preschools in the area because at four years old, it was time for Kian to be around other kids.

I thought about myself a little too and called a cosmetology school. I used to do hair out of my house in high school and enjoyed doing it, but I wasn't sure if I had the patience for that anymore. I could get the same amount of money from a nigga with a hell of a lot less time and work. That's if I ever decided to date men again.

I also called a few law firms to find out about being a paralegal. I could do that while I was in school part time in the morning. I just didn't know if college was for me anymore. I didn't want to wait three more years to begin a career. But I guess if I didn't start then, I would've never started. I just didn't know who I thought I was fooling, I couldn't live without men. I was just going to be celibate for a little while.

I called the cosmetology school and a new class was beginning in two weeks. The only thing was, I needed

All That Glitters

$600, which was half the tuition, by the end of the next week. I could go full time and be finished in six months. Then, I would have a job making my own money. I'd finally be independent, strong, and a sistah ready for the next phase just like Monet said. I laughed. That reminded me that I should call Monet to see how she was doing. She answered on the first ring.

"Monet?"

"Who's this?" she snapped.

"Mika girl, what's up?"

"Oh, hi! I'm doing alright." She didn't sound like it. "Would you believe that Ty still hasn't come home?"

"Stop lying."

"I'm for real girl. I haven't seen his ass since Sunday when I left Chesapeake. I thought he was still in down there, but when I went to the bank yesterday the muthafucka had closed our accounts already! He took ALL the money out! You should've seen me in that bank cursing everybody out."

"Damn, Monet. How come they let him close a joint account by himself?"

"That's what I was bitchin' about. They said we had the type of account where only one of our signatures was needed. I can't believe his bitch ass would do some pussy shit like that! He could've been a real man and told me to my face. When I left that bank I was ready to kill somebody, you hear me? I called Tamar to find out where Ty was, and he said he didn't know. He's another bitch-ass nigga and I know he's puttin' shit in Ty's head. Well, I guess Tamar found another girl for him. That's alright though because all his shit is going to the Salvation Army. His clothes anyway. His mink coats and his jewelry are going straight to the pawn shop. He done took this shit too fuckin' far. And it's a good thing this month's rent is paid because I'd be fucked for real. I got a little stash but I'm gonna have to do something quick." There was a long pause and I figured she was crying. "I want him to come

Ericka M. Williams

139

home," She whined.

I felt really bad for Monet and mad at Tamar for not try-ing to help her. "All of this over what happened Saturday?" I asked in shock.

"He must've had another chick on the side and just wants to use Saturday as an excuse for breakin' up with me. I think he's in New York."

"Well, don't let him play games with your head," I lec-tured. "Saturday wasn't even your fault. You know how nig-gas like to make you think you did something wrong when they're the ones who are dead wrong? But, if you want him back, maybe you should go all out and give it one last try." I thought about using my own advice. Like going to lay on Mark's lawn or handcuffing myself to the banister of his porch until he talked to me.

"Monet, call his family. Call someone who will get a message to him and tell him the least he owes you is a sit down. What if you sell all his shit and then he comes back a week later? He really gon' bust yo' ass then."

"Yeah...I don't know. A part of me just wants to let it go. That's why you always keep a cutie on the side. I got me a honey. I've been talking to him for about a month. I guess I saw this shit coming. But, I didn't sleep with him because I was trying to give me and Ty an honest chance, but tonight I'm gonna do that nigga lovely, right in Ty's fuckin' bed. You think I'm not?"

"You better change the locks before you do some shit like that, girl. What you got a death wish? I agree that you should get yours Mo, but damn, be careful...Do what you gotta do 'cuz you don't need the stress."

"I damn sure don't. So what's up with you and Tamar?"

"I can't lie, I'm feelin' him."

"Oh, wait, that's my other line," Monet said. She put me on hold for a few minutes before clicking back over. " Mika, that's that his mother right there, let me call you back!" She hung up before I could say okay. I couldn't believe that he had taken all the money out of the bank.

Damn, every time you think your shit is bad somebody else's shit is even worse. I returned to watching TV while Kian brought a million and one toys out of his room and into the living room. I laid around all day watching TV. I couldn't eat. The coke had me losing my appetite, and probably losing weight. Between that and the stress from missing Mark, I was gonna end up looking like Kiki.

I continued the same routine for the rest of the week, not going out, not getting dressed and running upstairs to Dawniece's. I must have spent about $500, buying two forties a day. I thought about how I had ripped Kiki that day in the park, and now look at me. See, *watch how you do people, 'cuz it just might come back to you.* I didn't feel like doing anything or going anywhere. I told myself that this was okay until Friday, then I would have to get my shit together.

━━━━━━━━━━━━━━

I got up Friday morning and took Kian to the two schools that I considered sending him to. Both schools were nice, but one had the nerve to be charging $350.00 a week. The other one was more reasonable. It was $120.00 a week, and I knew I wouldn't find anything cheaper. I would have to call Danny and tell him that he was either gonna have to start giving me more money, or the judge would be coming.

When I got back home, Shani was sitting there looking like she'd been waiting for me. "Well, how do you feel about it?"

"About what?" I asked.

"Mark," she said, folding her arms.

"I feel like I want him back. I want him more than I ever have. I feel like I'm ready to be what he wanted me to be. I took a chance with Tamar because I figured I would either be with him, or with Mark. I was just trying to make sure I wanted to be with Mark." I couldn't believe I was opening up to Shani, and giving her a chance to say, I told you so.

Ericka M. Williams

"You should've already known that Mark was the one for you. Nothing ever pleases you. And you just met Tamar, so why was he already on the same level as Mark? Or is it his money?"

I just looked at her and turned my head. One more comment and I was gonna curse her ass out.

"So now what are you going to do, be with Tamar and fly to Virginia every weekend?" She was being sarcastic like my mother.

"No, because I'm pushing his Lexus truck," I shot back.

"The key word is *'his'* Mika. What happened with Tamar anyway?"

"I had fun down there, but I don't know how we're going to make it work with him being down there and me up here."

"Is it his money that you like or him?"

"Shani, there's more to life than money. I mean, I like a man that is about his business, that knows how to make money, but the money can't be what makes him. He's gotta have personality, he's gotta keep me interested or I'm just gonna trick on him and bounce. I like Tamar. He's special, he's different than most guys with money. He's caring."

"What does he do?" She looked suspicious.

"He has a soul food restaurant and a towing business, but I don't know exactly what else. What I don't know won't hurt me."

"That's not always true Mika. You have a son to think about."

"I know, but it's not that serious yet."

"Well, Mika, please take your time this time. Maybe Mark was just here to help you get over Danny, you never know. Just slow down. You're always moving so fast and you never take time to think about your choices, you just make them. It may not be *that serious* to you, but this man gave you his car to drive. Do you think he would do that with any girl?"

I shook my head. "No."

"And please stop sniffin' that shit."

My eyes grew to the size of an eight ball. "What are you talking about Shani?"

"Mika, I know. Please stop. It's really bad for you...I've been meaning to bring it up, but I didn't know how. I'm worried. That stuff can kill you, Mika."

"I know Shani, but it hasn't been a lot. How the hell did you know?"

"You left a straw in the bathroom one day."

"Well, don't worry, I got it under control."

"Mika, I want you to stop," she demanded.

"Okay Shani, lemme just get over Mark."

"When are you going to stop leaning on people and things all the time and lean on yourself. Mika, you are a strong girl. Believe in your own strength."

"Okay Shani, but just bear with me. I feel like my life is going down the drain."

"Well, that shit ain't helping."

She left my room, and I immediately took out my bill from under my mattress and opened it up. I closed it swiftly. Then opened it again, and finished what was in there. Soon, I was high as a kite and imagined that Mark was about to come and ring the doorbell. I laid back and kept listening, thinking I heard the buzzer. *I'm buggin' that nigga ain't thinkin' about me anymore.* I screamed! Then I cried!

At that point, I was done, and refused to go back upstairs. It was only 5:30 p.m. and I didn't know what to do with myself. I couldn't keep frontin' like I knew everything. I needed help. I needed some answers. "God, I need you right now. I'm sorry for being everything I'm not supposed to be. A liar, a cheater, and a player. I haven't been real and I've been exposed. The games are tired and so am I. I'm no better than these tired men. I'm a tired broad," I prayed.

I was glad when my long time friend, Janae called to see if Kian could spend the night with her son Brandon. Janae was like family, so I didn't mind. Our parents had

Ericka M. Williams

been friends for years, and we were tight when they were all still together. I hadn't spoken to her in a couple of weeks, but was happy to know she was on the way.

By the time Janae arrived, Kian was completely packed. Janae tried to make small talk by asking me when I was gonna go with her to church; but I just lead them to the door with an expression that said I didn't want to be bothered. When they left, I watched TV for a while, dozing off and on. I'd pick up the phone, only to hang it back up, about fifty times. I got ready to call Mark and then changed my mind time and time again. I finally fell asleep about 7:00 p.m.

Soon, I was back up again. I just couldn't sleep. I called Asia but she wasn't feeling well. I asked her if she was going out later and she said no because she was sick. She said that she had been home sick for the last two days and that she was going to the doctor on Monday to finally see if she was actually pregnant.

I then called one of my straight and narrow friends, Salima, but she wasn't home. We had gone to high school together and although she didn't like the crowd I ran with, we always remained cool. I called my friend Maya, who was Salima's best friend, and she said that her and Salima were going to the Jazz Cafe to see Maxwell, Musiq, Angie Stone, and Jill Scott later that evening. I wasn't a big jazz fan, but I loved those artists. Mark listened to Jazz and always tried to get me into it. Good, something to do. I told her to pick me up and she said for me to be ready at 9:30 p.m.

I continued with what had become my daily routine, laying around. I ate for the first time in two days. When Janae called to see if Kian could stay for two nights, I got excited. I took a shower about eight o'clock and when I got out the phone rang. I took a deep breath, closed my eyes refusing to check the caller ID and prayed that it was Mark.

"Hello?"

"How's my wife doing?" It was Tamar.

"Damn, I'd hate to be your wife if you're only gonna call her once a week. Then, you give me ten seconds of conversation."

"I'm sorry baby. I've been busy trying to tighten things up so I can come and spend this weekend with you, without any interruptions. You wanna go to Atlantic City?"

"Yeah, when are you coming, Friday? Where's Ty?"

"Why, that ain't got nothin' to do with you," he snapped.

"It doesn't have anything to do with you either. Why did you talk him into staying down there?"

"Ty is a grown man. I didn't make him do anything."

"Come on Tamar, Monet is real upset."

"Mika, don't get involved in that."

"But…"

"What did I say baby, that's not your concern."

"Okay."

"Good. I'll be up there Thursday okay? But I'll call you tomorrow."

"Okay Daddy. I can't wait to see you, bye."

I got downstairs at 9:30 sharp, and Maya and Salima were pulling up like clockwork. I didn't think I was really going to enjoy myself, but it was worth a try.

When we walked in the club, the atmosphere was just like in the movie *Mo' Better Blues*. It was a smoke-filled, dimly-lit place filled with small tables and a bar. The crowd was mixed and mature, but it was relaxed and real cool and mellow. We found a nice table near the front and sat down. There was a band playing that I'd never heard of before, but they sounded good.

This real good-looking man was next to us, playing his invisible sax to the music. He was moving his fingers like he was really playing an instrument and tapping his feet. His woman was staring at him like she could eat him right in front of us. The jazz scene was cool. I could get into it. There were more young people there than I had expected. There were quite a few clean-cut cuties and some of them were dateless. I wasn't out on the prowl though. I was just

Ericka M. Williams

there to relax. I stayed in my seat while Salima and Maya went to dance with these two guys. How do you dance to Jazz? I wondered.

When the band was done, I hurried to find the bathroom because I didn't want to miss the show. On my way, the worst thing in the world happened. I was walking past a table and couldn't believe my eyes. Mark was sitting at this cozy little table for two with a BITCH! As soon as I saw him, he looked up and I stopped dead in my tracks. I took a deep breath, told myself not to make a scene, and walked over to them. As usual, I lost my cool.

"I see you're having a hard time getting over me. Who's this Mark?"

"Mika, this is Chanel. Chanel, Mika."

"And how long have you been seeing her, Mark?" I kept my voice as low as possible. "You were probably fuckin' her the whole time you had me thinking you were waiting for me." I looked around to see if people were paying attention and they weren't.

"Mika, why don't you sit down. This is not City Lights, they'll put you out."

Now he was trying to play me for this chick. Damn, this felt like déjà vu. I played him for Tamar, now he was gonna play me for her.

"Sit down for what? Excuse me uhm, Cherrelle..." I knew that wasn't her name. "How long have you been seeing Mark?" I hoped she didn't get smart and make me have to knock her out in the spot.

"Well, sweetheart, why do you want to know? Are you Mark's girlfriend?"

Oh, the bitch was trying to play Miss Sophisticated Lady. She must've been Tiffany's sister. Mark gave me a smirk as if to say, 'You would've been able to say yes a week ago, but whatcha gonna say now.' He almost had a grin on his face.

"No, I'm not his girl, but we just broke up, so I want to know how long you've been seeing him?" I kept my composure, but my heart was broken. I wanted to cry on the spot.

"We met Tuesday night. Is that okay with you?"

"Look honey, you don't have to get smart. Mark and I have some things to straighten out," I replied.

Mark got up, excused himself, and took me by the arm. We walked over to the bar.

"Mika, how you gonna start with that girl? She didn't do anything to you. And how you gonna question me? You can do your thing, but I can't do mine?"

"You made it seem like you weren't seeing anybody else."

"I wasn't until you fucked up," he bragged.

"Oh, so I can't get another chance? If you loved me like you claimed you did you wouldn't be able to walk away so easily."

"How much do you think I'm supposed to take without getting fed up? How long have we been messing around, six months? That's beside the point, I have to go. I can't leave her sitting there like that."

"Oh, so you're gonna put that bitch in front of me? After all that we've been through?" I asked.

"I thought the same thing last week. I gotta go," he responded. He started to walk away and I grabbed his arm with force. I was desperate.

"Mark, take her home so we can talk."

"Nah," he said bluntly. I thought I was going to explode.

"What? Well, fuck you then. You'll be back."

"Yeah, we'll see. Mika, you need to grow up." He walked away and I rushed to the bathroom and into a stall where I quietly sobbed. I had wanted him to do exactly as I said, *take that bitch home and be with me.* I was shocked that he had turned me down. My ego and my heart were both in pain. All I knew was that I had to get out of there. *How could I stay knowing that he was across the room romancing another chick?*

I got myself together and went back to the table. I had

Ericka M. Williams

147

missed 'Musiq', he was leaving the stage. Maya and Salima were smiling and still clapping at the performance when I returned.

"Where've you been?" Maya asked.

"I gotta go. Can you take me home now, please?"

"Why, what's wrong Mika?" I held back my tears.

"Mark is here with another girl."

"Let's go!" Maya said. "I know you can't stay here. You'll bug the fuck out. As soon as Maxwell goes off we're out! As long as he doesn't ask me to go home with him." She laughed, but I wasn't in a joking mood.

Salima disagreed. "Mika, you better stay here and start flirting and make him jealous! All these good looking men, girl get on your job. Show your ass. I bet you he'll take that girl home and be right at your doorstep. If you leave he'll know that he's got you."

I didn't feel like playing any games. Games were what got me into this mess in the first place. I didn't know what to do. I just wanted him back, but it didn't look good. *Would leaving and showing him that I was upset make him come back? Showing my ass would not be a good idea, under the circumstances, I have done that enough.* Salima interrupted my thoughts.

"Oh well, I guess we're staying because he's leaving." I looked over and saw that Mark and his date were walking toward the door. I wanted to run after him and grab him. I wanted to beg him to let her go, so he could stay with me. I wanted to tell him how much I missed him. Instead, I watched them walk out together.

I never thought I would see Mark with another woman. I got smashed after the show. I had about five drinks. I was talking to some guy, just so he would buy my drinks. He wasn't even sexy, so it was hard to even pretend that I was interested in him. I didn't want nothin' from him, and I was sure he could tell. I shot him the wrong phone number and left.

Chapter 14

NOT ENOUGH

The next morning, I had a stiff hangover, of course. I laid in the bed for hours, before deciding to pick up the phone to call Mark. I was highly disappointed when his voice mail came on at his house and on his cell. "Damn, he must've spent the night with that girl!" I yelled. The thought of it hurt me to my heart.

When the phone rang. I jumped. I just knew it was Mark calling me back!

"Hello."

"Mommy, I'm on my way home," Kian said.

"Alright Kian, I love you." I was sort of disappointed that it wasn't Mark. I hung up and the phone rang again.

"Yeah?"

"What kind of way is that to answer the phone? What's your problem, baby girl?"

"Hi Daddy. I'm having love problems," I revealed to my father.

"What else is new? I keep telling you *love don't love nobody.*" He loved to quote words from Motown Era songs.

"How are you Daddy? Where've you been?"

"Oh, I've been doing some travelin', takin' care of business." You would think he was a secret agent as much business as he *claimed* he always took care of. "How's my boy? And Shani?"

"Everybody's fine."

"Well, I'm gonna come by because I'm going out of

town tonight and I wanna see y'all. So how's your mother, still evil?"

"Don't call her that. She has a right to be bitter, you hurt her."

"What did I do so bad that she's gonna hate me for the rest of my life? She's gonna let her anger take her to an early grave. It's not good to always be mad. It's negative energy. You got anything to eat over there?" he asked.

He just ignored what I said. "Daddy, do you hear what I'm saying to you?"

"Oh, yeah yeah...I know. All right, I'll see you in a little while." He hung up. The truth hurts, I guess. Obviously, he was never going to own up to the fact that he destroyed our family. I loved my father, but he was such a typical man, always hiding from the truth. He knew he wasn't working when he used to disappear for days. One time he didn't come home or even call for a whole week. My mother was a nervous wreck, and cried everyday. She thought he was dead. Then when he came home he had the nerve to come in like nothing had happened. One thing I decided, based on what I just said to my father, was that I should at least apologize for what I did to Mark. I always treated him like he should've just accepted my ways. My father was a trip, and obviously, I was a lot like him.

Several guys had told me I thought I was a man, a nigga, a dude. That I think I could do what a man could. *Why couldn't I? That was it! It was Daddy's fault that I treated Mark so bad.* I knew I was blaming other people, but I also knew my father was a part of the reason I was so out of control. There I go blaming other people again, but I know they were a part of the reason I was so out of control. The doorbell rang and I answered it.

Janae walked in with Kian. "Mika how have you been doing? Since I've had this new job, I haven't been able to check on you as much. Is everything all right?"

"Everything is everything Janae. Life is life. It ain't always how you want it to be."

"True Mika, but sometimes we need to share our burdens with God."

Janae was always preaching to me. For a moment, I stared at her petite body envisioning her with a robe on behind the pulpit. "Janae, I pray. I talk to God."

"But Mika do you serve him? Do you try to learn his word?" she asked, peering over her glasses. "Or do you just ask him to listen and be around when you need him to be, or want him to do what you want?"

"I don't know Janae. I just ask for strength." From then on, I wasn't being very receptive to her so she stayed for a few more minutes. On her way out she said, "Mika, just come with me to church. Try it. I've been asking you for long enough. Just come."

I let her out without really listening to what she was saying. I closed the door and turned my attention to Kian.

"Hi Boo." I picked him up and gave him a kiss. "Did you miss your Mommy?"

"Yes. Mommy, I wanted to come home because I know you're sad since Mark doesn't come around anymore."

I stared at him and shook my head. I couldn't believe this was my four year old talking. But at least my son had my back. He was feeling my pain.

"Good, you want to make your Mommy feel better. Thank you. Grandpa's coming to see you today." Kian loved my father a lot and I was happy about that because my father felt like everybody hated him. I was glad that my son had his father and his grandfather in his life. I never understood a man who didn't value and cherish his children. I vowed to never let the streets teach my son about false manhood. I didn't want my son growing up thinking that being a man meant shooting somebody, because they stepped on his foot or some dumb shit, to defend some false honor. That was why I knew Kian needed a male figure in his life.

I wish my father had realized it. He thought his job was done, that girls were for their mothers. I grew up looking for a father figure in my man, which wasn't good. When the doorbell rang, Kian ran to the door at top speed. "Say Hi to Grandpa!" I said, as I swung the door open. Surprisingly, my mother was the one who walked in.

"Grandpa? Oh, is Super Fly coming to visit?" she asked. *Let the sarcasm begin.*

"Ma, no arguing today please?"

"I'm not going to argue, but he better not try to talk to me and be all buddy, buddy."

Damn, there was no throwing in the towel when it came to her and my father. I walked into the kitchen. I knew exactly what the day would be like. The doorbell rang. I heard my mother open the door.

"Hello Jackie...I said hello Jackie," I heard my father say.

I never heard a reply before he came in the kitchen.

"Hi Daddy!" I was happy to see him. Even though he was a rolling stone, he was still my Poppa. I didn't know where he lived or what his number was, or if he even had a phone. I only new cell phone numbers, and they got cut off often. When I needed to get in touch with him, I'd call my Aunt, where he stayed sometimes, and she gave him the message. He was still addicted to the streets, runnin' around chasing old dreams. It was sad.

Daddy walked into the room to show Kian how to play with the dart game he'd just bought him. That's one thing he always did though, gave nice gifts and money. I guess he used to think it would make up for him being a ghost.

I walked into the living room where my mother was watching TV.

"Where's Shani?" she asked me.

"I don't know, she must've gone out early this morning. Just as I finished my sentence, Shani and Fuquan came through the door. My father got up and hugged Shani and shook Fu's hand. Fuquan told him about a rally that they had just come from and invited him to join them one day.

"I don't know why you're telling him, Daddy don't know

nothin' about any righteous people," I said jokingly. Everybody laughed.

Then my mother sarcastically said, "They don't sell liquor at the rallies so he's not gonna go there." We laughed at him again.

"See why I don't come around? You all treat me so bad."

"You treat yourself bad, look at you, Joe. You look like shit. You still rippin' and runnin' the streets I see," my mother taunted.

"Well if I had a woman to take care of me I wouldn't look so bad. Would you like to volunteer?"

"No thanks. I spent enough time worryin' about yo' ass."

"Aw, give him another shot Miss Jackie," Fu said, and my mother gave him a dirty look.

"You better take him to the Mosque, so he can find a good obedient Muslim sista. But he'll probably destroy her life too."

"Look Jackie, I'm tired of you blaming me." My father's tone became more serious. "You weren't the easiest damn person to live with either. You ain't never happy about nothing, always bitchin' and complainin'. I gave you a nice house, you had cars to drive, fur coats on your back. You didn't even have to work," my father said.

"And I had women calling my house and hotel receipts and heart-aches too, not to mention, the whole town knowing that my husband was seeing a woman who lived two blocks away. That was just one of them. You ain't shit and I should have never waisted my life on you!" my mother yelled.

I didn't want to hear their bullshit. I realized that Danny and I sounded just like that. I was almost in tears and I didn't want Kian to see me, so I went into my room. I heard them screaming at the top of their lungs, and ran out when I heard everyone else screaming. I ran out and my mother had a knife to my father's throat. Kian was crying and Shani was wedged in between them.

Ericka M. Williams

153

I screamed, "Stop! When are you two gonna realize how much damage you've done to your kids!" I turned to my father so that he could see the hurt in my eyes. "Daddy, do you know that I will do anything to hurt somebody so that I won't get hurt because of how much you hurt Ma? And Shani is so scared to live because she believes she can pretend that life is supposed to be perfect!"

He lowered his head, but my mother stared me in the face. She couldn't believe I had thoughts about anything other than my men. "And you, Mommy, you don't know how to forgive! That's why I'm doing the same shit to my son, letting him see me hate his father. Ma, Daddy is human! Forgive him to give your own heart some peace. And Daddy, recognize what you've done and own up to it! You don't even feel sorry for wrecking our family." I was sobbing.

My mother dropped the knife and my father walked out. My mother didn't cry or show any emotion. I picked Kian up, and took him in my room. I heard my mother say, "It's his fault," as she headed to the door. It was just like her, and Shani, to always be the innocent victims. Me and Kian laid down on my bed and he fell asleep. I watched Boomerang, for the millionth time.

━━━━━━━━━━━━━━━━━

I woke up Monday to Kian jumping on me. "Mommy, don't I start school today?"

"Yes, you do," I said, excitedly. When we got dressed, I fixed him some breakfast, and we headed out the door to go and meet his new teacher. When we arrived at the school, my baby didn't even cry when I left.

I spent the day filling out applications for colleges in the Tri-State Area, New York, New Jersey, and Connecticut. It felt good to be doing something, 'cuz my life needed some turning around. I was tired of wasting it away. I'd wasted nearly four years, being Danny's sidekick, and rippin' and runnin' the streets. But I still wanted to see Tamar, so I called him.

"Yo baby? Were you thinkin' about Daddy?" he answered in his sexiest voice.

"Yes Daddy." I smiled.

"What's up girl?" Tamar asked.

"Nothing much. When are you coming up here?"

"I told you Thursday."

"It's only two days from now. Did you make reservations for Atlantic City?" I asked.

"Oh shit, I forgot. Can you call for us?"

"Okay baby. And remind me to talk to you about some-thing too."

"Okay." I heard his phone click.

I called this spot about ten miles from the boardwalk. We had reservations at a deluxe hotel. It was right outside of Atlantic City. I couldn't wait because I was feeling Tamar bad all of a sudden. I missed Mark, but I could get down with Tamar because he looked more like the Prince Charming that I'd been waiting for.

When Thursday finally came, I got a facial, along with my nails and toes done. I even bought new lingerie and worked out in front of the television for an hour. I took Kian out to dinner at Friday's before taking him to my mother's house because she wanted him to spend the night. She was off on Fridays, and it was Danny's weekend to get him anyway.

I got dressed and went upstairs to see Dawniece. She was fucked up when she opened the door. When I walked in, three girls were there getting high. I didn't want to sit with them, but I didn't want to go back downstairs either. It was dark in there and everybody looked crazy. I would just stay for a few minutes and Tamar could call me on my cell when he was downstairs. I had to make sure he didn't pick up on anything, but I couldn't go all the way to Atlantic City without a package because that shit made the sex better. I wanted to be down there fucking for days, and turning his ass out. I'd loss one dude, and damn sure wasn't about to lose another.

I sat down and once I started, my mouth got the runs. I needed a drink to bring it down a bit. Dawniece had some Hennessy compliments of the house. I ended up getting drunk from four straight drinks. No soda, no chaser.

Minutes later, my phone rang, but even though I was fucked up, I put my game face on. I smiled when Tamar told me he was out front.

I hurried down, only to see him looking good as ever.

"What's up baby?" I asked. When I hopped in the car, I planted a huge kiss on his lips.

"Damn baby, whatchu been drinking?"

"Hennessy."

"Come on, that's not cool having your breath smellin' like that. At least put some gum or a mint in your mouth."

"I'm sorry baby. Excuse me, I was probably a little nervous knowing I was about to see you." I smiled.

"Nervous? You? You weren't nervous two weekends ago," he countered.

"Because, it was spontaneous…this was planned. And I didn't care then. I mean, I didn't know how it was going to go and I figured whatever happened just happened. Now, I'm hoping this works out…Have you heard from Ya-Ya?"

"Yeah, she came down trying to get back with me." I felt a lump in my stomach. "So, what's up, you with me or what?" he asked.

"Yeah, I'm with you," I responded, playing with my hair.

"And you look fucked up. What did you drink a whole bottle? You ain't gonna be doing that now that you my girl, you only drink when you're with me."

I looked at him with an attitude. "You buggin'! I'm a grown woman."

"Nah, it seems like you a grown girl. You need some direction. Where we going?" he asked, obviously irritated with me.

"We're staying in May's Landing which is about fifteen

156   *All That Glitters*

minutes from the boardwalk."

"Have you ever stayed there before?" He looked at me like he knew I wasn't to be trusted. "I don't wanna lay up anywhere you already been with another cat." He stroked my cheek and gave me a serious look. "Mika, I'm really feelin' you, and I'll keep telling you if I have to."

"I know," I said, with a slight smile.

"See, I can't be real with you huh? I gotta play games? I'm tired of the games, but you seem like you the one that wants the bullshit girl, not me."

"Nah, I'm serious," I said. "I feel the same way. We just gotta make sure it's not just a beginning thing. You know, we fall in and out of love real fast."

"How do we make sure of that?" he asked, like I had a blueprint.

"Keep it real." I smiled, and leaned my seat all the way back.

We hit Atlantic City about an hour later. When we got to the room, I was all smiles 'cuz the room was plush. The bed seemed even larger than a king size and sat on a platform with three steps. The roman type column stands around it, looked like a scene out of Russell Simmons episode of 'Cribs'. Everything was gold, from the bathroom fixtures, to the door handles. I loved the huge Plasma screen TV that took up the whole wall, and the beautiful marble bathrooms. I felt like Tamar needed the crown that the character in the 'Burger King' commercials wore because the room was breathtaking. Hell, there was no need to go the casino. There were so many places to have sex that we could've stayed in the room the entire time.

I quickly undressed, and sat my naked body in the hot Jacuzzi waiting for Tamar. He took out a bottle of Cristal and unbuckled his pants. I felt like this was real. This wasn't just a pay day. I felt like this could really become something. I thought about Mark. I loved him still but maybe we just weren't meant to be. I felt sorry for hurting him, but would I have ever been happy with him? I needed a man in my life, not a boy, because I was a woman. I had always been taken care of. Every man I've had had taken care of me. Mark couldn't do that. I think it would've always been a problem because he wasn't even in the position to take care of himself. Especially since he still lived with his mother.

"What's on your mind shorty?" Tamar asked, breaking my trance.

"You."

"I better be." He slipped his fine, sexy ass in the tub and right up between my legs. I stood up and got out.

"Where the fuck you goin'? I just got in here."

"Damn, do you have to curse at me?" I snapped.

"I'm sorry, I ain't mean it like that."

"I have to go to the bathroom." I lied.

I rushed to the downstairs bathroom. I had put my stash up under a towel in the closet next to the bathroom. I grabbed my package and went in the bathroom and closed the door. I opened up the bill, picked up the straw, and took four big hits. Before I even got back upstairs I was feelin' it. It was a good feeling. I felt okay, not bugged out, but you never could predict where a hit would take you. Sometimes it took you to paradise, other times it took you to hell and you didn't always feel like you were gonna make it back from there alive.

When I got back, Tamar was stretched out, head back with his arms spread out on the sides. I slid in the water, between his legs. That was all she wrote. We did it in the tub, from the tub to the couch downstairs, and then to the bed upstairs. We were fuckin' hard, but it was all love. It was intimate. It wasn't just a fuckfest, I knew it in my heart, this was my man. We caressed. We hugged. We kissed. We fell asleep and woke up in each other's arms, and made love over and over again.

I gave him a massage while he slept. I also woke him up by sucking his dick, and then we did it again. I rode on top, on the side, on my knees, you name it, he gave it to me that way. I was gonna make sure that when he left this time, that he was leaving the woman that he loved, and he would soon return.

I got up and ordered him some room service just before giving him a bath and putting lotion all over his body. I showed him the type of wife that I was going to be. I was sprung. If I had rose petals, I would have dropped them before his feet as he walked out of that hotel to the truck.

We spent the next three days, winning and losing games and at the different casinos. I was in love by Sunday and he was too. Neither one of us said it, and I was glad. I wasn't about to say it, but if he had, I wouldn't have believed it so soon. But I knew. He wasn't goin' any-where. I had given him great love, and conversation, topped off with mad humor.

He talked about Ya Ya and I listened. He told me that he didn't want to be with her anymore. He also said that she didn't grow as a person and he knew that part of it was his fault because he didn't make her do anything. She did-n't have to work and all he did was give her everything she wanted, and she was not mature enough to handle it. All she wanted to do was hang out with her friends, get high all day, and sleep. I wasn't gonna make the same mistake she made. He was mine now and I was keepin' the prize.

When we got back from A.C., Tamar wanted to come inside my house, but I wasn't sure if it was time for him to meet Kian yet. With all the drama that was going on lately, I wasn't ready to bring another man in his life.

"Can I meet the fam?" Tamar asked.

I just looked at him.

"Oh what? You don't want me to meet your son? How are we gonna be together if I don't meet your son?"

He waited for a response, but I still didn't answer.

"So, I guess it ain't really like that between us huh? That was game you was tellin' me about us bein' together? Well, don't get it twisted baby, I'm out the game, but I can get right back in. I got mad chicks that want me to be

Ericka M. Williams

Daddy," he continued.

"Hold on, why you speedin'?" I did want him to meet Kian. I just didn't want Kian being exposed to another man so soon. "Okay, listen, I just stopped seeing somebody."

He looked shocked. "Oh, you ain't tell me that." He gave me a funny look.

"Well, I did. He broke up with me when I came back from Virginia because Kian's father found out and told him. Anyway, we ain't together anymore, so now I just don't want to expose Kian to another man right now, especially if you and I don't work out."

"I can understand that, but I just wanted to come up and see how my baby is living."

Damn, I wasn't used to this, a real man acting like that with me. Most niggas were too busy to give a damn. "Okay, come up," I said.

"Are you sure, baby? I don't want to cause any problems?"

"I'm sure, Daddy," I responded extending my hand.

When we went upstairs, everybody was home, including my mother. I introduced Tamar to everybody and the nigga got shook. He was looking all nervous, not like his usual cool and confident self. He tried to smile and say yes instead of yeah and talk all proper. I laughed at him behind his back.

My mother's stern disposition would make anybody scared. She looked him up and down and asked him too many personal questions. She came out and asked him what he did and how many kids he had. There was no shame in her game, and it was embarrassing because by the way she was acting, anyone would've thought that I was a teenager. She made it very clear if she didn't like you, she wouldn't even be nice just for the purpose of keeping the air clear of tension.

He was polite though, but when we went in my room he said, "I'm out. I got some business uptown. If I don't leave tonight, can I stay here?"

160 *All That Glitters*

"Tamar, I just introduced you to them, how you gonna stay here that fast. I don't really do that with Kian here."

"So are we gonna stay at a hotel?"

"We can but I'll have to be back before Shani leaves for work, so I can take Kian to school."

"Oh that reminds me…I'm taking the Lex, so I can check it out and make sure you ain't do no damage. Here are the keys to the Nav, so be easy. Don't have a whole bunch of bitches in the truck. I'll be back at ten."

He gave me a kiss and six hundred dollars. Six was his favorite number. I'd hit the jackpot and you couldn't tell me shit. As I continued to think about my new man, my mother had to bring me back to earth.

"So, he said he's from Harlem right?" my mother asked, standing in my doorway. "And what does he do again? I know he can't work a legitimate job."

"Why can't he? Ma, please don't start."

"What does he do? He just gave you a brand new Lexus truck. Ain't no nine to five job doing that. What does he drive, a Mercedes?"

"I never said he had a regular job. Ma, he's an entrepreneur."

"Uh huh. You think we're stupid. What makes you so naïve. No, you ain't naïve, you just playing dumb. Girl, you have a son."

I took Kian's hand, helped him put his coat and sneakers on and we went downstairs. When he saw the Navigator, he started buggin'.

"Ooh, Mommy, is this ours?"

"No, it's Tamar's. He took the Lexus that's not good enough for you."

"Oh yeah, that's right. The Lexus is gone?"

"He took it for a drive. Listen boo, Tamar wants to be with me. What do you think about that?"

"What about Mark, Mommy? He loves you. He told me he wants to marry you."

I got a lump in my throat. Damn, I still loved Mark. *What*

did I do?

"Look, you're too young to really understand but Boo...Mark was not ready for us to be a family. I mean, he was, and he wanted to be with us, but we were too much for him right now. He is not ready to support a family. He couldn't take care of us like a man is supposed to take care of his family."

I shut the door hoping he'd change the conversation. Instead, he said nothing at all. He was quiet for a long time. We drove straight to Asia's house, 'cuz I wanted to show off, since her ass was always showing off. I rang the doorbell, but nobody answered. I called her on her cell phone and she still didn't answer, so I left her a message.

"Girl, call me back. I got big stories," I bragged.

Kian and I rode around about an hour, showing off. Finally Asia called. "Yo, I'm in love," I yelled into the phone.

"Listen, I'm in the hospital," Asia said sadly.

"What!?"

"Yeah, I told you I was coming to the doctor to see if I was pregnant."

"Yeah, and?"

"Well, I'm not pregnant, but they wanna run some tests on me."

"For what?"

"Because they think I might have a tumor on my ovary that caused me not to get my period..."

"Oh God, Asia." I tried to be calm, but couldn't.

"So that's why I'm staying, they think it might be cancerous."

"Where are you?" I asked.

"At Medical, room 613."

"I'm on my way!" I yelled.

Chapter 15

SCARY

I entered the hospital, nervous as hell with the heels from my new Gucci shoes making loud noises down the hall. When I walked in the room, Asia was sound asleep. I sat and watched TV, waiting for her to wake up. I didn't know what I would say to her, so I was glad she was sleeping. Asia was like my sister and I was very worried. *Cancer at 24!* Damn, I tried to think positive and tell myself it was nothing, and that she would be fine, but every now and then bad thoughts found their way in my head.

"What's up girl?" she said, catching me off guard.

I looked at her for a minute and then got up and gave her a tight hug. "Nothin'. How you feelin'?"

"All right. Just scared."

"I know. You'll be all right...so tell me what happened?"

"I went to the doctor this morning. I told him that I thought I was pregnant because I've been sick, but that I'd been losing weight instead of gaining it. He took a urine test and it came back negative and then he took an X-ray. All he said was for me to drive to the hospital and he would meet me here because he saw something. That's all he said. Then when I got here, they gave me a room and he came up and told me...that I shouldn't worry because it might not be Cancer."

"So will all the results be in by Thursday?" I asked sadly.

"I guess." A tear rolled down her cheek and I started

crying with her. We cried for a little while, but didn't say much.

"Did you call your mother?" I asked.

"No, I didn't want to call her at work," Asia responded.

"All right, so let me go to your house. What do you want from there?"

"Just some sweats and some underwear. Oh and bring me that book that's on the bed. I'm reading this good book," she replied.

"All right, I'll be back." She gave me her house keys and I left. I drove to her house with speed, and when I got there, I rushed and got her stuff before her mother or sister came home. I jetted back to the hospital, but just sat in the parking lot thinking for awhile. I didn't want to go back, but I had to be there for her.

Minutes later, I walked back into the hospital room and Asia was on the phone. She hung up instantly, like she didn't want me to hear her conversation.

"Who was that?" I asked suspiciously.

"Nobody," she replied.

I knew she was lying, but didn't sweat it.

"So what's up with Tamar?" she asked.

"Yo, I'm in love. He's what I've been looking for since Danny fucked me over. He's the truth baby."

"So I guess you're over Mark?"

"I'm saying, I can't just say fuck him like that. We've been together ever since me and Danny broke up. He was really there for me…And I think if one of us was more stable we would have been able to make it. It's just that neither one of us could help the other. ..Now I'm worried about bringing another man into Kian's life."

"Girl, please. Do you."

"Asia, I can't just do me. Whatever I do affects me and Kian. And Kian comes first. If Tamar is not going to be good for Kian, I'm not going to be with him. You'll see when you have kids. Unless you gonna be a triflin' mother who don't give a shit about what she does that affect her kids.

Kids nowadays are raising themselves 'cuz their parents are too busy worrying about themselves."

"Oh here we go, Miss Philosopher. Just make sure that nigga Tamar gets a divorce," Asia replied.

I looked at her like she was crazy. "What! What the fuck do you mean a divorce?!"

"He's married to that girl, Ya Ya."

"What are you talking about Asia?" My face turned beet red!

"What did I just say?"

"I can't believe you knew some shit like that and didn't even tell me. What kind of friend does that? See that's why we always fallin' out Asia. You always bein' foul." I was mad as hell, and she knew it.

"Look Mika, I don't wanna hear that shit. I'm sittin' in the hospital and you worried about some nigga. He's married point blank. Don't fuckin' get mad at me."

"That's not the point. You should've told me when you found out." Asia always did shit like that. She didn't care about anybody.

"No, his ass should've told you. Besides, I just found out when you walked in the door."

I was quiet. I was dying to call Tamar, but I decided to wait until I left the room. I wasn't gonna make her happy by arguing with him in front of her. We sat there and watched TV and ate, while nurses came in every so often. When Peaches, one of Asia's good friends finally came in, I left and went straight home.

I decided against calling Tamar for the moment, afraid of what the outcome would be. I called Mark instead, and left a message. "Mark, please call me it's really important."

I called my mother and her voice mail came on too. "Ma, call me when you get home." I cried, but prayed for the best and tried to be strong and not think the worst. Kian kept asking me what was wrong. "Baby, Asia's sick and she's in the hospital. I'm worried about her."

Just as I was explaining, Shani came in followed by

Danny. It was nine-thirty, so I took my anger about Asia's situation out on Danny. "Uhm, what are you doing here? You didn't call first. You don't even call him on the weekends when he's not with you...he hasn't spoken to you since last Saturday."

"That's why I came by to tell him that I've been out of town," Danny answered. *He was just like my damn father.*

"Shani, come in the kitchen and let Danny spend a minute with his son." As soon as she saw my eyes she knew there was something more going on than my usual 'Danny anger'.

"Mika, what's wrong?"

"It's Asia. She has a tumor on her ovary."

"What!?" Shani asked, with her hand over her mouth.

"Yeah, I'm buggin'."

"Is it Cancer? Or they don't know yet?"

"They don't know." I cried and she hugged me and told me that I could lay down, if I wanted, and she would watch Kian for the rest of the night.

I walked past Danny and Kian in the living room and went to my room to lay down. I called Dior. I needed to fuss with somebody. After a few rings, he finally answered.

"Dior, why you ain't tell me Tamar was married?"

"Oh shit, I thought you knew. But Yo, he ain't wit' her though. I know that for a fact."

"So he should have told me. I'll talk to you later." I hung up, and called Tamar next, of course he didn't answer. "I guess you're with your wife, you married muthafucka!" I screamed on his voice mail.

As soon as I hung up the phone, there was a knock at my door. "Who is it?"

"Me," asshole said.

"What do you want?" I asked. He didn't even bother to answer me before he walked in and closed the door. I should've locked it.

"Shani told me about Asia. You alright?"

"Like you care?"

166   *All That Glitters*

"Mika don't start this shit, you know I care about you," Danny responded.

"Oh yeah. So is that why you purposely fucked shit up between me and Mark."

"Come on, I didn't try to...Nah, I'll be straight up. I did it to get back at you."

"For what? What did I do to you? You're the one who broke up with me."

"I don't know. It was my first time seeing you with somebody since we broke up, and it fucked my head up that day," he admitted.

"That's selfish. You have somebody, Danny. Why fuck up my shit?"

"You fucked up your own shit. Why did you play that kid like that? He really liked you. What, he doesn't have enough cheese for you?"

"What? Look Danny my girl might be dying, so I don't have time for your stupid shit, so can you just leave? And Mark loves me, don't get it twisted."

"Nah, I didn't come in here to argue with you. I wanted to make sure you're okay. So, let's start all over. Did you eat?"

"No, why are you gonna go get me something to eat?" I asked.

"No I'm gonna take you out to eat, let's go."

Uh-oh, I knew exactly what he had in mind. "Nah, that's alright. I'm okay."

"Come on, Mika. We have to start getting along for Kian, and I want to be here for you," he said sincerely.

"Why?"

"Come on, why does everything have to be a big discussion. Let's go." He looked at his watch.

"Why are you rushin' me? You gotta get home to Tiffany by a certain time?" I asked with an attitude.

"Shut up girl and come on. You know I don't answer to nobody, I get answered to."

"Your poor girl. She don't know what she got herself

Ericka M. Williams   167

into. Oh well, better her than me that's for sure." I meant that too.

We went to the South Street Seaport to eat. We talked about old times, good and bad, and I continued to throw my sarcastic remarks in, here and there. I didn't ask him anything about his life without me, especially not anything about Tiffany. I didn't want to know. He asked me questions about me though.

"So what's up with you and Mark?"

I looked at him and rolled my eyes. "Why?"

"Because I'm tryin' to make conversation. Why are you so mean?"

"Because you know you still care and you wanna act all cool like you don't. Make conversation about something else. Me and you ain't friends like that."

He gave me a sincere look, "We should be. We've been through too much together not to be friends," Danny replied.

"No, we've been through too much together to only be friends, we should've been married a long time ago. Plus, you don't want to just be friends. You want to have me and whoever else, and I'm not seeing you like that. I put too much time into you to be sharing you. I'd rather leave you alone and get over you than to hold on to something that's been over. I'm not allowing anymore shit into my life that's not good for me or my son."

"OUR son!" he shouted.

"Well since you brought it up you should've showed your son that a man is one who stays with his family."

"Mika, I really didn't mean to hurt you, but you kept pushing me to get married, and I knew I wasn't ready for that. What I don't understand is why you'll fuck with niggas who you know have other girls, but you won't see me. That kid Tamar, got mad bitches."

I had the deer caught in headlights look. Everybody knew about Tamar but me. "I don't care. I don't have feelings for him, like I did for you. But I'm not your yo-yo."

"Alright, well can we stop talking about it before you get an attitude and wanna go home."

We settled down with the negative talk and decided to drink and enjoy each other's company until the food came. We ordered several more drinks, and before long we were drunk and finally getting along. I knew we would end up in bed together, but not because he wanted to, but because I did. Not because I still loved him, but because I no longer did. If I still wanted to be with him, I wouldn't be able to handle a one night stand. It would upset me too much because it would bring back too many memories and feelings. All those times I was with him after we broke up, did me more harm than good. My hopes of getting him back would never be fulfilled. I wanted to do it that night to see what would happen. To see if I could walk away from it with no problem. Then I would really know that I was over him. I also wanted to do it just to get back at his bitch since she thought he wouldn't fuck with me. Plus, Tamar tried to play me.

"So come on, let's go to your house," Danny finally said. He tried not to smile while I kicked a little game.

"Nah, let's go to your house. I'm not letting Kian even think that we're together. It's not good for him to see us messin' around one minute and not speakin' the next."

"That's true. So let's go to the hotel."

"Whatever."

I didn't know why I was even going because I wasn't the least bit interested in him. This was all payback. For who, I wasn't sure. When we got in the room, I felt like I wanted to call the whole thing off. Then suddenly, Danny grabbed me and started kissing me, but it felt like a piece of sand paper being rubbed on my tongue. It wasn't soft and sensual, but hard and disgusting to me. His hands ran all over my body, but nothing happened. No sensation, no thrills, nothing! He squeezed on my nipples and pulled them out of my bra and started sucking them. But again nothing. I let him undress me and once he was done, I laid on my back and watched him undress. It amazed me that he seemed so cool with it all. I acted like I was cool, but on the inside, I boiled with hate. Something that used to be so special to me was rotten. He grabbed his dick and started jerking it in front of me. I grabbed him and put the condom on, then pulled him on top of me. When I tried to stick his dick in, I had to force it because I wasn't even wet. I pumped on him hard and fast so he would come quick, luckily he did. As soon as I felt his last jerk, I pushed him off of me and got up. I wanted to get as far away from him as I could. He thought he was gonna have an all-nighter, but he was wrong. I played him and quickly got dressed.

"Danny, take me home," I ordered.

"Why? Come on Mika, don't be so tense. Stay the night with me."

"Your girl is at your house, go get round two from her."

"See, you're just being like this because you think that nothing is gonna come out of this. Why don't we take it slow, we could become close again. At least this is a start."

"A start? What do you mean?" I asked with a confused expression.

"I wanna start spending time with you, so we can try to get it back to how it used to be," he responded.

"While you have a girl at home, right? See what I mean you're so full of shit. And then what?"

"Then maybe we can get back together."

"Still playing those mind games huh? Save it for your girl 'cuz I'm not tryin' to hear it," I said headed to the door.

"Do you still love me, Mika?"

I hesitated for a minute, "No."

"Yes you do. Tell me you still love me," he said, following me out the door.

He drove me home in silence, and I got out without giving him the kiss that he wanted. I really couldn't stand him. I walked in the house, took my clothes off, and picked up the phone. I dialed Danny's home number and Tiffany answered.

"Your man is on his way home with a dirty dick. You can suck my pussy juice off him if you want to sweetie." I hung up and laughed.

I knew he would be mad, but could care less. I knew she wouldn't break up with him, but I just wanted her to know that she wasn't all that. Besides, I wasn't ever giving Danny a reason to think that I was still waiting for him. I checked my messages to see if Mark had returned my calls, and he didn't. *Oh well, maybe it's time to move on from that relationship* too. For some reason, I felt stronger than ever before.

Chapter 16

THE BOMB

I woke up Monday and took Kian to school and headed back to the hospital. I went to see Asia and thank God, she was in a better mood. I stayed with her most of the day until about two o'clock before going home. I didn't even check my messages until I got in the house. Tamar had left five messages.

Beep: "Yo, Mika, call me baby. We gotta talk." **Beep:** "Baby, call me. You ain't even ask me what was up, before leaving that fucked up message, what type a shit is that? Yo, I'm ready to come back out there." **Beep:** "Yo, don't fuck up a good thing, over some bullshit you heard in the street. I'm out." **Beep:** "It's Monday morning. You ain't answer your phone all night. What the fuck is up? Yo, I'm about to be out. I wanna see you before I go…Yo, if you don't call me before I leave, fuck it, and you know what that means." Was he serious? **Beep:** "Fuck it man, I might as well get Ya-Ya and bring her back down with me, you playing kid games and shit. So fuckin' what we married, I'm filing for divorce, and I wanted to surprise you."

I listened to the messages over and over again. *I wanted to hear him beg. Then a thought hit me. I should've been a woman about it, and let him come back the night before and talked to him face to face.* I picked up the phone and called back.

"Yo Mika, man. Where the fuck you at?" Tamar asked.

"I'm home."

"I'll be there in a half hour. Who's there?"

"Nobody, but I gotta pick Kian up from school by six o'clock at the latest."

"It's three thirty now. Hold tight baby."

I was excited. Why, I don't know. Clearly, I was being a fool. I took a bubble bath and put on some cute pink terry cloth short shorts and a pink tight t-shirt with the New York City skyline in silver studs spread across it. It was teasing attire.

He got there early, and when I opened the door he hugged me real tight. Was this nigga gonna be a fatal attraction stalker type nigga?

"Listen baby, I was gonna tell you, but I wanted us to do us first. I ain't want that to turn you away. I filed for divorce today." I didn't know what the fuck to say. "Mika, look man this soft shit ain't even me. I'd normally say fuck a bitch if she starts that beefin' shit, but you, I'm wide the fuck open. You ain't gettin' rid of me that fast so you might as well forget it. I'm makin' you wifey."

He pulled a box out of his pocket and got on his knee. He then opened the box, took out a three-carat princess cut engagement ring, and slipped it on my finger. "As soon as my divorce is over, I want you to marry me. I know you are the one for me. You feisty, you strong, and you smart. I can't get no better than that. I want you to wear this ring and when we get the papers we can go pick out a fatter rock, whichever one you want." I looked down at that ring and figured fuck it, let's see how it goes down. He knew he had to come with something major.

"Look, I'm tired of playin' wifey. I wanna be somebody's wife for real."

"Baby just be patient. Let the divorce go through and you can plan the biggest wedding you ever dreamed of. Look at you, you ain't all that mad. Look how you came to the door, looking good enough to eat." He grabbed my ass and pulled me close to him and sucked on my lip. "And you ain't got no underwear on neither. It's on." He pulled my

Ericka M. Williams

173

shorts down, got back on his knees and had a shake for lunch. When I finished cuming in his mouth, he zipped down his zipper and stuck his toolie in. We stood up against the wall, right in the hallway by the front door. It was beyond good. We were bangin up against the wall when we heard the front door open. It was a good thing I put the chain on the door.

"Mika, open the door," Shani yelled.

Tamar was shook. He pulled his dick out of me, zipped up his pants, and looked at me like it was the police coming through the door. I motioned for him to go in my room and close the door. I pulled my shorts up and took the chain off before opening the door. Shani came in like she was the police, looking around, casing the joint.

"What the hell are you doing Mika?"

"Chillin'," I said, with a devilish grin.

As I walked toward my room Fuquan came in behind her and said, "Getting' her groove on."

"Shut up Fuquan...Don't you work? Or do you just follow Shani around all day?"

"Don't you worry about me, go finish handlin' your business. Eanie, Meanie, Miney, Mo...Is it Danny, Mark, Tamar, or a new beau?" I smacked him on the back. "Ssh, he might hear you."

I went in the room and noticed Tamar like a little boy who had got caught looking at a naked lady. I laughed at him as we laid on my bed. I looked at him and asked, "Tamar, why you couldn't just be real with me from the beginning? How long were you married?"

"Three years."

"When will the divorce be officially over?"

"I don't know, I'll ask my lawyer. But yo, that's a small thing man. I mean I know how you feel but worry about me and you. You got me now, keep it like that. Don't make me want another girl. Make me *stay* open."

"Oh, you act like it's the girl's fault when a man cheats."

"Sometimes it is. They get too comfortable and don't do

nothin' that they did to get you, to keep you. A man needs to stay interested and a real woman knows how to keep her man interested. Ya-Ya got too comfortable and the shit got stale."

"Well, I don't plan on letting that happen…But I don't know how this is going to work with you living in VA," I said.

"Why don't you and your son move down there with me?" he asked. "I mean we are engaged now."

I shook my head. "Baby, I've been here all my life."

"So it's time for you to make moves."

"Yo, slow down. We're going 90 in a 5 mile zone."

"You don't like the ride?" Tamar asked.

"I'm lovin' it. And that Lex is me. I love it.

"Well, I'm takin' it down tonight, keep the Nav till the weekend, then drive it down."

"I got Kian this weekend."

"Bring him. You said you wanna make sure I'm good enough for him," he responded with a huge smile.

"I didn't say it like that. My son comes first. If you and him don't bond, I can't be with you."

"I understand. So that's what you need to do. You and him come down this weekend and I'll get my son…Yo, you can pick my son up and he can ride down with you."

"His mother won't say nothin'?" I looked at him like he was crazy.

"What is she gonna say?"

We talked until 5:30 p.m., then went to pick up Kian. We went to Red Lobster for dinner and Tamar basically spent the whole time talking to Kian and trying to break the ice. They laughed and joked. I was glad they hit it off, but that was just dinner. Kian liked anybody who took him to Red Lobster. He was like his mother, he loved seafood. We went to the mall after that and Tamar wanted to buy Kian some sneakers, but I told him not to. I didn't want Kian to be bribed. I had money in my pocket, so I bought his sneakers. We left the mall around eight o'clock because I had to get Kian ready for bed. Tamar said he had to run to

New York and promised that he'd be back to chill with me.

I called Tamar about an hour later to tell him to bring a bottle when he came back so we could have a sweet good-bye party, but he didn't answer. That was the second night, I'd called him and he didn't answer, but I left a nice message, "Call me baby."

After I hung up, I went upstairs to see Dawniece. I got a forty and went in my room and locked the door. I must've-done too much too fast because I had a bad episode. Fifteen minutes after I started, I was buggin' real bad. My heart was pounding and I got so scared. I tried to mentally bring the high down by focusing on other things, but it did-n't work. I went into the bathroom and every step from my room to the bathroom, my brain told me would be my last. My mind kept telling me I was about to die. I started curs-ing myself out in my head. "You done did it now bitch, you wanna die, well your wish is gonna come true, you fuckin' cokehead bitch!"

I ran a hot bubble bath to try to relax my nerves as I shook uncontrollably. I was about to pass out. I prayed over and over. I slid in the warm water and looked down at my chest. I could see my heart beating, and it was so fast that all I could do was cry.

"Lord, please. I'm tired of doing this. Please don't take me Lord. I need to stop. Help me Lord. Please help me Lord. Don't let me die." I wanted to call Shani, but I just sat there fighting to live. I splashed the water on my face and slowly tried to stand up. I cried and sat back down in the water. I stood up and stretched my arms up to the ceiling. "Please Lord, why Lord? Please don't take me from Kian, he needs me. Oh my God, help me."

I sat back down in the water for the third time. "Okay, calm yourself down. Relax," I kept saying to myself. You're gonna be okay. Fight for your life. Breathe slow and deep. Relax. I heard the phone in my room ringing. I couldn't even get up to answer it. I just sat there feeling like a crazy person. I couldn't get myself together. It seemed like an

All That Glitters

hour before I could get up and go in my room. When I made it back to my room, I was groggy. It was near twelve o'clock. *Damn, I sat there for two hours.* I must've blacked out because it didn't feel like I was in there that long. I felt like I had taken sleeping pills. As soon as I laid down on my bed, my heart started pounding again. I got up again because I was scared. I quickly took the package and flushed it down the toilet. That was the last thing I wanted to see at the moment. I made some tea to help me relax and a few minutes later, I checked my phone and caller ID. Tamar had called at 11:30 p.m., but he didn't leave a message. I picked up the phone and called him back.

"Where were you at?" he asked.

"Drinking some tea," I responded in a nonchalant tone.

"Yo, why you sound like that? What's wrong?" he asked.

"I don't feel well. Where were you?"

"In the hospital visiting my Aunt. That's why I couldn't answer. I'm glad you didn't curse me out on the message."

"I was about to," I said softly.

"Yo, I'm comin' over there, I don't like how you sound."

"Nah, I'm going to sleep. I thought you were going back down."

"Oh now you tryin' to get rid of me?"

"Tamar, I just don't feel good. Stay till tomorrow and I'll see you before you leave."

"Alright, I'm coming early in the morning."

"Where are you gonna stay tonight?" I asked.

"With my aunt. I'll show it to you tomorrow. See you tomorrow baby."

"Goodnight Daddy," I said wanting to go to sleep. I felt like I had lost ten pounds over the last thirty minutes. That shit wore me down, I ain't fuckin' wit' that shit anymore. Enough is enough.

Ericka M. Williams 177

On Wednesday morning, I left the house early so I could go and get some clothes for work, before going to see Asia. I finally landed a job as a paralegal in Hackensack, only five minutes away. I couldn't wait for Monday to start. This was the start that I needed. After arriving at the hospital, I looked over at Asia who had a nervous look on her face since her test results were in. We just sat there waiting. At about 10:15 a.m. two doctors finally came in.

"Hello, Asia Jackson," one of them said coldly. They both looked like they were bringing bad news.

"Hi," Asia said, with a scared smile and less hopeful voice.

"Are you immediate family?" one of the doctor's asked me. I told them I was because I knew I would have to leave the room if I wasn't. Asia's mother still hadn't gotten there.

"Okay, we've run a series of tests over the last few days to see if there were any other magligant tumors, and if there were any other problems we should be concerned about."

Asia nodded and waited. The other doctor started where the first one left off. "Well, your tumors came back benign, which is negative for cancer..."

"Yes!" I yelled as the doctor looked at me. I didn't care, I was happy.

I looked at Asia who was smiling from ear to ear.

He continued. "...however, your blood test came back positive for Aquired Immune Deficiency Syndrome."

For a split second there was silence and then Asia started screaming, "No! Oh my God, no! Please don't tell me I have AIDS!"

I started shaking my head. I covered my mouth and started sobbing. I couldn't get up and go over to her because I felt like it was a dream, or that I was outside of the room looking in through a two-way mirror. Asia continued to scream as the doctor's looked at her like they wanted her to shut up. As I tried to take what little strength I

All That Glitters

had to get up, and hug her, her mother came running through the door.

"What's going on in here? Asia what's wrong?"

"Oh, Ma!"

Damn, how could she tell her mother? Her mother would die.

"What is going on? Somebody tell me what the hell is going on in here!" her mother continued to ask.

Finally, the doctors attempted to help. "Uhm, Ms. Jackson, may we talk to you outside while your other daughter calms Asia down?"

I got up and walked to the bed. My eyes were so flooded that I was seeing blurred visions. I made it to the bed and Asia grabbed me. I hugged her and she held onto me so tight, her whole body shook. Her mother went outside and within two seconds she was screaming, too. She came back in and fell to her knees.

"Lord, please Lord. Don't do this to me Lord? Oh, my. Oh, I can't go on with this Lord. Please make them wrong..." Ms. Jackson cried.

I blocked everything out so I wouldn't lose my mind right then and there. I couldn't look at Asia or Miss Ann. I stared into space in disbelief. I couldn't believe what was happening. I started thinking of the sexual encounters that I'd been having over the past year. I tried my best to recall all the 'raw' encounters. My mind started racing. Even if I had used a condom, how would I know that there wasn't a microscopic hole in it that allowed some semen into my body? What if condoms had broken without me knowing? What if using the same straw to sniff with had allowed some of Asia's mucus to enter my nostrils? What if Tamar has it? Oh my God, what if I have it too?

I started crying hysterically. We were all being punished. What have I done to myself, thinking I was so muthafuckin' slick and fast? Thinking I could do whatever I wanted to do. I felt the vomit rising from my stomach to my throat. I ran into the bathroom in her room. I made it to the toilet bowl

Ericka M. Williams

179

just in time to throw up. I heard Asia moaning, "Mika, not me! I got it! I got AIDS! I'm gonna die!"

I stayed on my knees for several minutes. I sat down next to the toilet and had to lean over it two or three more times. The spit was all over my shirt. I wiped my mouth with my sleeve and then my eyes. The party was over! *And was it really worth it? Was it all that much fun?* To be here now with the end of the world on top of my head?

"Mika, come here!" Asia yelled.

I had to gather myself. I looked at my pale face in the mirror. I splashed some water on my face, and before I could make it to her, she was standing in the doorway holding onto the introveneous stand for dear life. I looked in her eyes. "Why Mika?"she asked.

I shrugged my shoulders, smoothed my hair back, and walked over and put my arms around her. I walked Asia back to the bed and helped her get in it without saying a word. I had to take an HIV test ASAP. I didn't know what the hell to say to her, and didn't know if I was even in a position to, because I could have it too.

My mind was in a daze. I had to snap out of it. Something had to be wrong, this couldn't be happening to her. I jumped when her mother put her hand on my shoulder. She had tears in her eyes.

"Mika, go get those doctors, I want another test taken. I don't know how they can bring that kind of news and just leave."

I was glad that she was going to take control of the situation. She went over to Asia. "Come on, baby, calm down now. We're gonna get to the bottom of this. We can't fall apart now, everything is going to be fine. Yes, the Lord wouldn't do this, no sir. There's got to be a mistake."

I walked out of the room. I was glad that she asked me to leave. I needed to get away for a minute. I went to the nurses' station and asked for the doctors. "Excuse me, my sister is in room..." Nobody paid attention, so I spoke a little louder. "Excuse me, can you page the two doctors that were in room 613?"

"You'll have to wait," one of the nurses said, without even looking at me. I stopped myself from jumping over the desk and slapping the shit outta her.

"Look bitch, the two doctors who obviously don't give a shit just gave my sister a diagnosis and walked out. We want some muthafuckin' answers!"

The nurse took one look at me and paged the doctors right away. When they came back, Asia and I sat quietly while her mother did all the talking.

She took a deep breath. "Okay...first of all, I would like to know your names." When they told her, she wrote them down. Her voice was calm but shaky. "Okay, can you tell me what steps will be taken now?"

"Well, Asia appears to be in the early stages of full-blown AIDS," one doctor said.

Asia sunk down in the bed and started crying quietly. Her mother fell into a chair.

In my mind I asked God "Why?" like fifty times. "Why God? Why?"

They continued, "See, when people don't get routine AIDS tests they can be walking around with HIV and not even know it. Then when they get the virus, all we can do is treat whatever illnesses they come down with. There are some experimental drugs that are being used on AIDS patients that attempt to reverse the onset of the disease and we can look into those. However, the key is to take very good care of the body. Nutrition plays a big role in fighting off illnesses the body can't fight on its own. But we'll have another test taken first."

"Thank you," Ms. Jackson said hopelessly.

The doctors said they would come back the next day before Asia went home. When they left we didn't say anything for a few minutes. Asia was all cried out for the moment. She wiped her face and sat up. "Ma, why is this happening to me?"

"I don't know baby. I don't know. Do you want some-

Ericka M. Williams

thing to eat or drink? I'm going to the cafeteria."

"No," Asia said quietly.

"What about you Mika?"

"No thank you Miss Ann." I could tell that she was getting ready to cry. She walked out and Asia broke down again.

"Mika please tell me this is a dream." I looked at her through blurry eyes and then looked at the ground. "Mika, my life is over," she whined.

"Asia please...Let's just see what happens. Come on girl, we've gotta be strong. You know we're gonna be with you through whatever. Let's at least hold our heads until the second test comes back. Okay? You never know, they could've made a mistake."

"I don't think so, Mika. I mean in the back of my mind I was scared this was gonna happen. When I started losing weight, I guess AIDS was always in the back of my mind. I've really been feeling sick. I guess fuckin' around with no good niggas got my ass no fuckin' where! I should've listened to my mother."

Just then, a nurse stuck her head in and waved me out. Apparently Miss Ann fainted, and needed a ride home. She didn't want Asia to know, so I agreed to take her home. I ran back into Asia's room, kissed her on the forehead, and grabbed Miss Ann's pocketbook. I told her that her mom would be busy wth the doctors for a while, and I'd be back tomorrow.

I took Miss Ann home. Neither of us said anything in the car, but I told her I would call her later on. After dropping her off, I went to get Kian from school, and thanked God for him the moment I saw him. I gave him a hug and squeezed him real tight. When we got home he asked me about Asia.

"Mommy, how's Auntie Asia?"

My voice cracked. "She's okay Boo. She'll probably be home tomorrow."

I was acting as normal as I could. When we got home, I

called Miss Ann to see how she was doing, but nobody answered. I figured she probably went back to the hospital. Kian and I were watching TV when the phone rang.

"Hello."

"How's my wife doing?" Tamar asked.

I started crying when I heard his voice.

"What's wrong baby?"

"My girlfriend…Asia…Oh my God, I can't believe this…My girl got that shit," I responded.

"Sweetie, what's wrong baby girl?"

"She has AIDS. Ohhh, I'm gonna be sick." I looked at Kian. "Go take a bath."

"Mommy, can you give me a bath?" Kian asked.

I yelled. "Boy, you about to be five in a couple of months. Go take a damn bath."

He held his head down and walked out the room.

"Yeah, I wish you were here. I need a hug." I took out the package, I'd got from Dawneice's and took a hit. Every time I tried to stop some shit happens to make me run back to it. "Did you ever have an AIDS test?" I asked him with concern.

"What? I ain't no homo or fiend, and I ain't got no cold or nothin' so why are you buggin'?"

"You don't have to be gay or on drugs…I can't believe you just said that ignorant shit."

"Hold up, who you talkin' to like that?" he barked.

"Tamar, I'll call you back."

"Before you hang up, what's up with me hearing that you sniffin' that coke too? This chick in your building is going around saying you coppin' from her like every other day. Is that true? 'Cause I ain't marryin' another cokehead bitch."

"No Tamar," I said, without even trying to sound convincing. I didn't even care about that right now. This nigga needs to take an HIV test. "Can you please take an HIV test and bring me the results when you come back up? And please don't get mad or offended that I'm asking you. If it's

Ericka M. Williams

gonna be me and you we at least owe it to each other to know that neither one of us brought that shit to the table." I was waiting for him to act like a dick about it.

"Yeah, I'll do it. And when I come up, you'll take a drug test right?"

"Yeah."

"Okay baby, call me back…Oh wait, when you gon' take your HIV test?"

"Tomorrow."

"Okay, I love you baby."

"I love you too Tamar."

I hung up and kept going over today in my mind. Yo, Asia had AIDS and I might of had it too. I only used protection selectively, and as much as I don't want to have a test, I was gonna have to. It could prolong my life. Shani came in, and I paused for a short moment until the tears started rolling down my face.

"What is it Mika?"

I just sat there.

"It's AIDS isn't it?" Fu said. As much as I wanted to tell him to mind his fuckin' business and that he wasn't one of the girls. I just nodded my head.

"Oh Mika, I'm sorry." Shani came over and hugged me and I moved away.

"I'm sorry Shani but if you hug me I'm going to cry even more. I've been crying all day. Today had to be the craziest day of my life. You should've seen how happy we were when they said it wasn't Cancer. Then two seconds later they told her she had full-blown AIDS. Then they just walked out. Then Miss Ann fainted. Oh my God, I cannot believe this shit is happening."

"Well, who gave it to her, does she know?" Shani asked.

"Not yet, she just found out...Can you watch Kian for a little while? I'm going to take a nap."

I didn't even wait for a reply before I walked into my room and got bent.

All That Glitters

Kian woke me up about ten the next morning after missing school. I jumped up and called Asia's room.

"What's up girl, how you feelin'?" I asked.

"Alright, I was hoping I would wake up in my bed after a terrible nightmare about me havin' AIDS, but I guess not huh?"

I didn't say anything. "Did your mother come back to the hospital last night?"

"Yeah, why?"

"Just asking. So when are you going home?"

"After they take the second test."

"Do you want me to come over?"

"Nah, you don't have to. I'll call you later."

"All right."

I hung up and Danny called a little while later. He said he wanted to take Kian away, even though it was my weekend. He sounded like he had an attitude. I guess he was mad about me calling Tiffany. I was going to say no because Kian and I were supposed to go stay with Tamar, but I said okay. I needed to be with Tamar alone, so he could make me feel better.

"I'll be there in thirty," he said.

"Get him ready now!" I screamed for no reason. "It's 10:00 in the morning!"

"So."

"Where are you taking him?"

"To D.C."

"For what?" I asked.

"Because I want to."

"Whatever. Is your girl going too?"

"Why? You want to call and harass her? Yo, what did you do that for?" he asked like he was hurt.

"I guess because you came here with that same bullshit about us getting back together knowing you didn't mean a

damn thing you said. Instead of asking me why ask yourself why you were with me. You have a girl. I guess she's
not all that huh?"

"You see I didn't leave her for you, so she must be
somethin'."

I slammed the phone down, and got Kian dressed.
Twenty minutes later, the doorbell rang. I opened it and
that bastard was standing in my doorway with his bitch.
Had this been a year ago I would've flipped my wig. I probably would've dropped, to my knees, at his feet and cried,
"How can you do this to me?" like some bitch in a soap
opera. Instead, I moved Kian swiftly to the door, so they
couldn't come in. I gave Kian a hug and kiss goodbye, and
told him to be good. I closed the door gently and smiled! I
didn't pay either one of the bastards any mind.

I wanted to speak to my best friend, Mark. I felt bad, but
I couldn't dwell on what I did wrong. I did bad things, but I
wasn't a bad person. I had to change for myself and I had
to forgive myself. I asked the Lord for forgiveness, and the
ability to learn from my mistakes and move on. I prayed
that He was listening.

Chapter 17

DANGEROUS

I packed my bag, went upstairs and got a forty. I asked Dawniece if she was spreading my business, and of course she lied and said no. I knew she wasn't gonna say yes. After all, I was putting money in her pocket.

When I arrived at the clinic, I was so high. I was sure the nurse who took my blood assumed that my lover had broken the news because I was acting like I already knew the results. I went back home and took three more hours getting high before I got on the road to VA. I wrote Shani a note telling her that I was going to Tamar's. I didn't know where the hell I was going after I got past D.C, so I kept calling Tamar. I didn't even know how I made it down there. I was high out of my mind and paranoid the whole way.

I stopped at a hotel to get myself together. I ended up getting stuck there for two more hours trying to get myself together. If he would've seen me that way, I'm sure he would've known that I was lying to him the night before on the phone. I hoped he wouldn't push the issue about giving me a drug test once he saw how upset I was. I took five showers before I brought it down and was able to call him to meet me somewhere familiar. When he met me on the highway, he must have thought I looked crazy from crying because he didn't say anything.

When we got to his house, he treated me so good. We just stayed in the bed for the rest of the night, while Les brought in whatever I wanted. I didn't talk about Asia, but Tamar said when I was ready to talk he would listen. We watched movies and just held each other. At about three in the morning his phone rang. He jumped up and said he had to go out, but didn't tell me why. After all the drama I was going through, I could care less. I went back to sleep.

I awoke around five in the morning, to a chrome plated .357 gun in my face. I looked up and two cats with hoods had Tamar going in his bedroom safe. They held me down with force. It took me a few minutes to realize what was going on, and when I did, I lost it. I scrambled across the bed like a junkie going cold turkey. I started crying and Tamar kept telling me to shut up. I kept begging and telling them that I had a son. My heart was in my throat. All I could see was Kian at my funeral. I started shaking uncontrollably. The nigga with the gun on me starting yelling, and told me over and over me to calm down. "I'm a put a muthafuckin' bullet through your pussy bitch!" he said.

I cried even more and began to rock back and forth.

Tamar opened the safe and passed them five stacks of cash. He was talking the whole time like he was okay, "Yo, y'all better not let me find out who you are," he said real calmly. I was thinking that would give them all the more reason to bury him and me right then and there. Suddenly, they walked out of the room.

"I love you baby, don't worry. Don't call the police," he said to me. "Don't move, stay right where you are. I'll be all right." Tamar looked so serious, not scared at all. What the fuck? Was he that used to this shit? He was too fucking calm for me.

"Tamar, please, why y'all gotta take him? He gave you the money?" I begged.

"Shut the fuck up trick," the last guy out the room shouted, and closed the door behind him.

They walked down the hall and then I didn't hear anything. One of them came back in the room without Tamar. He tied me to the bed post with thick rope, so I knew for sure he was getting ready to rape me. I heard a commotion in the hallway and then a gunshot. I started screaming, but no noise came out of my mouth. The guy ran out of the room and down the hall! I just knew Tamar was dead. I heard footsteps running down the stairs. *Where was the muthafuckin' police?* I laid there shaking, and tied up for about two hours until I heard two people come back in the house. Suddenly, Tamar walked in the room like nothing happened. He changed his clothes, and put them in a plastic bag. I tried to put my arms out for him to come toward the bed, but couldn't move. *Couldn't he see that I was tied up?*

"Baby, you alright," he asked loosening the rope. Listen you and Dee Dee need to go to my mother's house," he said, as he untied me.

"What happened Tamar?"

"Do what the fuck I said. I'll be there in about two hours." After pulling the ropes off, he turned around and left.

Seconds later, Dee Dee came in the room shook, as I was getting dressed. Neither one of us could talk. When I was done, we walked out the room and noticed blood in the hallway. What the fuck is going on?

Dee Dee drove us to Tamar's mother's house, who lived an hour away. I didn't know where I was. I felt like I had died and was watching this in a dark movie theater. I was scared out of my mind. When we got in the house and sat down, I asked Dee Dee what happened.

"I don't know. I was downstairs sleep. Les said he saw a nigga in the hallway with a gun to Tamar's back, so he took out his gun and shot the nigga and the other one ran out the door. Then he said something about Ty being shot."

"So they were in the house with us while we were sleeping. Oh my God!!! I wanna go home." I cried like a baby.

After two hours, Tamar and Les finally showed up and told us to follow them. And like two fools, we did. I was scared to ask any questions. We ended up going to a hotel about an hour away from his mother's house. We stayed in two adjoining rooms. When I got in the bed, Tamar walked in from next door.

"Listen baby, I'm so sorry. These niggas killed Ty, and was coming for me too."

"Tamar, you gotta get out the game. Oh my God! Kian could've been here." *I can't be with this dude. This was not the life for me anymore and definitely not my son.*

"Mika, don't leave me. I'm gonna make it better," Tamar said.

"How Tamar?"

He shook his head. "I don't know yet."

We hugged and slept in each other's arms that night. I was by my man's side and I didn't wanna leave. However, I wasn't going back to that house though.

First thing in the morning, Tamar and Les left to go take care of some business, while Dee Dee and I went shopping at a nearby mall. They had left us a thousand dollars each. Even though it was probably bribery, shopping sure took that shit off my mind. As we shopped, Dee Dee and I kept bringing it up, but then said we didn't want to talk about it. Dee Dee said she wanted to move away, and I agreed. Tamar was gonna have to move back North, or he could forget about me. Niggas didn't like niggas from up north comin' down south gettin' money. They have killed quite a few niggas that I knew. I could think of five right off the top of my head who called themselves going down south to hustle and came back up in body bags. It was gonna have to be retire or breakup, and I was serious.

When Tamar and Less came back, we all went out to dinner. They didn't tell us shit. We all tried to act like nothin' ever happened. The air was thick. I guess they had a lot on their minds.

Thankfully, I left Saturday around eight. I got home Sunday morning at 2:00 a.m. I was tired. I took the Lex home this time. Tamar promised me that he would tie up some ends down there and move back home. He said it would take him a month or two. But his move was under one condition. That Kian and I move in with him. I had the task of looking for a place. I also gave my one condition, it had to be in Jersey. *Damn, I need to call Monet. I wonder if she knew already.* I wasn't gonna call her until Monday. I prayed and thanked the Lord for saving my life. I picked up the phone and decided to call Janae. I was finally ready to go to church.

Chapter 18

AMEN

I woke up Sunday morning about 8:30 a.m. I made myself breakfast and got dressed in my best conservative gear. Janae called and said for me to be ready at 10:30 a.m. I waited downstairs at 10:25 sharp, because Janae was always on time. When we got there, we found good seats about three rows from the pulpit.

When the service started, I sat through the normal announcements, looking around at the different hats in front of me. When it was time to help the church pay their rent the choir sang. The choir was young and vibrant, their songs touched me. I joined the rest of the people who stood and clapped. The song was "Please be patient with me God is not through with me yet." The girl who was singing it, sang it for all of us. When the song was over, I sat down and thanked Janae for bringing me. I whispered in her ear, "Girl, I needed some good church music. That girl has a real powerful voice." She nodded in agreement. Then it was time for the Altar Call. The pastor called anyone who wanted to pray at the altar to come. Janae got up and grabbed my hand. I followed her to the altar and we knelt down. I bowed my head and closed my eyes...

Lord, first I want to thank you. Thank you for letting me see another day. Thank you for protecting me in Virginia. Thank you for my family and my son. Thank you for all that you have done for me.

Please know Lord that I am thankful, but I must ask something of you. I will never know why Asia had to get HIV, but please let her live for a long time. Please let her body be strong and fight it. Lord, I know I've done a lot of crazy things but please give me a chance to better myself. All I ask for is my health and a strong mind to succeed. Clear my mind from all the sh...I mean stuff that is negative and guide me towards a positive way of life. Show me how to be more open-minded. Lord, I think what I really need is a husband...

Janae nudged me. As I looked up and she was standing with everyone else ready to go back to their seats. I was embarrassed. I jumped up and walked back to the pew. Of course, the pastor didn't miss it and had to comment. "That's all right sister, you wasn't ready to say Amen. You had more praying to do than we did. That's alright." Everybody laughed and I blushed.

I didn't mind. I enjoyed my minute with God. I may not have gone to church every Sunday, but I did have God in my life. God had watched over me for years. I could've been crippled, retarded, dead, or a crackhead, but I wasn't. I could've been molested as a child but I wasn't. I had no control over all those things, so I knew it was God's work.

The choir sang another song that rocked the whole church. Just about everybody was on their feet dancing, clapping, and getting the holy ghost. Even after the song was over the piano and organ were still going for those who were still feelin' happy. Then it was time for the pastor's sermon and I wondered what he would talk about. He started with a scripture out of the Bible that I wasn't familiar with, but I listened anyway because I knew he would be putting it into real life terms. The more he talked, the more I thought about my situation. I knew it was time for a change. For forty-five minutes straight, I was hit with testimony after testimony, and cried at the end of the sermon. Janae put her arms around me, and I gave her a slight

Ericka M. Williams

smile.

I was filled with energy, and glad that I had gone to
church. The sermon always felt like it was made personally
for me. We walked outside and it was a beautiful sunny
day for the end of September. I took a deep breath and
promised myself that this would be the first day of my new
life. The fact that I was starting work the next day made it
even better. I always felt this way after church, but this time
I wasn't going to go home and let everything be the same.
I was going to try to live a positive and fulfilling life. I wanted to succeed in life. I no longer just wanted to exist. I
wanted my life to have some type of meaning.

"So, do you like my church?" Janae asked, as we
walked to her car.

"Yeah, I really enjoyed it. I love pastors who can put the
Bible into present day."

"Yeah, he's good. Do you want to go out to breakfast?"

"Yeah, but do you mind if I see if Asia wants to go,
she's been kind of depressed lately?"

"Of course not, call her."

I called her, but Miss Ann said she wasn't home. Dag,
where could she be? I hung up and a few seconds later
the phone rang. It was Miss Ann, whispering. "Mika, it's
Miss Ann. Asia is home but she's not taking any calls.
Mika, she's been staying in the bed, not eating. I don't
know what I'm gonna do."

"Do you want me to come over?"

"No because she'll know that I just told you she wasn't
here. I'm hoping that she'll snap out of it. She can't stop
wanting to live because of this." her mother almost
broke down.

"I know Miss Ann. She'll snap out of it." What else could
I say? "I'll come by. She's just in shock, you know how
stubborn she is. Don't worry, she'll fight it."

"I hope so baby. Let me go, she's coming downstairs."

"Okay Miss Ann." I still couldn't believe this was happening to my best friend.

All That Glitters

I told Janae that I was going to go by Asia's house instead of going to eat.

"Oh, okay, is she alright?"

"Yeah, her boyfriend got locked up so she's upset."

"Oh."

Janae dropped me off at my car and said that she would call me later. I drove over to Asia's doing at least 80 miles per hour. When I arrived, Miss Ann answered the door. She looked like she had aged since I last saw her. She gave me a hug and held me tighter and longer than usual. I gave her a kiss on the cheek. She whispered in my ear, "Mika, you've gotta talk to her. She still won't eat or get dressed. She's had the same pajamas on since Friday."

I clinched my arms tightly, and just looked around. The whole house was dreary. It had the feeling of death already. I told Miss Ann that I would go upstairs and talk to her, but I thought I would be doing the same thing if I were in her shoes. *How do you continue with your life when you've been told that it's over?* I asked how Asia's sister, Sariah, was taking the news and Miss Ann said that Sariah hadn't left Asia's side since she got home.

"Go on up there baby, I'll call y'all when breakfast is ready."

"Okay Miss Ann."

I went upstairs and opened Asia's room door slowly. Asia was under the covers and Sariah was sitting on the edge of the bed. She was happy to see me.

"Mika! I haven't seen you in so long. Come in!" Sariah came over to me and gave me a hug. She looked so grown to be only seventeen.

"Asia, how you feelin'?" I asked, trying to sound upbeat.

"Like I'm dying." She didn't even look at me. I got a chair and pulled it over to the side of the bed.

"What's up Asia, did I do something to you?"

"Why?"

"Because it seems like you're mad at me about something, what's wrong?"

Ericka M. Williams

"What's wrong Mika? You don't know? Should I be happy?"

"No, but you've gotta keep living your life. Fu's uncle lived for five years after he was full-blown. How do you know you can't live for ten? How do you know that there won't be a cure by then?" She shrugged her shoulders. "You gotta fight it with your mind."

"I don't know how. How do I plan things? I can't set long term goals."

Sariah shook her head. "Asia come on now, you go on telling yourself that you're going to make the most of every-day you have. I could die in a car accident tomorrow. Do you think you're the only one who is hurt that this is hap-pening?"

"Well, until you're in my shoes you can't talk."

"Well, taking it out on us is not going to change any-thing," Sariah said, angrily and stormed out of the room. I figured I should keep plugging.

"You know she's right Asia. We know we're not in your position, but you're not alone. Think of how your mother feels. She can't even get you to eat. Don't you think it's hurting her to see you not even try to fight and this is only the beginning Asia. Are you listening to me?" She looked away from the TV toward me.

"Yeah, I'm listening." I decided to give her a break and change the subject.

"So, have you spoken to Butch?" I asked with concern.

"No."

"Have you spoken to his mother?"

"She called to ask me to take her to the mall, but I told her that I took the rental car back."

I was running out of questions. "Are you still going with me to Tanesha's wedding next weekend?"

"I guess."

"Asia please stop with the one word answers."

"I have to tell Butch, I got it," she blurted out.

"Asia, I don't think you should tell anybody yet."

"Fuck it then, I'm not telling him, or anybody else shit. The nigga that gave it to me didn't say shit." She wiped a tear away.

"Maybe the person doesn't know," I said calmly.

"It could be Butch's fuckin' ass, you never know. Damn, how the fuck did this happen to me?"

"Well, you know I won't tell anybody."

"I know bitch." That was the Asia I knew.

"I decided today that I am a queen."

"Now who's acting crazy?"

"No, I'm for real Asia. I'm changing my life."

"All right bitch, if you say so."

I couldn't blame her for not taking me serious, but eventually she would. Miss Ann knocked on the door and stuck her head in, "Girls, come and eat." I loved Miss Ann's cooking, especially on Sundays, because she always made full course meals. I ate and left to go home to get ready for my first day of work.

Chapter 19

WAKING UP

When I got home Kian was in the living room with Danny, and Shani was in the kitchen cooking. I picked Kian up, gave him a kiss and went into my room to change my clothes. Someone knocked at my door.

"What do you want now?" I asked, knowing that it was Danny.

"I gotta talk to you, open the door."

"Wait a second, I'm changin' my clothes."

"Oh, like I've never seen you naked before," he countered. "Before is over, and the other night *didn't mean shit*, so wait." I put on some sweats with a T-shirt and opened the door. He came in and sat on my bed.

"Can you sit in the chair?"

"Mika, stop acting silly," he smirked.

"What do you want, damn, you're like a splinter. Every time I try to get you out of my system you keep diggin' deeper and deeper...You get under my skin like no other man I've ever known."

"That's because you've never loved another man like you loved me."

"How the fu..." No, I'm not gonna curse and get excited. I'm a new woman now. "How do you know?"

"Because I was your first."

"That's what I told you," I said, sarcastically.

"Well, I know you're going to hate me when I tell you this but I'd rather tell you than for you to hear it on the street...I'm getting married."

My heart stopped. "What!" I swung open the door. "Get the fuck out!" *There goes my three minutes of calmness.*

"Mika, sit down." He went to grab me and I pulled away. I ran to the bathroom. I started crying quietly so he couldn't hear me. I heard Shani tell him that she was taking Kian to the store so that we could talk. When she left, he knocked on the bathroom door. I cleared my throat and tried to sound like I wasn't crying.

"Damn, can I go to the bathroom in peace? I'll be out in a minute." I wiped my eyes and washed off my face. It's a shame that I couldn't let my emotions show with someone who I once loved. It was always something with him, and it seemed like he enjoyed making me upset. I wasn't mad because he was marrying her now, but because he didn't marry me before. I opened the door and sat on the couch in the living room.

"Alright, so you're getting married, can you leave now? I'm sure she's claiming to be pregnant, right?"

"As a matter of fact, she is pregnant. I went with her to the doctor," he said reluctantly.

I could feel the anger running through my body. "Oh, but you couldn't marry me when I was pregnant right? Did you know this on Monday when you were talking your greatest shit?"

"No," I really wanted us to work on our relationship."

"Yeah, so after she gets a call that you were with me, all of a sudden she's pregnant, how convenient. Well, I wish I knew then what I know now 'cuz this would have been your first child."

"Mika, don't say that. You know you don't regret having Kian."

"No, but I regret having him by you. You were with me for six years and you couldn't marry me, but this other girl comes along and all of a sudden you're ready to get married. You know it's a good thing my mother raised me to be strong because if she hadn't, I probably would've killed

Ericka M. Williams

myself over you."

Danny didn't say anything. He just looked at me like he knew I couldn't take any more defeat.

"You tell 'Miss Thing' that she can forget it if she thinks she's going to be calling any shots when it comes to my son," I shouted while my finger moved back and forth. "You will have him every other weekend like always. As for you, you think you're leaving the same little girl you left at twenty-three, well I'm going on twenty-five and a lot of things are changing in my life, and you are the one who is gonna miss out. The only thing we have to deal with each other about is Kian, that's it. Do not ask me to go anywhere with you, do not ask me for a kiss, and don't come here without calling. And don't think you're gonna stop taking care of him or I'll be taking you straight to court. Remember, Kian is your first!"

"Mika, come on, I wouldn't treat him any different. That's why we took him away this weekend, so I could tell him."

"And what did you tell him?" I asked.

"That he's lucky because now he's gonna have two families instead of one."

I gave him a look of death. "Does he know that Daddy is going to be somebody else's Daddy too?"

"No, Tiffany thought we shouldn't put too much on him at one time. But I'm sure he wants a little brother or sister."

"Do you think for yourself, or does Tiffany have your nuts in a headlock?" I stood with my hands on my hips wondering if he realized that Tiffany was starting to control him.

"Come on now, you know ain't no woman runnin' this show."

"Goodbye, Danny, and good luck. I hope you find marriage fulfilling so you can stay the hell away from me." I opened the door.

"Mika, think about what I said alright."

"Is that what you want to teach your son, that he can

have as many women as he wants? Grow up Danny, there's more to life than fuckin' different broads." I slammed the door.

I was shocked. I hoped that the marriage would keep him out of my life, but the way he was acting, it didn't seem like it would stop him from doing anything.

Danny was going to do whatever he wanted, regardless of who he might hurt. I was distraught, but then I thought, *tomorrow my new life begins...But tonight I'm gettin' me a package.* How much can one person take?

I went upstairs to see Dawniece. When I walked in, she was looking crazy, as usual and had a get high crew sitting around. This nosy ass bitch from the next building was in there named Tiesha. I didn't want to be in there with her, but fuck it. She couldn't say shit, she was doin' the same thing. She was smoking crack with Dawniece.

"Hey Mika. Yo, I heard you fuckin' with Tamar from Harlem. He got you that Lexus truck?" Tiesha ain't waste no time trying to get in my business.

"Why?" I snapped.

"Oh nah, I was just asking. This girl I know knows his girl."

"Ex," I shot back, "and?"

"Damn, what's your problem?" she asked.

"Nah, I'm just tired of muthafuckas. Every time my phone rings nowadays it's somebody tellin' me some shit they heard about me. Bitches need to stop sweatin' me and get their life together. Stop suckin' my dick 'cause I ain't payin' them for it."

"Fuck 'em Mika. I don't give a shit what a hoe say about me. She ain't payin' my bills," Dawniece said, while she was putting her crack in her weed blunt.

"Yeah but Dawniece…You're tellin' people that I be comin' up here coppin' shit from you? Because my sister, of all people, already said somethin' to me about me gettin' high and my sister don't know nobody in the streets. Nobody that would know shit like that."

Ericka M. Williams

"Hell no. I told you that already. This is a sanctuary girl. Whoever comes here is safe. Now as far as somebody who may have been here when you came, I don't know. That's why I had to stop letting certain people chill…They just get they shit and I make 'em bounce. I don't need no cops runnin' up in this joint."

"Well, give me a forty, nah, make it a sixty." I gave her sixty dollars and headed to the door. I didn't even speak to the two girls who were there because I didn't need to meet nobody else. Enough people knew me and half of them were phony anyway."

———————————

I was laying in the bed frozen and fucked up by the time Kian and Shani came back. My heart was jumping outside of my chest. Every time I took a breath I prayed to take another one. I was scared to breathe too hard. I thought my heart would just explode. Kian came in my room concerned.

"You okay Mommy?" He crawled into bed with me, sneakers and all. I looked at him and he looked blurry. "Mommy! Mommy! What's wrong?" I was fading in and out. I guess I was blacking out or something. I could hear him but then again, I couldn't. It seemed unreal. "Auntie!" he screamed.

Shani came running in my room. Before I knew it she had me in the shower with all my clothes off. The cold water didn't even feel cold. I could hear Kian crying, asking her what was wrong with me. She made him go into the living room and I could hear him screaming. I swear that brought me back to life more than the water. How could I do this to my son? Make myself die, so he could hate me for the rest of his life. "Shani, I'm addicted." I started balling. Now the water was freezing. "Lord, please! Help me!"

"Mika, you have to get help. You have to get help,"

Shani cried. "Look at you. You look like you've lost twenty pounds in the last two months. You're gonna die over men? Are you gonna let Mark and Danny kill you?"

"Shani, get me out of this freezing water! That's what's gonna kill me." We started laughing. I put a towel around my wet body and went out to the hall. Kian ran up to me and put his little arms around my waist.

"Mommy, please don't drink no more, was it the drinks Mommy?"

"Yes baby, I promise I won't drink no more. Just promise me you won't drink when you get older or do drugs."

"I promise Mommy."

I turned to Shani and asked, "Why didn't you say something about my weight before?"

She looked at me with a cold expression. "I was waiting for you to love yourself."

Shani sent Kian to his room so she could talk to me alone. Before she could say anything…I stared, "I don't know, Shani. I'm getting soft in my old age. Asia has AIDS, Danny is getting married and having a baby, I betrayed Mark and he hates me, and now I have a muthafuckin' drug habit?"

"You also have a beautiful son, a great personality, a strong spirit, and a family who loves you like crazy. Mika we may criticize you, but you are the life of this family. You have the never ending spark, you just have to use it to light the right things, don't keep the bad shit alive, turn this shit around. I don't want to come to your funeral." She couldn't contain herself. She started crying and left the room. I was going after her, but Kian ran out his room.

"Hey Boo!" He looked sad. "Don't worry Mommy's okay. Hey, are you happy that your Daddy's getting married?"

He shook his head. "No."

"Why not Boo Boo?"

"Because, how come he's not marrying you Mommy?"

"Because baby, your mommy and daddy don't love each other anymore...And we don't get along. You don't

Ericka M. Williams

203

want us always arguing and fighting right?" He shook his head again. "So, we have to stay away from each other because we don't agree on a lot of things. But we both love you. What's wrong with Tiffany, you don't want her to marry your Daddy?"

"No. She's no fun. She doesn't like to play games and stuff. All she wants to do is hold Daddy's hand and kiss him all the time." My stomach tightened.

"Well, that's what people do when they love each other. One day you are going to fall in love with a girl and always want to hold her hand."

"No I'm not. I'm going to marry you when I get older."

"Aw, my baby loves me so much," I said, rubbing his back.

========

I had to wake up at seven a.m. the next morning, to start my new life. Holding down a job would take some getting used to. I had to drop Kian off at school and be in Hackensack by 9:30 a.m. I was a little nervous, and didn't know why. Either it would work or it wouldn't. I met my supervisor and the girl who was going to train me. They were both white, but they didn't seem prejudice. The afternoon went by quickly, and it was three o'clock before I knew it. On Mondays the firm closed at three-thirty, so all we did after lunch was go over some of the cases that I had to review that morning. I was supposed to become familiar with the firm's most successful and challenging wins and losses and the attorneys' styles. It was a moderately sized firm, so I worked under four lawyers. Two white men, a white woman and a black man. I had met everyone except the black man, he had a court date. As I left the office this guy who looked about thirty-five, walked in. I knew it was *'him'* and man did he look good. I didn't look him in the eye. I told myself not to look. Just as he passed I looked up and into his eyes. Damn, I love me some men. I was like a man magnet. I could never pass up a handsome face. He stopped dead in his tracks.

"Excuse me Miss, are you my new assistant?"

"If your name is Kevin Styles then yes."

"In the flesh."

I chuckled and thought, *how corny*.

"Well let's take some time and get acquainted tomorrow," he said, looking me up and down.

"Okay."

"Where are you from, Darling?"

"Englewood."

"Oh yeah?"

"Uh, yeah."*What did that mean?* I didn't feel like standing in the doorway of my new job trying to figure out if my boss was already trying to hit on me, or if he was just trying to be nice. I wanted to go. I never liked older men anyway. A light bulb went off in my head...*maybe that's what I need, an older man*. I laughed. *What the hell was wrong with me?* This was a new job and this was my boss. *Could trouble leave me alone for one damn day?*

"I'm sorry, but I really have to go and pick up my son. I will be in tomorrow at nine-thirty as directed by Shirley." I caught him off guard.

"Oh." He did a fake chuckle. "I'm sorry. I'm being rude keeping you past your hours without offering any overtime. It was nice meeting you. I'll see you in the morning, pretty."

"Mika," I said, with a funny look.

"I'm sorry, Mika." He put his hand out and I put my hand in his. He shook it. I would've been ready to file for sexual harassment if he had kissed it.

The next morning I woke up worried to death. I tried to dress myself up real nice and stay optimistic. I was scheduled to get my test results after work. I wanted to call in sick to work, but couldn't do that on my second day. It wouldn't have looked good. Besides, it seemed like a real

Ericka M. Williams

interesting job. I was really interested in court cases. Even at home I liked watching Court TV.

As I prayed in the car before going in, Mr. Styles knocked on the hood and interrupted me. What the hell did he think I was doing, sleeping? I gave a fake smile and waved.

I walked into the office, and Shirley handed me a stack of paperwork that included five cases from the day before, that needed to be re-read. As I walked away with paperwork up to my neck, Kevin came out of his office. "Miss Turner? May I call you Mika?"

"Yes."

"I'd like to do our preliminary meeting now. Please step into my office."

Was this man going to attack me? He just seemed horny as hell. First, we talked about my job description, then I had to hear his specific requirements. Although I was responsible for four lawyers, they were going to rotate me. Of course I would be working with him first. I was trying to listen to everything he was saying, but my mind kept drifting to my test results.

"Mika, are you okay? Is this too much for you all at once?"

"No, I'll be able to handle it. I'm interested in law. I'm sorry, I've just got a lot on my mind."

"No, we can take a break. Enough of the professional stuff. Tell me about you, not your resume."

"You tell me about you. You're not my boss during a break." He laughed.

"I'm divorced with two kids and I live in Teaneck."

"How old are you?"

"Thirty-six, and you?"

"About to be twenty-five." He laughed.

"Oh, you're laughing at me?"

"No, I just remember how confusing and dramatic twenty-five was. You are probably going through a lot of personal turmoil. That's why you seem so serious. Don't worry, the thirties are much smoother. I know we are in a working relationship, but you really seem like something heavy is on your mind. Do you want to go out for drinks after work?"

I looked at him like I was offended because I was. I stuttered... "uuhhhha."

"Listen, I'm not going to take advantage of you because I'm your boss. I wouldn't try to jeopardize your job, you said you have a son. I would just like to break the ice a bit. It may help our working relationship if we get to know each other.

"I'm married." I didn't even sound convincing.

"Stop lying."

"Okay, I've never been out with an older man before."

"So give it a try. First of all, it won't be a date. It's going out with a co-worker."

"I don't know. Maybe. But I have something to do right after work. It depends." I really didn't think that would be a good idea, but I didn't want him being hard on me at work because I turned him down for an innocent outing. Damn, he was really good-looking. Tall, dark, and handsome with a helluva body under that suit.

"Okay, okay, I won't ask you anymore. Put my number in your cell, and if you finish what you have to do early, just give me a holler." I put his number in my phone.

I walked back out to my cubicle and spent most of my day reading. I didn't even take lunch because I wanted to leave at three-thirty instead of my scheduled time. Shirley said that was fine.

Before I knew it, I was parked outside of the clinic after work, balling. I didn't know why I was crying. I guess because I was scared to go in. I wiped my tears and said, "Fuck it, if I do have it, sitting here won't make it go away." I walked in to the lab, gave my name, sat down and waited.

They called my name fifteen minutes later, which felt like an hour. I sat down with the heavy-set nurse and my file. She looked at me with a disapproving look, and tapped her pen on the desk for about a minute straight.

Ericka M. Williams

"Miss Turner, you're negative for HIV antibodies. Congratulations," she finally said.

"Jesus! Thank you! Thank you Miss!" I ran out of the office rapidly. I was going to give Tamar an honest chance, but I could've used a friend. Maybe Kevin would be just that.

I drove home thinking about what I would do for the rest of the day. I had an urge to see Dawniece, but fought it. Damn, is this shit going to kill me? I almost fuckin' died yesterday...I decided not to even go near my house. I picked up Kian and went by Asia's.

Tamar called as I was pulling in her driveway. I told Kian to go ring the doorbell. "Hey Daddy. I've been worried about you. My test was negative!"

"Good. Everything is going to be okay. We got each other. We're gonna be good. Baby, I want to be with you, so I'm gonna give this all up for you. I'm just working things out down here. My mother wants to stay down here and keep the restaurant and my sister is keeping the salon. I already spoke to my man at the bank in Jersey. I'm gonna open my trucking business up there. I'm coming baby. Just be good 'til I get there."

"I will."

"Have you found us a spot yet?" he asked. I didn't answer. "See, you not handlin' your business."

"Is your family gonna be safe down there?" I changed the subject.

"Yeah man. I'm tellin' you it wasn't no personal beef with me. Ty came down here thinkin' he knew the deal. He lucky they killed his ass, 'cuz I would have after that dumb shit he did."

"What did he do?"

"Come on now, it ain't for your ears. I know you are concerned and that's why you want to know. What did I tell you. Your only business is taking care of me. Can you do that?"

My baby was so smooth. I blushed. "Yes Daddy."

"Alright, 'cuz that's what I plan on doing. Taking care of you and Kian."

"Alright, I'm at Asia's, I'll call you when I get home."

"Okay, Baby cakes."

I went inside with Asia and Kian. Kian was already playing with Sariah's son, so I went into Asia's room. Asia said she'd be taking a lot of tests the next day, so she wanted to just relax for the rest of the day. She pulled out a folded bill, took a hit and held it out for me. I didn't want any, so I shook my head. When she placed the bill on the dresser, I just ignored it.

"Well, you seem like you're in a good mood today." I smiled at the only best friend I'd ever known.

"I'm trying to think positive, Mika," Asia responded.

"Well I'm glad girl. You sound better."

"Yeah. Well, I got a date tonight."

"What?" I went over to the dresser, picked up the bill that contained the coke, but put it back down. *Damn, I need to get out of here.* "A date? Is that good?"

"Oh, so I'm not supposed to go out?" Asia said with a frown.

"I didn't mean it like that girl. I thought you weren't feeling well." I didn't know what else to say.

She rolled her eyes slightly. "No girl, I feel fine."

"So who are you going out with?"

"Plum."

"Who's Plum?"

"I told you before, a young cutie."

"So, what if he wants some sex?"

"Oh, now I can't have sex!?" Asia shouted. Obviously, she was offended.

"I'm just asking, damn," I replied.

"I want some sex! Never mind what he wants. It's not like I didn't do it with him before."

"Did you use a condom?" I asked.

She held her held down. "No."

"Well, are you gonna use something now?" I didn't want

to get her mad, but I was hoping she wasn't going to go on a homicide mission.

"I'll tell him to, but he might not listen."

"Asia!"

"Look Mika, I don't want to hear it. He may be the one who gave it to me. Plus we did it already so he probably already got it anyway."

I guess I got her mad but I couldn't believe she would let him sleep with her if he didn't want to wear a rubber. I thought about taking a hit, but how could I with the the way God was blessing my life? I could've been dead the night before and I could've been given a death sentence that day. I didn't go home to stay away from it, and the shit found me anyway. That shit was the devil and I was fighting against it.

"Asia, come on now. Don't be like that," I begged.

"Fuck that, whoever gave it to me didn't give a damn about my life," she snapped. "And fuck you too!"

All I could do was shake my head. I finally gave up and left. I hated being mad at my girl.

I woke up the next morning sluggishly, and even though I still wasn't use to the new routine, I managed to get to work on time. As soon as I arrived, I went to my desk and quietly did my work. Every day I learned a new task, so it was very interesting. All throughout the day, I kept my eye on the clock and hoped that nobody noticed that I was a timekeeper. I couldn't have been happier when it was time to get off. The day was long, but productive. As I was leaving work, someone pulled up behind me, while I was getting into the car. When I turned around, I noticed that it was, Kevin, who was driving a pearl white Range Rover.

"Hey lady," he said, rolling down the window.

I smiled. Kevin always seemed like he was up to no good, lawyer or not. It's funny how I felt comfortable around criminals, but was scared of an honest businessman.

"You always come right in the nick of time, huh?" I said.

"You know it. I'm like a poet, babydoll." Oh boy, what was that? A seventies pick up line? "You wanna go get something to eat?" he asked with a huge smile across his face.

"No thank you."

"Aw, come on girl, I'm not gonna bite you."

"I didn't say you would, but I have to pick up my son," I replied.

"Okay so let's go get him then. You're looking very pretty today. Is it because you thought you might see me?" he asked.

I let out a slight laugh, but left his question hanging.

"So did you delete my number from your phone?" he questioned.

"Yeah, I did."

He looked surprised by my answer. "Well, at least you were honest."

"I'm just joking. I still have it."

"Well having it and not using it is just like throwing it away, so I hope you decide to use it. Mika look, I'm not going to kidnap you."

"I know, 'cuz I'd have to kill you."

"So, why does a pretty girl like you seem so sad?"

"Because I am?" I got smart with him, but not intentionally.

"Did I say sad, I should've said mean," he joked.

"I'm sorry, I didn't mean it like that."

"Well, as gorgeous as you are lady, you shouldn't have a care in the world. Whatever the problem is, put it to the side because you have the whole world at your fingertips."

I sighed. "Yeah? So, why can't I grab it?"

"Are you reaching or are you waiting for it to come to you?"

"I don't know. I never really thought about what I wanted to do with my life, not seriously. I feel like I should have

Ericka M. Williams

stayed in college. I guess life is just kickin' my ass right now, reality is smacking me in my face."

"So, how's your love life?" he blurted out.

"I can't go into that right now, but let me ask you a question. Why did you and your wife break up?"

"Because she wanted to run the streets," he shot back. "She only wanted to be a mother and wife part-time."

"How long were you married?" I asked.

"Four years."

"So now what are you going to do?" I asked, feeling sorry for the brother. He wasn't all that bad, I started thinking.

"Find a black woman to marry. I don't like the dating scene. I'm a family man."

"Why only a black woman?" I was testing him.

"Because there is no other creature on this earth for a black man than a Black Pearl. Now, can I have some information on your personal status? Are you in a relationship?"

"A new one that I just started, but it's long distance right now."

"Are you faithful?"

"Yeah. I have a four year old son. He's the only good thing in my life right now." I took a seat with the door open and he stood behind it. I had begun to feel real comfortable with Kevin.

"So, you are not with your son's father?" he asked.

"No, I'm another statistic. I'm not with my baby's father. My last boyfriend left me."

"A real man wouldn't leave such a prize."

"Oh, I wasn't such a prize at the time. I was selfish and inconsiderate. I pushed his love to the limit. I was like your wife. I wanted to play games and make him wait for me to come around."

"Don't worry, God may have something better planned for you. Did you learn your lesson?"

"Yeah, I did...I hope. Maybe God does have something better planned for me. Time will tell." It seemed as if he was insinuating something, but I wasn't going to feed into it. I was enjoying our conversation, so I wasn't really trying to go there. Although he was handsome and had a good job, I wanted to be faithful to Tamar. Cheating didn't pay. I wasn't used to Kevin's type, and had mixed feelings about him. He was too nice, yet strong, older but still down, and aggressive yet patient. He wasn't pushy, but in a subtle way let me know that he wanted to see more of me outside of work.

We finished talking and I told him I'd see him the next day at work. As soon as I got home, I called Mark to tell him that he'd better stop playing around and playing hard to get because I was getting serious in a relationship. Like he cared. I didn't even know why I did that anyway. I guess 'cuz Tamar hadn't called as much, and I didn't really believe all his promises.

Mark's answering machine came on and I hung up. I wanted to cry, but I didn't. I got ready for the next day and realized that I had become a homebody. It wasn't bad though, I wasn't missin' nothin' in the street, but bullshit and drama. Being alone wasn't bad either, it's just that I couldn't wait to have someone laying next to me every night. I started watching Boomerang until I fell asleep.

Chapter 20

THANK GOD

I woke up Wednesday morning and got both myself and Kian ready. Work was getting more and more interesting because there were some juicy cases on our roster. I'd read about a case that Kevin won where his client was accused of kidnapping his son's mother. He found out that she had the whole thing set up to send her son's father to jail. Now she was in jail. I'd also read about another girl, who owned a boutique and her husband ended up killing her. Her husband and another accomplice ended up being charged for murder, and unsurprisingly Kevin won that case too. I found myself becoming attracted to him. His clout in the courtroom was a true turn on. When I got off of work, I was tempted to call Kevin, but I decided not to.

For some reason, I'd been feeling so lonely lately. I was going to a wedding on Sunday and didn't even have a date. *Damn, what is the world coming to?* Me without a date? As usual, Tamar said he couldn't come to town that weekend so I called to see if Dior was out of jail yet. He ended up answering on the first ring.

"I thought you were in the County?"

"I came home Monday. It was some bullshit, as usual. You know how it is. They wanna keep a brotha in the penal system," he joked.

"What happened?"

"I'll tell you another time. I'm on my way out. Call me later," Dior replied.

"Wait! I want you to go with me to Tanesha's wedd[ing] on Sunday. We grew up together, so I gotta show my s[up]port."

"What?! You don't have a man to take? Yo, the worl[d] getting ready to blow. Oh that reminds me, I gotta talk to you…Niggas are saying you gettin' high and buggin' over that kid Mark and that you got stuck up in VA with Tamar. What the fuck is goin' on wit' you man, you aight?"

"Where did you hear all of this?"

"Yo, are you alright man? Are you sniffin' that shit? Come on now, that ain't you. You finally let Asia bring you down for real? She been trying to get you to fall off cause you prettier than her. Yo, Asia is not your friend. She be hatin' on you, talkin' mad shit about you, but you don't want to believe it. Mika, you buggin'.'"

"Damn, Dior, you believe everything you hear, huh? Asia is my friend!"

"Yeah, okay…we gon' talk Sunday 'cuz I got something to tell you about your man."

"Tell me now," I whined.

"Nah."

"Then why did you bring it up. I hate when people do that, why even bring it up?"

"Fall back, he's diggin' you, I just got something to tell you, relax."

"Oh, that reminds me…you remember that kid that Asia used to fuck with…Aaron?" I knew what he was going to say.

"Yeah, why?" I asked reluctantly.

"That nigga died from AIDS. You better tell your girl to get a test."

I felt sick on the stomach. Was Asia gonna die too? "You're lying!" I tried to sound surprised. "Damn…well me and her aren't really speaking right now, tell me about it Sunday."

"What time do you want me to scoop you?"

"Come at 1:00 p.m. and please don't be late," I ordered.

Ericka M. Williams

ight. I'll be there. See ya baby. Oh, can I get some
poo like a real date?"

"Bye Dior." I hung up.

I called Asia to tell her about Aaron and no one
answered. I called her cell and again, no answer. I just
hung up. I was so worried that I couldn't sleep all night. I
called the next day and the recording came on saying that
the number had been changed, to a nonpublished number
and her cell was off. I was pissed. I'd heard that Asia was
being a wild child around town, gettin' with any nigga with a
lil' paper. I needed her to know about Aaron.

Tanesha's reception was off the hook. The hall was
even nicer than the church. When Dior and I sat down, I
admired the expensive looking favors that were placed
neatly on the table. I was especially impressed with the
crystal champagne glasses. Tanesha had outdone herself. I
couldn't help but to be jealous, and wonder when my day
was coming. I was happy for her, but when was I going to
find Mr. Right? Tamar clearly had too much fuckin' drama.

Ironically, we were seated with people from our high
school. Asia's name was on the table, but she wasn't there.
My eyes scanned the room looking for her, but instead
zoomed in on Kevin. I was shocked to see him, but since I
didn't know if he was there with someone, I just waved and
got up to go to the bathroom. Swiftly, he snuck behind me
and grabbed my hand.

"Hey baby girl, where you runnin' off to? You look drop-
dead gorgeous girl." He gave me a hug and kissed me on
my cheek. "I don't want to get you in any trouble, are you
here with someone?"

"Just my friend. Who are you here with?"

"My family. The groom is my cousin," he revealed.

"Damn, it's a small world. Tanesha and I went to high
school together."

"I didn't see you at the wedding. Come with me, I v
you to meet my family and my kids." He took me by the
hand to meet his mother, his brothers and his sisters.
Kevin's kids were cute. Again, I couldn't help but to be jea
ous because he looked happy as well. I sat and talked to
him for a few minutes before the newlyweds finally arrived.
I knew it was time to be seated. I promised him I would
save him a dance, and walked back to my seat.

As the wedding party was announced, I dreamed about
my own wedding, but couldn't make out the groom's face.
Eanie, Meanie, Miney, Mo…Tamar, Mark, Kevin, or no?
Tamar had given me an engagement ring, but was I really
engaged? Even more important, he was still married. He
was trying to buy time as far as I was concerned. I needed
a man who was ready for a total commitment. Kevin
seemed like a good man even though he also seemed like
a horny ass bastard. Nothing could be better than having a
wonderful family and raising beautiful children with a good
black man.

Just as the bride and groom entered all choked up, Asia
and Plum walked in like they were the center of attention. I
guess they were trying to be with their matching mink jackets on, even though it wasn't cold enough yet.

"Hey Mika, where you been homie? I been tryin' to call
you. Oh, hi Dior," she said nonchalantly.

"Asia, please. You ain't even call me and give me your
new number."

"I changed my number 'cuz I'm being faithful, and I
don't want none of my old men callin' me. I'm being good,
right baby." She put her arm around Plum's neck and
pulled him close to her. He grinned and kissed her on the
cheek. She was so full of shit, and snifflin' every two seconds. The other four guest at the table looked at her like
she was crazy.

"Oh, Dior this is Plum, my baby." They gave each other
nods.

"Mika, I have so much to tell you. I'm sorry I haven't

Ericka M. Williams   217

ed. I was mad about a few things, but we'll talk about
t later." She waved her hand like it wasn't that impor-
nt. "Girlllll…we just came back from Atlantic City. Plum
won seven thousand. You like our jackets?" She was talking fast as hell.

I nodded at everything she was saying and just looked
at her. My girl, my road dog, was a different person. She
wasn't the same. She went on about their trip and how
Plum was going to buy her a diamond ring. She was
embarrassing; talking loud like everybody at the table was
dying to hear her conversation. I was glad when it was time
to get up and get our food. Hearing her talk shit was getting on me and Dior's nerves. When we got in line, he
asked me if I had told her about Aaron. I told him I couldn't
get in touch with her.

"Yo Mika, I hate to say it, but she probably got that shit,"
Dior said.

"I hope not," I commented.

"Well, I hope Shorty rock is protecting himself because
he looks like he's only twelve years old…Asia is dead outta
order comin' to someone's wedding all coked up and talkin'
shit. I ain't never seen her act like that. She's always been
crazy, but always classy. She ain't fly no more."

"Look, enough about her, I gotta rap to you."

"What," I asked hoping the news wasn't too bad.

"Tamar knows that you fucked fat ass Jarrod! Damn,
Mika was you on money that hard?"

I lowered my head.

"He told me he wouldn't say nothing 'cuz he's done his
dirt too. I just wanted you to know."

"Enough, here comes Asia," I said, hoping he would
shut up around big mouth.

"Ooh Mika, Tanesha looks so pretty. Congratulations
girl!"

"Asia, stop yellin' across the room and go over there.
It's bad enough you all fired up."

"Fuck you Mika, see that's what I'm talkin' about. Come

All That Glitters

on Plum, let's go get some more drinks. Mika must ‧
because she don't have a date." She took Plum's ha‧
walked over to the bridal party's table to show off. I jus‧
rolled my eyes at her.

After I finished eating, Kevin came and convinced me‧
dance with him. I stayed with him the rest of the night. Dic‧
was busy talking to an ex-girlfriend from high school, and
Asia was in and out of the bathroom, so nobody else was
paying me any attention. Near the end of the night, Kevin
popped an uneasy question.

"Do you want to come with me and the kids back to my
place?" Kevin asked.

Right now I need somebody to talk to. "Sure, why not."
It was a good thing that Kian was with my mother, so I did-
n't have to rush home.

<hr />

Kevin's house was laid out and very neat. We watched
two movies with the kids, and then he sent them to bed. He
opened a bottle of wine, put some jazz on, and we played
backgammon. I won forty dollars from him and noticed that
it was getting late.

"Kevin, I'm gonna go home now."

"How are you gonna get there? I guess you'll have to
stay." I looked at him like, *Don't even try it.*

"I'm just kidding, I'll pay for your cab. You know I'd take
you home if the kids weren't here. "Did you enjoy yourself
or did we bore you to death?"

"I had a really nice time. I love your kids, they are so
funny."

"Can I do one thing for you before you leave?"

"What is that?" I asked.

"Can I eat your pussy?"

His question caught me off guard, and I immediately
thought about Tamar. *Would that be cheating?* I didn't want
to cheat on Tamar, but I thought about how good it would

Ericka M. Williams 219

ly feel.

just want to taste you. I won't act different toward you
work and I won't ask to sleep with you when I'm done. I
nt you to release some tension that you are holding," he
ontinued.

Damn, that sounds like a good reason to say yes. I
knew I would be mad if Tamar let a chick suck his dick, but
he wasn't gonna find out anyway. His ass was all the way
in VA. I pulled my pants down and took one leg out and
laid back on the couch. He ate it nice and slow. It only took
me about three minutes before I came. I felt no shame. I
pulled my pants back up, and asked him to call my cab. I
acted like it never happened.

We sat quietly looking at each other for a few minutes.
He finally blurted out, "When can I see you again?"

"When do you want to see me again?" I replied as the
cab blew its horn. Before he could answer I jumped up.
"Call me tomorrow night, and we'll talk. I won't be in the
office tomorrow."

He said okay, walked me to the door and kissed me on
my lips. I hope he wasn't going to be open too fast. I was
just looking for a friend to keep me out of trouble and away
from the drugs. As I got in the cab, I thought about what
was going on in my life. *Confusion.*

Chapter 21

SISTA LOVE

Three days later, I sat at my desk, when my cell phone rang. I figured it wasn't Tamar, because his calls were becoming less frequent.

"Hello?" I answered.

"Hello Mika."

When I heard her voice, I knew something was wrong. "Miss Ann, is everything alright?"

"No baby, Asia's in the hospital!"

My heart dropped. "Is it serious Miss Ann?"

"I'm not sure. She went this morning with a 104 temperature. They say she has a very bad infection."

"Is she coherent?" My voice became shaky.

"Off and on, but overall she's delirious."

I closed my eyes and sighed. "What room is she in?"

"Room 728...I should let you know, you're going to have to wear a mask, a gown, and gloves...She's been quarantined."

"So how are you Miss Ann?" I knew the answer to that.

"Baby, I'm hopeless. I don't know what to do. I just ask the good Lord not to take my baby yet."

"She'll be fine." I hoped. "I'm going to go and see her and I'll call you this evening...Get some rest Miss Ann."

I hung up and cried like a baby. Then, I prayed. I started mumbling to myself, "Damn Asia, you're like my sister. You can't die." I banged on the desk. "We've been through too much together! I instantly took the rest of the day off and

...raight to the hospital.

...ce inside the hospital, I felt awful. I didn't want to put ...gloves and mask on because I didn't want Asia to feel ...comfortable, but I had to. I walked in, and she was under ...plastic tent. She had tubes coming out of her nose, ...mouth, and arms. It was too much for me. I instantly broke down. Tears flooded my eyes, and my heart sank. My loud-sobbing woke her up. I rushed to the side of the bed, and took her hand. "Oh Asia..." I squeezed her hand.

"I know, I look fucked up...don't I?" Only Asia could make a joke at a time like that.

"You better get well." I ordered. "And when you do, your lifestyle has to change Asia. You know that right?" I wiped my eyes.

"Yeah," she said, in between coughing.

"You've been actin' crazy...you've been on a mission to kill yourself and you need to be on a mission to stay healthy and alive." I wiped the tear that rolled down her cheek. "It was Aaron, he died."

"How do you know?" she asked.

"Dior told me."

"You didn't tell him, did you?"

"Hell no, I didn't tell him. You're lucky you're sick because I would fuck you up for asking me something like that. I didn't tell anyone except Shani and my mother. I may have been mad at you, but I would never betray you like that... I love you stupid."

"Please Mika, don't get sentimental on me."

"What are you going to do about it?"

"Well since you insist, let's get a good cry out. I love you too girl. I wish I would have been more like you instead of trying to make you like me. You're going to be alright, Mika. Keep strivin', your dreams will come true. And...you'll get your Prince Charmimg too...So who was the guy you left with at the reception?"

"That's Kevin, one of my bosses at my job."

"Yo, I'm not sane anymore, but I'm still well enough to

All That Glitters

know a good catch when I see one. So what's up him?"

I couldn't believe Asia was still interested in men time like this. I shook my head and answered, "Nothir really. I went with him and his kids to his house. He's cool...I don't know, I feel like he's an older brother."

"Girl, you're buggin'. That man is fine with a capital F. You better do your thing. You have a handsome older man with a house? A lawyer?"

"Yeah. But I took this ring from Tamar." I held my hand up so she could get a good look. "I'm supposed to be moving in with him."

"Girl, do I have to smack some sense into your head? Forget about Tamar, he is stuck in the streets. And forget about Mark too, he's nice but he's still a kid. I know that's what's holding you back. I thought you wanted a real man? I thought you were thinking about marriage? Mark ain't ready for all that and Tamar can't unless he wants to go to jail for polygamy."

"But I love them both."

She shook her head. "Mika, you are a lovable person. That's why it's so easy for you to love. I bet you'll love this man too. You only want Mark now because he left you. When you had him you didn't want him. You got caught up with Tamar because of the money. Lawyer or drug dealer? Sounds like a simple choice to make to me. Give this guy Kevin a chance until Tamar comes up here, then decide. Fuck Mark, he ain't even coming back for yo ass."

"Mark is not like that, I keep telling you. He has more respect than that."

"He may have respect, but he doesn't have a house." We both started laughing. I was really glad that she was in a good mood. It made the visit so much easier.

"Asia, you're strong...that should tell you something...But, I'm getting ready to look for a townhouse for me, Tamar, and Kian. "

"What?"

, I told him I would. I'm gonna try it with him. I
ait 'til he comes up here. I really want it to work."
will Mika. And don't let that bitch come in between

"I'm not, she fucked up. She better not try to get him
ck now. She should've done her thing when she had
im." She started crying out of nowhere. I was speechless.
"Asia just don't give up."

"I'm trying not to girl, but I'm in some vicious shit. There
aren't any survivors."

"There are a lot of people who live for a long time
because they take very good care of themselves...Just
don't give up."

We sat silent for a few minutes. I turned toward the TV
and when I looked back at her, she was sound asleep. I
watched her for a few minutes wishing this was all a
dream. Instead, it was a straight up nightmare. I kissed her
on the cheek and quietly left the room. On the other side of
the door, I stood stiff. I stepped out of the protective gear,
and tossed it in the trash can next to me. I tried to stop the
tears from falling, but was unsuccessful. The walls seem to
have closed in on me on my way out. I rushed to go get
Kian.

I regained my composure by the time I got Kian, but I
needed to talk to someone sensible. I called Kevin when I
got home, to keep me from going upstairs to Dawniece's
house.

"What's up?" I asked in a low voice.

"How are you Pretty Girl?" he said, in a sexy-like voice.

"I'm okay. Well, not really. I just came from seeing my
girl in the hospital."

"Who's in the hospital?"

"My girlfriend. She has AIDS," I responded in a low
tone.

"Oh...is she okay? I mean, you know?"

"I don't know."

"You wanna come over?"

I thought he'd never ask. I took Kian, and we spent the evening at his place. I told Kian he was my boss, and we had to go over some things for work. He played with Kevin's kids, and they hit it off well. I really just needed to talk and stay away from Dawniece. I was stressed. It was so terrible seeing Asia like that. I'm glad I was able to act normal because I just couldn't stop picturing it in my mind.

"Mika, what's on your mind?" Kevin asked like a concerned father.

"I don't know...the problems of the world have me stressed. We're not safe from anything. If it's not AIDS, it's Cancer, or violence!"

"And there's nothing you can do about it so why worry? When it's your time, it's your time. You have to capture the moment and try to live everyday like it's your last. And you have to make as many of your dreams come true as you can." He clinched my chin and looked deep into my face. "Mika, you have to thank God for everyday he gives you. If you keep thinking that way you're going to lose your mind and become one of those people who are scared to go outside. You will be peaking out of the curtains with a gun in your hand like Malcolm X." We started laughing. "I know what you need. See if you can get someone to watch Kian tomorrow evening. I want to take you somewhere."

I smiled in agreement. Kevin and I were getting along very well. I just didn't want to use him, but I felt like I was. His case kept him from the office so I would only see him coming and going, which was good. He took my hand and kissed it.

"What was that for?"

"I just wanted to make you feel special." He grinned.

"For what?"

"Because you deserve to."

"Thank you. Thank you for being a friend because that's

Ericka M. Williams   225

what I need right now. Thank you for putting up with me. I know I can be bitchy."

"You're a piece a cake, you just play that role like you're hard."

"I'm just depressed...I can't stand seeing my girl sick." I thought back to the way Asia looked.

"I know it's hard for you Mika, but you have to be strong...Stay away from the drama in your life, keep it simple. The streets will only take you down."

"It's just that...life is starting to hit me...I never had a care in the world...But I can't deny that things have been better for me than they have been. It's just my girl..."

"It's good when it smacks you in the face. That way you straighten up. Mika you are a beautiful person. Good things will come to you. You're probably just too stubborn and hard-headed sometimes. So, Mika do you like me?" he said out of the blue.

"Yeah, you're cool. You're different than my usual type. You're respectful and you seem like you really care about people." Kevin moved a little closer which was my cue to leave. "But you know what? I'm gonna take it slow. I've been speedin' all my life. I'm about to go home and get me and Kian ready for bed."

"Can I do something for you before you leave?" My face said it all. "Don't worry, I just want to give you a foot rub."

"Oh you can definitely give me a foot rub." I took my shoes off and put my feet on his lap. He got up and came back with some oil. He rubbed the oil into my legs and feet and gave me the best foot rub of my life. He finished with a nice peck on the top of both of my feet. *Damn, I need to make a fast break.*

We hugged and I went home. I felt better and I was too tired to go see Dawniece. The fact that I had to get up early for work was another deterrent. I couldn't sleep all day after being up all night, and I would never want Kevin to find out that I was doing that. Kian went straight to bed after telling me he had a good time with Kevin's kids.

The next day Kevin called and told me where to meet him. I parked my car in a lot and got in the Range Rover with him. The back seat of the truck had a dozen roses and two balloons for me. I was shocked when Kevin kissed me, and handed me a wrapped box. It was some Dolce & Gabana perfume, one of my favorites.

"Thank you Kevin, this is really nice of you."

"No problem, Baby Girl, I just want you to feel better...but don't thank me yet."

He drove to this place called Tease Me. It was a black owned beauty spa. It was decorated with African art and African-American photography. Mint Condition's song, *'Pretty Brown Eyes'* played as we walked in. He gave the receptionist my name and told her that he had made an appointment for me earlier that morning. She told him to take a seat in the waiting room and told me to follow her. I was excited even though I didn't know where I was going. I was taken to a small room and given an Afrocentric silk robe to change into. Then a big, black, beautiful man gave me a full body massage, which instantly filled my body with ease.

I felt like a new person when it was over. All I needed then was a good piece, but I wasn't giving Kevin any. I was waiting for my man to come up here. When I got dressed I was told that the robe was mine to keep. I wondered how much he had paid for all of that. On the way out I grabbed a menu, and realized he'd spent some money!

"So, how do you feel?" he asked.

I felt horny, but said, "Good as candy." He started laughing.

"Did I tell you that you tasted like candy that night?"

I wasn't going to feed into that. Besides, I felt like a queen at the moment. "Thank you. I needed that. I'm gonna try to do that once a month."

Ericka M. Williams   227

"You should. Everyone deserves to be pampered. So, where do you want to go now? Are you hungry?" he asked.

I rubbed my stomach. "I'm starving."

"Do you like Italian food?"

"Uh huh."

We went to Fort Lee to a small Italian restaurant. It was nice, nothing extravagant. I was glad because I didn't want him spending any more money on me that day. I felt funny with him spending all that money knowing that I wasn't giving him any sex. I didn't want him to think I was trying to jerk him because I wasn't. I wasn't concerned with the money. Kevin made me feel good, not just sexy. He didn't just see me as a piece of ass. I was glad that I'd made friends with him. He was supportive and someone to talk to. I was curious though about what he was looking for. I put down my fork.

"So Kevin, why are you spending all this money on me?"

"Because I can afford to."

"But why are you?"

"Because I like you Mika...I see things in you that I don't think you see in yourself yet."

"And what is that Mr. Fortune Teller?"

"Well Miss Feisty, your sharp tongue is a sign of intelligence, however you are very sarcastic. Your brain is quick and you're very observant and analytical. You portray yourself as hard, but you could be as gentle as a kitten if someone would just pick you up and hold you. And it's so cute because you try to act like you're untouchable. You're strong though and you've been through a lot. I can tell by the way you talk about men, like you're such an expert on the subject. People who are not mentally on your level will not be able to understand your profoundness. Your soul is deep sista. It's very attractive. You would actually make a great lawyer, did you ever think of that?"

I couldn't help but blush, he dropped a helluva drink that time. I was that great! "I honestly have been thinking

All That Glitters

about that."

"Shirley and Paula have said that you are doing great analyzing the cases. You are almost ready for your first new case. You will have to do the investigating to help me get ready."

"I'm ready." I grinned too hard.

"Almost."

"Damn, you sure have a way with words."

"I love verbal intercourse. A woman who cannot converse and relate is boring outside of bed so she better at least have that going for her."

"So what about that?"

"What...sex? Oh baby believe me I'm a lover too. I'm not just into conversation." He smiled. "I'm just careful about who I try to get in the bed with."

"So why haven't you tried me?" I asked.

"I haven't tried to sleep with you because in the condition that you're in right now, I would just be taking advantage. You are hurt and unhappy, you don't need a stiff dick you need some pampering. I don't mind doing it for you either. Don't get me wrong. I would love to have a fine piece like you, but only when you're ready."

"So, what if I'm never ready for that with you?"

"I'll still value our friendship and I'll have to respect it because more importantly, we work together."

"So where are you getting your sex from for now?" I caught myself after I said it. I didn't want to sound like I was interested.

"I have friends." I wanted to leave it at that, but he shared more. "I've met a lot of women since my separation, and some women just don't have it all upstairs. They're lost. You, you're intriguing. You're radiant. You have a positive energy that makes you glow. You...are an African princess who will soon be a queen."

"When?" I giggled.

"When you spend some more time getting to know yourself and what you want out of life for sure..."

Ericka M. Williams

"I believe I've done that already."

"Well then you're closer than you think. It all comes with wisdom and experience. Once you love yourself, then you become loveable."

We were done eating and I was ready to go home. I had to think about all that he'd said. I made up an excuse that I had to get home, so he dropped me off at my car. When I got home, I went upstairs and called Tamar immediately, but as usual his voice mail came on. I didn't feel like leaving a message. I had a rough couple of days.

I thought about what Kevin did for me, and what he said. I was scared to fall for him. He seemed too good to be true and damn sure talked a good game. I was so confused. I wanted real love this time, not some temporary fake love. Kevin caused me to do something I hadn't done in years. I took out my journal and began to write.

As I got in the bed to get more comfortable, Shani knocked on my door.

"Yeah," I answered.

"Can I come in?" she asked.

"Sure."

Shani walked in and sat on the edge of my bed. She looked at me for a few minutes before speaking. "I know you're stressed out over your friend, I just wanted to tell you that I'm proud of you lil sis. Keep up the good work." She got up and as she approached the door to leave, I stopped her.

"Shani?"

"What is it now, you brat? One compliment isn't enough for you tonight," she said jokingly.

"Can I have a hug?"

Shani came toward me with her arms opened wide. "No matter what, always remember, Mommy and I love you." She grabbed me and gave me a bear hug. I hugged her back real tight. I had to realize that all my family wanted was the best for me. I loved my mother for being strong, but I couldn't deal with her negative energy. It was painful not to have a relationship with her, but until we could some common ground, I kept my distance and loved h from afar. My dad was not around on a consistent basis I enjoyed when he did come around, because you never knew how much time someone will be here on this earth. But I damn sure loved my sista, with her annoying ass and all.

"I really came in here to tell you something else too," Shani said blushing.

"You're gonna be a sister-in-law."

What? I thought, *another fucking couple getting married before me?* Goddamn, am I ever gonna walk down the fucking aisle, or am I always gonna be a spectator?

I reached over and hugged her again. I couldn't gather any words quick enough to cover up what I was feeling.

"Fuquan and I are going to the Justice of the Peace next month on his birthday, because he said I was his greatest gift. You know, we don't need anything fancy, we just want to be together."

"Oh my God!," I was finally able to say. I still held on to her arms. "Shani, congratulations. I'm very happy for you." In my heart, I really was.

The phone rang breaking our mini embrace. I answered, "Hello."

"Where's Shani?" the voice roared. It was my mother.

"Right here. You all right Ma?" I asked in a worried voice.

"What you want to know for?"

"'Cuz, I'm hoping that you are taking care of yourself. Viral infections can be serious. I don't want to see you in the hospital again." I was giving it yet another try.

"Well, maybe you will be happy if you end up in the hospital like your best friend." *Damn, she hates me that much.* She couldn't bear to have a decent conversation with me ever. If she wasn't judging me, putting me down, or criticizing me, it just wasn't right.

"No, maybe you will," I fired back. "Then you can tell me

old me so. Then you can turn out to be right. God for-
if I get my life together, get married and end up happy.
at would just eat you up inside."

"Oh yeah, your big moving day is coming. Let's see
how this fiasco turns out. Uhm uhm uhm, girl you will never
learn until the Good Lord makes you!"

"I wish the *Good Lord* could give you some damn joy in
your heart."

"He gave me you, so I guess he was punishing me."

"I hate you! You are the most evil person I know. Damn,
can't you just be happy to be alive!"

Shani grabbed the phone from me and I walked away. I
refused to cry. We were just never going to get along. I
wanted a mother who was understanding, not a judge and
jury.

"Ma, why don't you give Mika a break. She's going
through a lot right now," I heard Shani whisper. Then, her
mouth dropped as she held the receiver. That figures, my
mother had hung up.

Chapter 22

ASIA, MY ASIA

I was awakened by a phone call at about 3 o'clock in the morning. I assumed it was Tamar when I answered.

"Hello."

"Mika, I'm gonna die tonight."

"Asia, please stop. Get some sleep, I'm coming over in the morning." I hung up before she had a chance to hear me cry.

I hurried to Asia's house before work the next morning, and when she opened the door I was stunned. She looked like she weighed about 80 lbs. Her eyes were sunken in her head. I wanted to hug her, but I knew that I would only feel bones, so I ignored what I saw.

"See silly, you're still here," I joked.

"Yeah...and?" She was bitter, but I understood. I couldn't take it personal. I ignored that too.

"How do you feel today? I see you're not in that wheelchair." She had been in a wheelchair for two weeks.

"Oh I feel great! I feel like going mountain climbing!"

"Still a comedian...so you don't stay in the chair all the time?"

"No, just on the days when I'm really weak or when my knees buckle and my legs give out on me." Damn. "How's my little man doing? You have to bring him by to see me before I..."

"Yeah yeah yeah, I know. I'll bring him by this weekend."

"People have been calling Peaches asking her if I got

Ericka M. Williams   233

'the package', nosey muthafuckas! Especially since Butch died." Butch had suddenly gotten sick and died in jail. "Do people ask you about me?" she asked me in a softer tone.

"Hell no because they know I'll curse their asses out. Plus, I haven't been talking to anyone. I've been keeping to myself." I smiled.

"To yourself or to your man?"

I started smiling. "I keep telling you, Kevin is not my man. We just enjoy each other's company and he keeps me out of trouble. We ain't doin' nothin'. Besides, Tamar will be here for good next month."

"Shit, you need to give him some before Tamar comes up here. He deserves it for all that he's done for you."

"Asia, I keep telling you I'm with Tamar? I'm trying to do right for once in my life."

"Girl, you crazy. That girl is pregnant by him?"

"What!!! When the fuck did you hear that?"

"Peaches told me."

"Oh my God." It was always something with his fuckin' ass. I whipped out my cell and punched the number keys as hard as I could. As usual, I called Tamar beefing. He didn't know what I was talking about. He said it was all a lie, and that he'd call me back. I was hot!

"So, Asia what do you do all day?" I said, trying not to think about Tamar.

"Sleep and watch TV. Peaches picks me up sometimes, or a lot of my family comes around. You don't!"

"Asia, don't say that. You were really losing your mind there for a minute. I couldn't mess with you. I wanted to fuck you up a couple of times...Like that time we were in that after hours spot waiting for Plum...and Tanesha's wedding. I could've strangled you."

"I know. I wasn't coping well...Shit, you don't know what it's like. I go through so much. At times I really do just want to die. Just always remember that I love you girl."

"I love you too." I got all choked up for a moment, so we sat quietly for a few minutes until I finally thought of something to say to change the subject. After talking for a few more minutes, I kissed her forehead and told her I was going to work. I thought about getting high on my way there, when visions of Asia entered my head. I knew that I had been blessed, and decided against it.

I spent most of the following week out shopping for our new place. Tamar all of a sudden seemed real excited. I never mentioned again to him about what Asia said about Yanira being pregnant. I'm sure it was all a lie.

Everything was going well, until I got the call that Asia was doing worse than before. I hurried to her house, knowing she wasn't going to live much longer. Miss Ann escorted me in her bed room, while massaging my shoulders for support. She knew I needed it. Asia was curled up in her hospital bed like a fetus, with a baby bottle in her mouth. Her hair was very thin,and I cried at the sight of my girl wearing an adult diapers. She couldn't talk anymore, so she only nodded her head and blinked her eyes to communicate with me. The disease had really eaten away at her in a rapid amount of time. I knew it would be the last time I would see her alive.

"Asia baby? Look who came to see you," Miss Ann said, as Asia looked up at us like a newborn baby wanting to be picked up. "Do you know who this is? If you know baby, blink twice."

Asia took a long time to blink. I was so glad to see her eyes open back up. She took a few seconds and blinked one more time.

"Asia, I love you," I said.

"Mika said she loves you. Do you love her?" She gave a quick two blinks.

"Oh Asia, you're still her girl," Miss Ann said pretending to be happy...

Asia had what looked like a slight smile in her eyes.

Ericka M. Williams　　　　235

She was propped up on her pillow. Miss Ann stroked what was left of her hair. "Asia, I'm moving very soon," I said. "Tamar and I found a nice townhouse on the other side of town. I'm going to marry him."

She just looked at me with a tear in her eye. She stopped sucking on the bottle and it slid down the pillow. Miss Ann told me she'd be right back. I had one last cry with my girl. "Asia, please talk, say something. I want to hear your voice again. Asia, please don't die." I just broke down! Tears rolled down her cheeks. I was sobbing when Miss Ann came back in the room.

"Mika, go in the bathroom and get yourself together. We don't want to see her suffer anymore. I ran out and couldn't go back in. I ran down the stairs and out of her house. I could hardly see the road as much as I cried on my way to pick up Kian.

When I got home,I went straight to Dawniece's. I bought a twenty like that was better than my usual forty. I went in my room while Kian played in his. Shani had already started cooking, and when she saw my face she knew to leave well enough alone. I did the whole twenty in about fifteen minutes, mostly because I was mad at myself for getting it. I just wanted to get it over with. My body must have liked the break over the last couple of weeks because it quickly rejected the coke. I was in the bathroom throwing up for nearly twenty minutes when Kian came to the bathroom door.

"Mommy, was you drinking again?"

"No baby, I wasn't drinking. My stomach is upset over Asia." I had already explained to him that Asia was terminally ill. "I don't think she is going to live much longer."

"Well, I know you're sad Mommy, but I don't want you to get sick too."

"Don't worry baby, I won't get what Asia has. I'm taking good care of myself okay?" *And wearing rubbers for the rest of my life,* I thought.

I got myself together and called Tamar. He cheered me

up a bit. "Baby, it won't be long now, until we're together under the same roof."

"I know," I said, "I need you by my side so badly."

"I know baby."

Damn, I think I really love Tamar. I hung up and went to bed, only to be awakened by the phone at about 1:00 a.m.

"Mika?" It was Miss Ann. My face turned colors.

"Uhhh…it's me," I said meekly.

"Baby, Asia went on to be with the Lord honey. She died right in my arms. She tried to hold me tight, but she just didn't have a bit of strength left in her."

I just dropped the phone and cried for hours. I laid there thinking about all the times I shared with Asia. I would miss her forever. Regardless of our ups and downs, she was my right hand, and now she was gone. I just kept reflecting on seeing her in that hospital bed, and glaring up at me blinking. At least she knew me right up until the end.

I didn't know how that was going to affect me. I knew I needed to be strong and not let that turn me back to the coke, but I was sure feeling the urge to get high.

I sat up in the bed and said out loud, "Asia, I'm sorry if I ever did anything to hurt you or made you feel like I wasn't your real friend. And I forgive you for all the times that you hurt me. You'll always be my friend. Asia my Asia, why'd you have to leave me?"

Chapter 23

CHOICES

The next day I felt terrible, and needed a shoulder to cry on. I knew Kevin was the only man who would be able to talk some sense into me. I called him, but got no answer. I figured I'd just go over to his house anyway. When I got there, his ex-wife answered the door wearing his robe. I looked like I'd seen a ghost. She smiled as wide as she could when she saw the shock on my face. I didn't turn around and leave because I wanted Kevin to know he didn't have to front on me, 'cuz it wasn't that serious. It was all good.

"Is Kevin here?" I asked.

"Kevin is sleeping," she said, like a mother speaking to a girl who was after her teenage son.

"Well, I need to talk to him." I really didn't pay her gloatin' ass any mind.

"Can't you see that we're busy?" she asked, in a sarcastic tone.

"No, tell him Mika is here." I just wanted to see the whole thing for myself and get his reaction. Instead of going to get him, she did something better. She escorted me into the bedroom where Kevin was laid out, flat on his back, butt-naked. She got in the bed next to him and kissed him, "Wake up baby. Somebody is here to see you."

He lifted his head up, stunned. "What?" He looked up, "Oh shit." He dropped his head back down on the bed.

"Bye Kevin," I smirked.

All That Glitters

I walked out, got in the car, and drove off. I didn't feel anything. I thought for a minute, and then busted out laughing. He couldn't say shit. I wasn't mad at him...how could I be? I felt sorry for him though 'cuz I'd heard from the ladies in the office that his bitch was a nut case. But love could have you like that. I'd been there myself. He probably liked me a lot, but couldn't get over her. Plus, I wasn't giving him no play. It was better that we didn't do anything because we had to work together.

For the next few days I stayed to myself until the day of Asia's funeral. Her funeral was packed, but Miss Ann had a closed casket because she knew that a lot of people would just be coming to either confirm or deny the rumors. Tamar was right by my side. He looked good, and seemed to be changing. His thugged out appearance was fading, taking on the attitude of a man I'd been waiting for all my life. After the funeral, I noticed Mark walking by like he didn't even know me. I wanted to speak, but Tamar was holding my hand tightly the entire time. *I can't believe Mark would be so disrespectful during a funeral.*

Strangely, a couple of hours later, I came home to a message on my answering machine. I couldn't believe the voice I heard. "Mika, it's Mark...Uhm, I need to talk to you. Give me a call." He left his number.

Why! Just when I was over him. What did he want? It was too heavy for me. I didn't know what to do. I wanted to call but then what? What if he wanted me? What if he didn't, and just called for something minor. Then I would've been mad. I was mad either way at the fucking nerve of him. All night I contemplated, but I didn't call. Every time the phone rang my stomach turned. I didn't want to screw things up with Tamar.

Mark called again the next morning, just as Tamar had gone out the door, so I answered, "Hello?"

Ericka M. Williams

"Why didn't you call me back?" he asked.

"Hello to you too, Mark." I was nervous.

"How've you been, Mika?"

"I was doing fine until you called."

"Why, is it like that?"

"Oh, you're going to play the dumb role. Okay, I tried to contact you how many times, and it was too much for you just to find out why I was calling?"

"I didn't want to talk to you," he replied.

"So why do you want to talk to me now?" I snapped.

"Let me come over and speak to you in person."

"When are you coming?" I asked as nonchalantly as I could.

"I'm coming now. Meet me downstairs in fifteen minutes."

I decided to at least hear him out. "Alright." I hung up and threw some tight jeans on. I wanted to look cute, but I didn't want it to look like I was trying to dress up for him. I fixed my hair extra special, and headed downstairs to wait for him.

When Mark pulled up in a new Maxima with expensive rims, my jaw dropped. He opened the door for me and I got in. I didn't want him to think that I was still driven by materialism, so I didn't ask about the car. He leaned over and kissed me on my lips, and then he just stared at me for a few minutes. I stared back. He looked good as shit and smelled even better. He looked like he'd put on a few pounds with the help of some weights. I was in trouble.

"So, what's been going on?" he asked nonchalantly.

"Nothing." I looked at him dead in the face. "Come on Mark, cut all the bullshit. What do you want?"

"You," he said sternly.

"I don't think so."

"Why don't you?" he responded, like he was shocked. "Mika, at first I told myself that it was over, I didn't want to want you. I went out, met people, but after a while I got bored because nobody was you. I kept trying to fight it, but all I could think about was being with you. That's when I knew I loved you for real."

"Are you sure it wasn't because things didn't work out with your little girlfriends?"

"No, the women I met were cool, some of them were fly as hell, but I kept finding little things that turned me off, so I stopped going out, and got my shit together so I could come back correct and finally have you all to myself." He leaned closer to me, and I moved further away. "Mika, you didn't want to be mine because you didn't think I had any-thing to offer you. I always wanted to give you whatever you wanted, and I felt like less than a man because I couldn't, so I enrolled in a training program at my job, worked real hard and got a promotion. I didn't do it for me, I did it for us."

I was shocked. I expected him to come to me with some bullshit excuse, I didn't expect that. "Mark...that's good, but I needed you and you abandoned me. You think because you're making a few more dollars a year that excuses it? I wanted you for you, not for what you could give me."

"Come on Mika, now you cut out the bullshit. You know I would've never left you if you were treating me right...Besides, I'm making twenty thousand more a year."

What could I say? I just nodded.

"Plus, you were the one who was wrong, but I'm the one asking you to take me back," he pleaded. The only thing I want from you is for you to realize that a man and woman have to work together to get the most out of the life they want. I love you, but if you're still on that *gold-digging* shit, then I'll just leave things the way they are."

I couldn't believe his arrogance, even though it was appealing. He was actually threatening to break up again before I even agreed to take him back. He had always been very modest and I wanted him to be more aggres-sive, but his new attitude was rather attractive. But the fact remained that I didn't know what the hell to do? I didn't know if I should tell him that I was with Tamar, the same person he broke up with me over?

"But Mark, so much time has passed...How do you know if I'm the same person you fell in love with? It's been months. How do I know that you're the same? You don't realize how much you hurt me." I started crying. "I really missed you. I realized that I loved you, but I couldn't believe you could be so cold to me. How could you just walk away and never look back? How do I know you won't do that again?"

"Mika, was I supposed to know that you loved me with what happened? You didn't even know you loved me so much until I left. Mika, if you do decide to be with me you have to realize that I won't be able to give you everything you want, whenever you want it, but I will be there for you and that should be enough. *Damn, I was feeling him.* You shouldn't have made me feel like less than a man just because I couldn't give you things, but I'm willing to forgive you if you'll forgive me. I'm sorry for hurting you, do you forgive me?"

"I do. Mark, I'm sorry too. I shouldn't have taken you for granted like that. I'm working now, and it feels good to do for myself. I'm working at a law firm as a paralegal. I'm going to go back to college too. See, you leaving was good for both of us."

"We both have grown, and now we can be better for each other. Now we can do our thang baby. Can I get an Amen?"

I was supposed to laugh at that, but I didn't. I just sat there. I did owe him a chance but what about Tamar?

"Mika, what's wrong?" I looked in his eyes. Damn, he looked so good. I could sure get with him right now...*No, I can't do that until I'm sure that I'm going to be with him, I can't lead him on.*

"I just need some time to think about it," I uttered. "I just don't want to get hurt again. But let me just ask a curious question...How do you know I didn't find someone else by now?"

"Who? A drug dealer, who you have no business being with? I'm not intimidated by that shit no more because that's not the life. What kind of future can a nigga like that offer for you and Kian? The chances of him staying alive, and out of jail are not that great and you know that...that's why it's time for you to cut that shit outta your life."

He reached over and put a chain around my neck with a sliding diamond heart pendant on it. I shouldn't have accepted it, but I did. *If I decide not to be with him, I'll give it back.*

"You said you've changed now prove it," he said, in a more serious tone.

We sat in the car and caught up on things. He told me about how he'd been working out at the gym, but I could clearly see that. I told him all about my new job, and how I'd learned so much over the past few months.

"Mark, I need some time. You needed time and so do I."

"I'll give you that. But don't miss out on a good thing again. You can't keep taking my feelings for granted."

"Mark, I had to keep living my life because I thought you were going on with yours. Just give me some time."

I gave him a kiss, stepped out of the car and went upstairs in a daze. When I reached the living room, I realized Shani and Kian were already sleeping. I laid in my bed and damn near went crazy trying to decide what I was going to do. Damn. Mark had changed. He seemed much more confident, and sure of himself. I hope it wasn't just because he had a new car. He did seem more like a man. He wasn't as passive as he used to be. He was even a little more cool. I could probably really be into him now, more than before, and it had nothing to do with the car.

A couple of days later Tamar came up for Monet's wedding. She was marrying the bank manager where Ty had

Ericka M. Williams

closed their accounts. They started dating after her fiasco in the bank and she said she did everything in her power to make him fall head over heals with her. He did, and within a few months, they were married. Tamar knew I was feeling some type of way wanting to be married and seeing how fast Monet had gotten a man to marry her, so at the reception he passed me an envelope with one of my Christmas gifts inside. I opened it, and found two tickets to Cancun. I was happy, but it wasn't our wedding.

Christmas eve, just before midnight, I removed the chain from my neck that Mark had given me. I remembered what he had said about waking up with it, but I knew I'd be waking up with Tamar. Tamar woke me up Christmas morning about six with breakfast in bed. It was Danny's year to have Kian for Christmas, so we were alone. The room service tray had three plates covered with stainless steel. He lifted one of the plates and it had a red box on it. He picked up the box.

"Mika, I know you still feel unsure about this, but I also know that we love each other. Regardless of all the drama that we have gone through in these three short months, our love is bigger than that. So I thought you deserved something bigger." He opened the box which contained a pear shaped five carat engagement ring. "I'm going to marry you." He leaned down and handed me an envelope from off of the floor.

I opened it up and read the document. It was proof the he had filed for divorce. I wrapped my arms around his neck and started crying. This was truly the man of my dreams.

"Tamar, I love you. And I know I can be stubborn, and mean..."

He cut me off, "Bitchy is a better word baby." I laughed.

"I know baby, and you have continued to show me, not just tell me, that you love me and you're here for me...When will everything be final?"

He cut me off again. "Soon."

"Can we do it in August? I always wanted a summer wedding."

"Whatever you want baby." I gave him a stern look. "Yes, baby, August 2003, you will be Mrs. Tamar Woodson." We set our date for August 23rd. I later found out that that was Tiffany's due date for her and Danny's baby. Never a dull moment, I swear.

Two weeks later we were moving into our townhouse. Tamar was putting together a bed, and I was putting some small boxes in the Lex. I heard a car pull up behind me. Suddenly, I heard a door slam and I turned around. It was Mark.

"Oh, so you moving in with that killer huh? That's the type of life you want for your son? I heard you're getting married too."

"Look Mark, I'm not going to do anything to hurt my son, just give him the family that he deserves."

"I must've been crazy to think that you could change! You still had me, but go 'head bitch, bury yourself!" Tamar came up just as Mark was yelling and walking toward me. Instantly, he ran up to Mark.

"Is there a problem Duke? Mika, who the fuck is this?" he asked, still standing right in front, glaring in Mark's face. Mark stood his ground.

"That's Mark baby."

"Oh, this is the cat I stole you from? Live with it Homey. You weren't ready."

"You can have that hoe!" Mark said, making sure he was in his car by the time he finished that statement.

"I ain't mad at you man. I would be hurt too, if I lost Mika. But the difference between me and you is, I know how to keep her."

Mark drove off with hate for me in his eyes. He made sure that he drove past me shaking his head.

Ericka M. Williams   245

I was a little hurt, but I looked for my answer from God. The one that stood by my side was the one for me. Tamar was the one for me!

Chapter 24

CONSEQUENCES

Tamar and I were in our home and I finally had the family life I always desired. Tamar had about three different businesses that were profitable: the restaurants, the trucking/towing company, and the spa that his sister ran in VA. We were 'poppin' and I was loved every minute of 'the good life'. We were *ghetto superstars.* It was a culture shock, though. Having a man right there and him not having to call before he came over was weird.

I was even more ecstatic when I spent about $100,000 thousand dollars on furniture for my new home. Our bedroom set was $10,000 by itself. We had a huge king sized bed with matching chaise lounges from Safavieh, a ritzy Mediterranean furniture company. Our entertainment center held a 56 inch flat screen and serious surround sound. I also had the bathroom done over so we could have a Jacuzzi in the floor, Scarface was the inspiration for that.

There were four bedrooms. Kian had a huge car bed that he loved, and a room that was decorated like the child of a Hollywood celebrity. Toys were everywhere. We also had a bedroom for Tamar Jr. that contained a bunk bed, and pictures of Michael Jordan all over the wall. He was a huge fan. My plush living and dining room furniture had also come from high end stores. Tamar had money to burn and I was sure setting fire to it.

Everything seemed to be perfect, with the exception of a few things. Turns out, Yanira was really pregnant with Tamar's baby, but at that point it didn't matter. I was in too deep, and I was also still fucked up over Asia dying. For some reason, I was still sneaking over to Dawniece's on the weekends that Tamar worked. It was a lot of pressure on me trying to handle life's issues.

We had started our life together and Tamar was getting ready to be a father, of a child by another woman. Despite this, I had no complaints because he was a good man and rental-father for Kian. The only time Tamar would hang out was when Dior would come around. Dior was my brother and I loved him, but started feeling that they were up to no good. One night while they were out I found about two hundred thousand dollars in cash, and like three bags of exquisite jewelry in our garage. It wasn't the type of jewelry that we wore. There were antique pieces and what looked like custom- made heirlooms. I knew it was some stuff that belonged to white people. There were brooches, pins, and rare gems. I questioned Tamar and he told me to mind my business. I started questioning, in my mind, if his businesses were what were bringing all that money in.

He came in that night and I sat on the couch crying.

"Baby, what's wrong?"

"Tamar, I thought the criminal shit was over."

"What are you talking about?" he asked with a straight face.

"I'm talking about the money and jewelry in the garage. What the fuck Tamar? You left the drug game to become a house burglar. Dior has been in and out of jail for years for that shit! All the cops around here…everybody and their mother know that that's what he does. That's what you are doing now?"

"Look Mika. I'm going to take care of you. You don't have to worry about things that don't concern you." He gave me a look that said-*don't ask any more questions.*

"Don't concern me? If you go to prison what am I gonna do? I can't hold this down alone."

"I have legitimate businesses; these cops out here don't even know who I am. They ain't got no reason to be watching me."

"If they are watching Dior, they are watching you! Oh my God, I thought all of this criminal shit was over for me. As far as I know you can be using your truck to transport drugs down south." He gave me a funny look.

"Mika, stop worrying. Everything is going to be fine. Are you happy?" I looked at my man and looked around my living room. I looked down at the ice on my fingers and my wrists and wiped my tears.

"Yes Tamar, I'm happy. But I want to have babies with you. I don't want this to be a temporary thing."

"It's not. We're getting married in a few months," he said convincingly. "And whenever the sperm hits the egg, we'll be having our first baby. Damn, be happy. I changed my life for you." He pulled me into his arms. "Stop being in your man's business. I keep telling you, everything is not for you to know. I'm taking care of home, that's what you said you wanted; now you got it. Go 'head in the room and let's start working on that baby. When I get in the room, I want you on the bed, ready."

I went to the bedroom and he went downstairs. It was a nice March night and he had on all black. I had been with Dior after he had robbed a house and that's what Tamar looked like. He went into the garage while I started taking my clothes off telling myself that he was probably just letting Dior keep his stash here. We always lie to ourselves when we don't want to believe what we already know. When we moved in Tamar specifically told me he had stopped selling drugs. I never thought he would do something like that. At that moment, I believed him.

A month later, I got a phone call from Peaches. She told me to turn on the news, quick! I had just gotten home from work. I saw Tamar and Dior's mug shots right in my face. There was a press conference on the local news stating that the two of them had been seen leaving the scene of a house that had been robbed. When the description of the Navigator was given, the cops pulled them over and found stolen property in the truck. They were charged with robbery, receiving stolen property, and transporting stolen property over state lines because the house was in Upstate New York and they were stopped re-entering New Jersey. His bail was a hundred thousand, his truck was impounded, and I thought my life was over. All of my friends were calling to make sure I was all right and praying on my downfall.

I had learned from Monet that I needed to keep a job, and stack some of my own money. I went into the stash we had at home, and bailed him out with $10,000 dollars, which was the required ten percent. When I saw Tamar, he swore that he wasn't robbing houses with Dior. He said Dior had asked for a ride, and Dior had the jewels on him. I believed him.

Little did we know, that the undercover police knew him well, they wanted to find out what he was about. So, over the next month this dirty cop named Clarkson Howell started asking all these people about Tamar and they were coming back telling me. The cop tried to tell Tamar that I was cheating on him with Dior to break up their friendship so that one would rat the other out. Anything *for a conviction.* That dirty ass cop tried to scandalize my name in the street. He even said that he'd fucked me before. He also constantly harassed me and my family. The detectives regularly parked by my house and fucked with us. Howell even pulled Shani over one day and questioned her about Tamar. Tamar tried to run his trucking business and they badgered his clients so badly, causing him to lose some of his biggest accounts. It was crazy.

When the trial came up, he pled not guilty and Dior took the blame. Dior had told them that Tamar was just giving him a ride and that he had acted alone. Dior was sentenced to three years in prison. Of course, Dior exonerating him didn't make the prosecutor drop the charges against Tamar. He had to go to trial anyway. They just wanted him to go broke on lawyer's fees. They waited until the very end and thousands of dollars later to drop the charges. Of course there was a little caption in the paper about it, but nobody called about that. People only liked it when you have a problem, not when you overcome one. Tamar promised me that this wouldn't happen again.

To rid ourselves from the stress, Tamar wanted to take me away for the weekend. We packed our bags, and were Virginia Beach bound. On the way there, we stopped pass to see his mother and sister because he needed to pick up some money from them.

As he drove, we talked about how things had been so crazy, yet we'd grown so close because of it. We talked about the good times and the bad times. We were happy that he didn't end up going to prison. I think he paid Dior off to say he had nothing to do with it, but that was Dior's choice to do it.

We were telling each other how much we loved one another, and how we couldn't wait to get married and have kids. I had already picked out my wedding dress. The bridesmaids and groomsmen were also chosen. It was going to go down in three short months, and I couldn't wait. I was FINALLY getting married!

We made it to Virginia Beach and checked in to a nice hotel. We chose one with a Jacuzzi of course, that was my only demand. After settling in, both Tamar and I decided to get in the bed early. With all the drama that was going on, I was extremely tired. Just as we feel into a deep sleep, we were startled by a loud noise. It was a hell of a wake up call.

"Oh my God! Tamar!" I yelled, as I jumped up. I was shocked to see five detectives with their guns drawn, coming in the door surrounding our bed. There were four white men and a white woman, staring down on us.

They grabbed Tamar out of the bed and handcuffed him. I screamed, "What is going on! Tamar! Tamar!"

Luckily, we were both in our pajamas. I would've been buggin' even more if I would've been butt-naked. I was

Ericka M. Williams

yanked up out of the bed and handcuffed by a female cop. I was in shock. I watched as they looked around and went through everything. I thought they were just making a mistake, or harassing us because we were black.

I tried to ask why I was being handcuffed, but they ignored me. Then I realized that Tamar was on the other side of the bed being awfully quiet. I stopped, turned around, and questioned him.

"Tamar, what's going on?" As he turned around, I could see the word GUILT all over his face.

He mouthed, "I'm sorry."

I shouted, "What!"

An officer asked me to be quiet, but before I could say another word, the taller officer removed a big bag of white powder, from Tamar's bag. When I saw that, I started crying. They stood him up and walked him out of the room.

I screamed, "Tamar! Why! Why Tamar! We're supposed to be getting married! Why did you do this to us?"

He was led outside between two officers, with his head lowered. Then it was my turn. They stood me up and started walking me out. We were allowed to slip some clothes on over what we already had on. All I could think about was my mother, Kian, Shani, and my father. *What on earth is going to happen to me? Am I going to go to prison?* I was scared to death but more shocked. I couldn't talk, cry, or think…I felt like a zombie walking down the corridor. When I got outside there were people watching as the police put us in separate cars, I kept thinking I'm going to jail! *After all my life of affiliating with criminals, I'm finally going to jail. Oh my God!*

I was put into a car with a male and female detective. They were talking, but I had no idea what they were saying. All I could hear was, "Womp Womp Womp Womp" like the teacher on the Charlie Brown. I was in a daze. I was there but I wasn't there. I wanted to see Tamar.

Thirty minutes later, they pulled up to a building and we got out. That's when I saw my furure husband. I was able

All That Glitters

to go over to him, and all I could say was, "Why."

He put his cuffed arms around my neck, and kissed me. "I'll tell them that you had nothing to do with this. It'll be all right, just trust me."

All I could say was, "Oh my God! I love you! I need you!"

They walked us inside. We were separated and read our rights. After I was read my rights, I was taken down a hall only to stand right next to my man while the Magistrate told us separately, what we were charged with…Posse-ssion of cocaine with intent to distribute.

After hearing my charge the detective told the Magistrate that Tamar had taken full responsibility for the possession of the narcotics, and claimed that I knew noth-ing of them. For a split second I thought I would be uncuffed and able to get in my car and hysterically drive home. The Magistrate stated that she was charging me anyway with possession of an illegal substance with intent to distribute. She told me to my face that she didn't believe that I didn't know he had the drugs, so I would have to prove it!

We were then taken to the county jail, fingerprinted, and photographed. We were able to talk and mouthed back and forth, here and there. We were still in the company of each other. I just knew my life was over, really over this time. We kept telling each other that we loved each other and he kept looking at me with those eyes saying he was sorry, and that he was gonna make sure that I was all right.

"What about you?" I mouthed. "I want you to be all right too? I want to go home, and I want you to go home with me"…He shook his head no. That wasn't going to happen.

"Just be strong baby. Be strong for me."

I wasn't going home and neither was he. They let me make my one phone call, so I called my mother.

"Hello," she answered.

"Ma, I'm in jail!"

"What! What happened! Oh, Lord have Mercy! What

Ericka M. Williams   253

happened!" She was screaming.

"Tamar had drugs and I didn't know." I was crying.

"Oh Lord have Mercy! No! Goddammnit, MIka! You hard-headed little bitch! I told you this was gonna happen but did you listen? No!"

"Ma, I'm sorry."

"Where are you?" she asked with a raised voice.

"In Virginia Beach!"

"Oh my God! Mika what have you done? Are they gonna let you come home?"

"Not 'till I go to court on Monday. I have to go in front of the judge on Monday."

"Tell Kian that our car broke down and we'll be back home Monday."

"You want me to tell Kian that lie, and they might keep your ass in there! Danny's gonna take this boy from us. He ain't gonna let us raise Kian. You happy now?" she roared. My mother sounded evil as hell. Here I was waiting to be arraigned and she already had me sent away losing custody of my son. How I wished I had a mother who would say, "God will work it out." Or, "We're coming down there. We're gonna get you the best lawyer and get you out of this mess. We won't let Danny take your son from you. Everything will be all right baby." That's not what I had because misery loves company, and she was miserable as hell.

I interrupted her as she rambled on, "Ma."

"What! Are you sure you're gonna be able to come home Monday?" She was crying and yelling at the same time.

"Well, Tamar took responsibility for everything and told them that I didn't know that he had the drugs…and the detective said that he would put in a word with the judge to let me go because he believes that I didn't have anything to do with it. Monday morning Tamar is gonna have to testify to the judge that he takes full responsibility and ask the judge to let me go." I sobbed uncontrollably. How could this

All That Glitters

be happening? My fairy tale was over.

An officer told me I had to get off the phone. My mother was crushed, but I didn't need her negative energy anyway. "Ma, I gotta go, I'll call you Monday, either way."

I hung up and was taken to a cell on the women's side with about six other stinkin', drug jonesin', cursin', fucked up women. I didn't care how much I thought I was 'bout it' before this, I immediately knew that I wasn't cut out for this shit. I wasn't a ride or die chick. I wasn't trying to be in jail with my man…But, what the fuck! I was in jail, with my man! And it was horrible.

By Saturday afternoon my cell was freezing, and I was on a metal slab, no bed. I only had a pillow and a thin ass blanket. I kept replaying them busting through the door, finding drugs, and arresting us. I tossed and turned for hours.

Finally a female officer brought me some food. I asked the guard what time it was and she told me 4:30 p.m. It felt like it should've been nine o'clock at night, time was standing still.

———

By the next morning, I felt like I had already been there a week and had lost twenty pounds stressin'. I had no idea that jail could be so depressing. I mean, you just couldn't imagine what being in there was like, until you experienced it. It is the absolute worst thing.

One girl was stinking up the whole jail with her period. It smelled like a dead animal. The other women were complaining so much that at about six that evening we were put in the bullpen while they bleached the walls and the floors. I didn't talk to anybody, and we were in one big cell together. They were all laughing and joking. I was thinking, *What the fuck is so funny, we're in jail.*

We were quickly put back into our individual cells and I agonized over my situation. I had a million questions and

Ericka M. Williams

no answers. A thousand thoughts went through my head. *Was I going home on Monday? Would I have to go to trial? Would I need bail money? What happened? What was Tamar doing with the drugs? Obviously he was selling them, but to who and how long had this been going on? What made the police come? Was he set up? Why didn't he tell me?"* Well, I wouldn't have gone with him if he had. *"How come this happened? Were we over? Would I end up doing time? Would he? How much? Would we ever get married? What would I tell Kian? How would I make it without Tamar? What about our townhouse? How much money did he have in the stash? What would everybody be saying? Why did this have to happen to us? Who set him up, obviously the person he was there to meet. Were we followed from Jersey?* I wanted to go home SO BAD! I looked around only to see, several bitches acting like it was an after-work networking event.

Everytime they asked me a question, I ignored them. Eventually, they ignored me too.

"Girl, you better make yourself throw up?" one woman said to an inmate.

"I know, but I keep feeling like it but nothin's coming up?"

"What you on Heroin?" she asked like it was normal medication.

"Yeah."

"That dope ain't no joke girl."

"I been tryin' to kick it, but it's hard. Every time I try, I get sick and I gotta cop a bag just to feel better."

"I know I was on it, but I lost my daughter so I got myself together before they took the rest of 'em."

I thought, *damn these people are crazy!* No wonder kids were so fucked up nowadays. I could barely concentrate because the women that I was surrounded by were acting like we were at a fuckin' spa retreat. I was totally disgusted.

I closed my eyes, and blocked out their voices. I couldn't believe the shit I was in. I sat in the cell with my back to the wall with a blanket over my trembling knees. I looked like a scared child hiding in the closet from an intruder who was ransacking my house. I couldn't make a sound, nor could I believe my ears. While they were talking and laughing, I was thinking about a damn lawyer.

═══════════════

Monday morning finally came, what felt like three years later, and we were put back in the bullpen. Some new women were brought in and they were coming from prison, for court. I was just in jail. I wouldn't last a day in prison. Those three days were the most horrible three days of my life. One of the new women, who looked to be about fifty, was talking to one of the younger lookin' girls that was brought out with me. She looked to be about seventeen. I didn't know if she was a dope head, the shooter, or the crackhead, I guess she wasn't any of the above because she had a story I hadn't heard yet.

"What you here for girl?" the older woman asked.

"I stabbed my boyfriend," the younger woman said.

"Why?"

"Because he did all the drugs without me," the new girl stated.

"Girl, you look so young. You strung already?"

"Yeah," the new girl replied.

"On what?"

"Dope and crack," she revealed. The room went silent.

"Dope and crack? You might as well just put a gun to your head and get it over with, damn, girl...life is that bad for you? You gonna wake up in twenty years, IF you don't wake up in a coffin, and ask yourself what you did with your life. You better get yourself together before you end up in jail all your life, like me...it ain't worth it. You gonna let your whole life pass you by. You got kids?" the older woman asked.

Ericka M. Williams

257

"Yeah, four."

"Well, think about your kids." The older woman shook her head and then looked at me up and down. "Now, you don't look like you belong in here. What you do?" Before I could answer the stinky dope head answered for me.

"She ain't talkin' to nobody. Her ass has been in here for two days and ain't said shit to nobody. I guess she's better than everybody."

I said damn right, in my mind, of course. I didn't want to waste my time talking to the creakhead, so I figured I would talk to the OG. She could probably tell me what I was lookin' at.

"My man had drugs in our hotel room and the detectives came in and found them," I finally replied to the older woman. I figured she'd be able to give me some sound advice.

"Aw girl. Where y'all from?"

"Jersey."

"Damn, girl. This is Virginia, the commonwealth state. They can do whatever they wanna do to you. And you gonna get trafficking."

I had to fight back the tears. "But he told them I ain't know. He took the blame," I responded.

"Girl, they don't give a damn. You ain't know?" She looked at me suspiciously and I shook my head. "You really ain't know?"

"I didn't know." I put my head down. What about Kian? I can't go to prison.

I was taken out of the holding cell and moved closer to the courtroom into an individual cell. A lady cop came to me with a message from Tamar. "Your boyfriend said he asked the judge to let you go because you really didn't know anything and you have a son to take care of." She gave me a blank stare.

I asked her what she thought the judge would do and she said the judge on the bench was pretty mean. She didn't look too optimistic. The news was getting worse and worse and I was very nervous. I looked a mess. I hadn't had a bath, or brushed my teeth. I couldn't brush my hair, my weave was jacked up and matted. I felt like a bum. I couldn't even see my man so that his comforting eyes could calm me down.

I was brought into the courtroom in handcuffs and watched all the people looking at me. I felt like a criminal. I walked in front of the judge and stood there while he read my charge...possession of cocaine, with intent to distribute.

He asked me how I chose to plead. I answered not guilty. The prosecutor told the judge that they would allow me to be released on my own recognizance based on the testimony of the last defendant. She said that I would have to return on July 31st for my arraignment. I had two months to go crazy worrying about whether I would be found guilty and sentenced to prison. She gave me a card for a public defender. I was confused, yet happy and sad all at the same time.

"Girl, God was shining down on you today. You are blessed. I thought for sure you were staying, but you're going home. I guess he believed your boyfriend, but this better be a lesson to you," the female cop preached.

She put her hand on my head. "Lord, guide this young lady that she never finds herself in this kind of predicament again. Let the charges be dropped against her. Show her that you are the final judge. Make a way for her Lord. Her son needs her with him."

I thanked her and saw the older lady I was talking to in the holding cell. She told me good luck and wished me the best.

I went to the clerk and received my paperwork and personal belongings. I was being released on my own without bail. I shouted, "Thank God! Thank God! Thank God! God is Sooo GOOD ALL THE TIME!"

Though I was still being charged with possession with intent to distribute, I still had to thank the LORD for helping me out. It wasn't over yet. I could still end up doing time.

Ericka M. Williams   259

The detective who arrested us came up to me and said that I should be okay as long as Tamar took full responsibility on the 31st. He said that I wouldn't be able to get the truck back because it was in Yanira Woodson's name, Tamar's wife. My jaw hung low. The officer could tell I was embarrased. "I had no idea," I said to him. He said they had given the money Tamar had on him to his legal wife. I told him about the upcoming divorce, but he just shot me a pitiful look. He gave me a huundred dollar bill and told me to take a cab outside to the train station.

I walked out into the bright sun, feeling like I'd lost the fight. I honestly looked like a crackhead. I had on the same clothes and hadn't bathed in damn near three days. Now I knew how homeless people felt. I must've been in survival mode because I didn't remember anything from the jail to the train. I got in a cab, asked to go to the train station, and got on a train headed straight to New York. I came back to life on the train, when the whole thing hit me. I had no cell phone to call anyone. It must've been confiscated or still in my truck, or better yet, Yanira's truck. Luckily, I had my house keys but that was all they gave back to me, and the jewelry that I had on at the time of my arrest.

I sat looking at my engagement ring. I knew that regardless of what happened, or how many lies he told me, except me doing time, I was going to stand by my man. I wouldn't forgive him if I had to be away from my son for years because I would never be able to explain to Kian, how mommy would be away from him for a long time. He would never forgive me for leaving him.

I was going to wait for Tamar because he deserved it and there wasn't another man on earth for me.

It was a long ride home. I kept going over and over what had happened. Tamar was going to jail. Although I was scared deep down, I felt that I would be all right because how would they prove that I knew? I was innocent. God was gonna bless and protect me, I hoped.

I made it to the Port Authority and took the bus across

All That Glitters

the George Washington Bridge to the corner of my street. It was dark, and I didn't want anyone to see me. I put the key in my front door and became hysterical before I even closed it behind me. I was bawling, screaming, crying, and begging the Lord to tell me Why! "Why Lord? Why? All I wanted was a family. What have I done so wrong?" I said out loud.

I got myself together, and thought, it's going to be a long two months in Hell waiting to find out what will be the outcome. Tamar is probably not going to be coming home. He took the weight, but I'm alone…again! My wedding is gonna have to be called off. How am I going to survive and maintain without Tamar? I can't afford all these bills on my own. I don't know how to run his business. I'm barely going to be able to pay the rent on our townhouse. I thought about the money and jewelry that I had found in the garage. I ran down there to see if it was still there. Surprisingly, no! Am I gonna have to find another nigga to hold me down until he gets out?

I panicked at the thought of my life headed down hill. "I gotta go see Kian," I screamed. I made the dreaded call to my mother's house. I didn't get a hello or a thank God you're home."

"Oh I see they let you out," she blurted.

"Ma, can I speak to Kian?"

"Who? Your son? Oh, the word is already out around town that you got arrested so Danny gladly came and got your beloved son who you lived your life for."

"What!" I fell to my knees. "He can't just take Kian like that! I've only been charged, I haven't been convicted! He has to take me to court." I cried like a baby. "He's all I have!"

"Oh really? Well, he went to family court early this morning and was granted temporary full custody, Miss Know-it-all! Looks like Officer Howell gave him the information about your arrest and the judge thought that was enough for you to have to ask for visitation to see your son!

You gotta go to court if you want to see Kian," she said proudly.

I slammed the phone down.

I thought about Kian, then Dawniece...I gotta go see Dawniece cuz my fairly tale life with Tamar was over.

All That Glitters

About the Author

Ericka M. Williams is the author of All That Glitters and a seventh-grade Language Arts teacher in New Jersey. She is a mother, an independent film director and actor. She also hosts a local cable talk show, "That's Just How it Is" in New Jersey where she lives.

Ericka was inspired to write All That Glitters when a very close cousin, Nadja Thompson, passed away in 1993. Ericka has spoken at AIDS awareness seminars, motivational conferences, and mentors many teenagers. Currently she is working on the sequel to All That Glitters, titled Shining Star. In addition, she is crafting a screenplay titled, "The Clique". Ericka M. Williams is an inspiration to many. She may be contacted at ericka.allthatglitters@yahoo.com and www.patersononline.net/ericka where she has an advice column titled, "Ask Ericka". Her voicemail is 212-201-9329.

Who Needs A Job When You're A Paper Doll

As a young girl Karen Whitaker dreamed of becoming rich and famous, promising to buy her mother that huge house on the hill with a Rolls Royce parked in the driveway. Her desire for material things turns into a grown woman's obsession with money, power and sex. Now of age, Karen possesses the brains of a scholar, beauty of a diamond, and a body that a Coca-Cola bottle would envy. She knows how to get what she wants even if it means taking advantage of those who trust her most. Greed and passion for tantalizing sex throttles her into compromising situations that may destroy her career and crumble her picture perfect relationship with a multi-millionaire. Take a journey into her intriguing story as demons from her past strike to unravel her fairytale life thread by thread. In the end, will she escape her dark clouds or be exposed as one money-hungry, conniving vixen?

Visit Nicolette Online @ www.myspace.com/paperdollthebook

ORDER FORM

MAIL TO:
PO Box 423
Brandywine, MD 20613
301-362-6508

FAX TO:
301-579-9913

Date	
Phone	
E-mail	

Ship to:	
Address:	
City & State:	Zip:
Attention:	

Make all checks and Money Orders payable to: **Life Changing Books**

Qty.	ISBN	Title	Release Date	Price
	0-9741394-0-8	A Life to Remember by Azarel	08/2003	$ 15.00
	0-9741394-1-6	Double Life by Tyrone Wallace	11/2004	$ 15.00
	0-9741394-5-9	Nothin' Personal by Tyrone Wallace	07/2006	$ 15.00
	0-9741394-2-4	Bruised by Azarel	07/2005	$ 15.00
	0-9741394-7-5	Bruised 2: The Ultimate Revenge by Azarel	10/2006	$ 15.00
	0-9741394-3-2	Secrets of a Housewife by J. Tremble	02/2006	$ 15.00
	0-9724003-5-4	I Shoulda Seen it Comin' by Danette Majette	01/2006	$ 15.00
	0-9741394-4-0	The Take Over by Tonya Ridley	04/2006	$ 15.00
	0-9741394-6-7	The Millionaire Mistress by Tiphani	11/2006	$ 15.00
	1-934230-99-5	More Secrets More Lies J. Tremble	02/2007	$ 15.00
	1-934230-98-7	Young Assassin by Mike G	03/2007	$ 15.00
	1-934230-95-2	A Private Affair by Mike Warren	05/2007	$ 15.00
	1-934230-94-4	All That Glitters by Ericka M. Williams	07/2007	$ 15.00
	0-9774575-2-4	The Streets Love No One by R.L.	05/2007	$ 15.00
	0-9774575-0-8	A Lovely Murder Down South by Paul Johnson	06/2006	$ 15.00
	0-9791068-2-8	Changing My Shoes by T.T. Bridgeman	05/2007	$ 15.00
	1-934230-93-6	Deep by Danette Majette	07/2007	$ 15.00
	1-934230-96-0	Flexin' & Sexin by K'wan, Anna J. & Others	06/2007	$ 15.00
	1-934230-92-8	Talk of the Town by Tonya Ridley	07/2007	$15.00
	0-9741394-9-1	Teenage Bluez	01/2006	$10.99
	0-9741394-8-3	Teenage Bluez II	12/2006	$10.99
			Total for Books:	$
		Shipping Charges (add $4.00 for 1-4 books*)		$
			Total Enclosed (add lines)	$

For credit card orders and orders for over 25 books please contact us @ orders@lifechangingbooks.net (cheaper rates for COD orders)

*Shipping and Handling on 5-20 books is $5.95. For 11 or more books, contact us for shipping rates. 240.691.4343

BAD GIRLZ OF FICTION

COMING JULY 2007

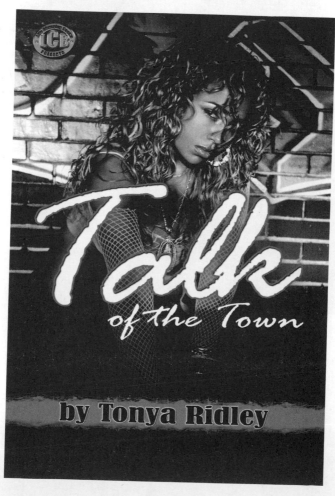

Talk
of the Town

by Tonya Ridley

BAD GIRLZ OF FICTION

COMING SEPTEMBER 2007

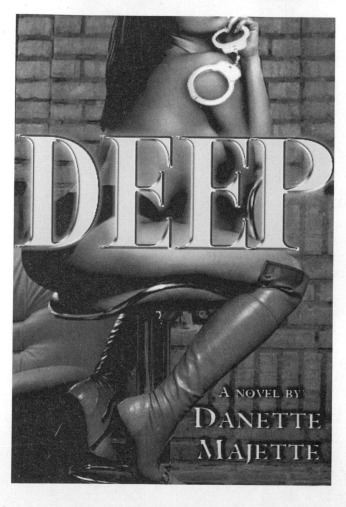